Karan Anshuman is a screenwriter and filmmaker based in Mumbai, India. He is the director of the 2015 film *Bangistan* and the creator and director of *Inside Edge,* India's first Amazon Original. An ex-film critic for *Mumbai Mirror,* he spends his time nerding out on film, trivia, science, and design. *Kashmirnāmā* is his debut novel.

KASHMIR NĀMĀ

What is the price of paradise?

KARAN ANSHUMAN

JAICO PUBLISHING HOUSE

Ahmedabad Bangalore Bhopal Bhubaneswar Chennai
Delhi Hyderabad Kolkata Lucknow Mumbai

DISCLAIMER

This is a work of fiction. Names, characters, businesses, places, events and incidents are either the products of the author's imagination or used in a fictitious manner.

Published by Jaico Publishing House
A-2 Jash Chambers, 7-A Sir Phirozshah Mehta Road
Fort, Mumbai - 400 001
jaicopub@jaicobooks.com
www.jaicobooks.com

KASHMIRNAMA
ISBN 978-93-86348-46-3

First Jaico Impression: 2017

Page design and layout: Special Effects, Mumbai

Printed by
Replika Press Pvt. Ltd.
310, 311, 444-45 EPIP, HSIIDC,
Kundli Industrial Area, Sonipat,
Haryana – 131028

For Zoë

LIST OF CHARACTERS

Vikram Rathore: NSG, Special Action Group Captain
Bani Rathore: His wife
Rajveer Yadav: NSG, Vikram's friend and colleague
Aditi Shenoy: Reporter, Capital News
Soumik Sen: Managing Editor, Capital News
Jamal: RAW agent
Bobby Bhullar: Indian arms dealer
Bhushan Pratap Singh: Bhullar's secretary
Lord Cecil: the Marquess of Hertshire
John Steele: Representative, BMD Plc

Javid Razaq: Kashmiri Goat Herd
Khurram Razaq: Javid's son
Shaukat: Khurram's friend

Indian Government
Jaywant Shirke: Prime Minister
LP Krishnamoorty: Minister for External Affairs
Ajit Seth: Minister for Home Affairs
Ajinkya Ranade: Defense Minister
Rajiv Modi: Communications' Minister
Usha Narayanan: Cabinet Secretary
Ravi Bhagwat: Chairman of Chiefs of Staff
Avinash Sadanand: Director General of the IPS
Jaswant Singh Garah: Chief of Army Staff
Obaid Sheikh: Chief Minister of Jammu and Kashmir

Pakistan Government

Inayat Nur Khan: Prime Minister
Mohammed al-Bashir: Minister of Foreign Affairs
Iklaq Mirza: Defence Minister
Liaqat Hussain: Director General of the ISI
Maqsood Malik: Army Chief

GLOSSARY

RIAF: Royal Indian Air Force

CoAS: Chief of Army Staff

NSG: National Security Guard, an Indian special forces unit

Tur: A light-armoured vehicle used by the NSG and the Armed Forces

MP: Member of Parliament

7 RCR: 7, Race Course Road, the official residence of the Indian Prime Minister

AI: Air India

AK: Automatic Kalashnikotv or AK-47, is an automatic assault rifle

C-4: A plastic explosive

HAL Tejas: Indian-made single-seat, single-jet engine, light combat aircraft (LCA)

Globemaster: A large military transport aircraft

IGIA: Indira Gandhi International Airport

RAW: Research and Analysis Wing, India's primary foreign intelligence service

ISI: Inter-Services Intelligence, Pakistan's premier intelligence agency

PIA: Pakistan International Airlines

PROLOGUE

OCTOBER 1947

Jawaharlal Nehru stormed down the black-and-white checkered marble corridor of the palace, his strides long and purposeful. He pushed through the door at the far end, swatting away the Maharaja's attendant with a mere glance, and came to a halt. Stepping to the side, he positioned himself against the wall, between a telephone atop an out-of-place wooden table and the exit; both within arm's reach. From this vantage point, he glowered at the mound of a man curled up in the middle of the oversized four-poster bed.

Hari Singh looked rather comfortable in his pyjamas. However, it was evident that his sleep – marked by a twitching face and dissonant snoring – was troubled. The white stubble on his enormous, usually clean-shaven chin, aged his appearance a great deal. The king – who had turned tail and fled his capital city as the adversary approached – had found the time to take an afternoon nap.

Nehru's companion and chief advisor, the unflappable VP Menon, who was left gasping for breath as he tried to keep up with the prime minister, went to work attempting to rouse Hari Singh.

The duo had landed in Srinagar to find the city abandoned by its Maharaja, who had made off with all his valuables and fleet of cars to Jammu. Menon had managed to procure a rusting Jeep and, with Nehru clutching on to the sides of the tattered passenger seat, they had chased the Maharaja southward. Despite the terrain and the resplendent view, the Prime Minister of India had barely blinked. His visit was shrouded in secrecy. Only Menon's name had been on the travel record. The mission was too important for Nehru to leave it to his confederate, even though Menon had a flawless track record. More than once on the four-hour journey, the PM wondered if his own presence was imperative. Was he acting out of personal spite? Had Jinnah left him no choice? Did Kashmir deserve to be taken by Pakistani tribesmen after all the dithering? No, he assured himself. He was acting in the best interests of the state, its people, and India. Hari Singh was an idiot. He had left Srinagar naked and vulnerable, putting a huge question mark on the legitimacy of his kingship. Sheikh Abdullah's unarmed volunteers were no match for the marauders from across the border. Srinagar would fall by midnight.

With matters reaching tipping point, there was no time for more thought. He had to meet the king and convince, cajole, or coerce him to do the job. But it was best that he told nobody. Only Dickie knew.

Hari Singh stirred and sat up in his bed with difficulty. Pearl- and diamond-laden necklaces around his neck shimmered with his sweat. Nehru was certain the king would have preferred to die in his sleep rather than make the difficult decision before him now. Menon conjured a sheet of typewritten paper and placed it before the Maharaja.

INSTRUMENT OF ACCESSION OF...

"You need to write Jammu and Kashmir State on the top," said Menon, holding out a black pen, its ink staining Hari Singh's trembling fingers as he accepted it. There was no point even reading it now.

On the dotted line, he slowly scribbled:

JAMMU..AND...KASHMIR STATE

The white space below, the largest available on the page, required his name.

Shriman Inder Mahinder Rajrajeswar Maharajadhiraj Shri Hari Singhji,

Jammu & Kashmir Naresh Tatha Tibbet adi Deshadhipati

Nehru huffed audibly as Hari Singh scrawled slowly into the margins, squeezing his title into multiple lines, taking almost a minute. Menon shot him a glance, his expression pleading the leader to keep his composure. This was Menon's territory. It had only been a couple of months since the Maharaja of Jodhpur – Hanawant Singh – had pointed a .22 calibre pistol at him in frustration after signing the document of accession. Menon had talked him down. This was a hallmark of Menon's manner. He went about dealing with more than five hundred princely states and their temperamental rulers with as pragmatic an approach as possible, taking away their titles, lands, and privileges with a single stroke of his pen. Kashmir was the last.

The Maharaja flipped the page and came upon the final blank spot on the document.

For the first time, Hari Singh turned and looked at Nehru. Stiff-necked, his body convulsed as it made the effort. Nehru stared back, arms behind his back, still unblinking. Then, an almost imperceptible nod.

Hari Singh signed at the bottom of the page.

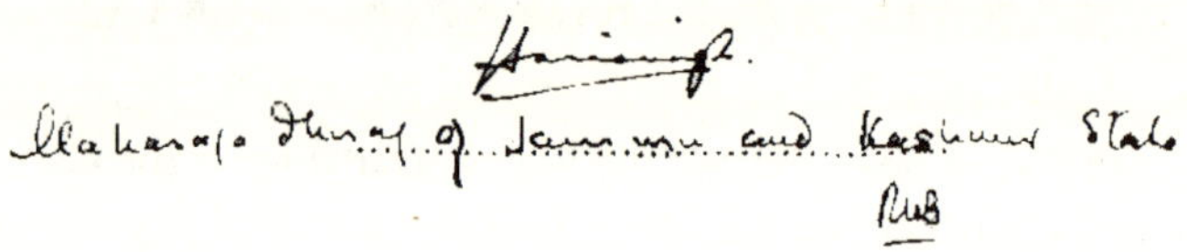

And just like that, over 200,000 square kilometres of the planet's most stunning, pristine territory exchanged hands.

Menon gently tweezed the document out of the Maharaja's hands and put it in his pocket. Nehru had already dialled the final digit on the phone. He only had to wait for a single ring before he heard his friend's familiar voice on the other end.

"Hello, Dickie? It is done."

In Delhi, Louis Mountbatten had waited impatiently at his desk all afternoon. There lay a formidable endeavour ahead. If Nehru and Menon were to find and convince Hari Singh to sign the Instrument of Accession, he'd need to mobilize a joint forces' airlift into Kashmir in a ridiculously short amount of time. Such an operation, ferrying thousands of troops in a hundred civilian and RIAF aircraft by first light tomorrow – code-named Operation JAK – was unprecedented in the history of international warfare.

Timing was crucial in this matter. If he pre-arranged such an airlift but Kashmir did not accede, the Pakistan government would come unhinged, accusing the Indians of plotting an illegal, premeditated military strike, and whatever public support the country had from the Kashmiris would vaporize. So Mountbatten waited, sitting at his desk and reviewing the steps of what needed to be done in either scenario over and over. That's when the phone rang.

"I'm on it. But you will have to speak with the service chiefs."

"I'm going to make the calls right now and head back. We only have hours to take back what we can of the state. Get those planes in the air!"

MONDAY

1

1030 HOURS

SQUAD Commander Vikram Rathore, Special Action Group Captain of the NSG, took off his black balaclava the moment he entered the wood-and-brick building on the banks of the Jhelum, in the heart of Srinagar. He took a deep breath. He could never see the point of the mask in the midst of an operation. Besides causing mild claustrophobia, it made him feel vulnerable at the back of his head, as if the gear blocked an instinctual sense of what was happening behind him.

Vikram led four other NSG commandos in the siege. The unit – called a "hit" – consisted of two pairs of commandos operating as partners and one man in charge of technical support; this was the smallest deployable unit.

Even though he'd only just turned thirty, Vikram was the most experienced of the five. He had met three of them for the first time at the start of the mission when they were briefed at Palam airbase. Only Rajveer Yadav, his deputy and partner in this mission, he knew well.

Yadav had been transferred to the Delhi HQ seven months ago. Even though they had spent long hours together in training and operating in one-off missions, their acquaintance had only turned to friendship when one evening, in search of a rumoured "perfect" butter chicken, they had decided to take a bottle of whisky with them and had driven all the way across Haryana, past the Punjab border. Hours later, losing the trail and all hope, they had ended up at a vegetarian dhaba. But when the last shot of the Black Label had been drained, they promised each other that they would stick with the mission in the long term: to find and savour the greatest butter chicken in North India.

And stick with the mission they did! Yadav even kept a diary and in it were over thirty entries so far. Over these familiar meals in unfamiliar places, Vikram and Raj shared their stories. Raj was a natural raconteur, and Vikram learned of his humble background and how he had found his calling at Sainik School. In turn, he offered his own story: the South Delhi rich kid from Defence Colony with private school education who rebelled against being groomed to take over his father's cloth mills and decided instead that his country needed him. It was an unlikely friendship, and right now, in this terror-ridden house in Srinagar, there was comfort in the fact that it was a friend and not a faceless colleague watching Vikram's back.

A search-and-rescue hostage operation, the mission had become far more complicated than anyone could have imagined in a matter of hours. An unknown number of terrorists had entered the house through the front door and taken a family of twelve – that of a pre-eminent doctor in the area – hostages and sealed every exit. The situation should not have gone beyond the control of the local police and stationed army.

That news coverage was selective and suppressed in Kashmir was an open secret. Army failures were off limits, and news of "disturbances" rarely found themselves to the front pages of national newspapers. This event was changing all that.

The terrorists were striving for drama.

Taking a leaf out of the Islamic State's MO, they had taken an unknown hostage, had him kneel in front of a phone camera and decapitated him. There was no hesitation, no indecision. The video clip of the execution, along with the terrorists' demands, had been promptly emailed to a slew of news channels.

A short deliberation – mostly over videoconference – between the members of the News Broadcasters' Association resulted in the decision not to air the footage. Moments later, however, the clip had leaked on Twitter and gone viral.

The government had no choice but to open up coverage to the national media. The logic: if you can't brush it under the carpet, showcase it.

The terrorists elected to call themselves 'fidayeens' and had among their hostages two children and five women. Their ultimatum was specific: call off the treaty signing between the Indo-Pak heads of states scheduled for Friday in the valley. Then, almost as an afterthought, they had appended a list of peripheral demands that were a combination of being tragically unambitious (free a local skirmisher from Srinagar Central Jail) or too naïve (full army retreat from J&K).

The channels doubled their effort in dispatching their top reporters and large crews to cover the crisis. The government response was slightly slower and the NSG 'copter reached ground zero in full view of a live television audience. The NBA cut off the feed at this point, as part of an agreement after 26/11 to show a delayed transmission during mission critical ops.

The commandos grouped on the terrace and, using C-4 to blow open the door leading to the landing, secured themselves in a concealed high position to plan their next move. One AK-wielding man had tried to creep up on them from the stairs leading up, but was met with instant fire. He escaped with a good enough look, Vikram suspected, at the strength of the squad.

Swinging into action, Vikram led the rest down the first two flights of stairs to the top floor of the wide three-storey house. The technical member stayed behind on the upper landing, after setting up communications and deploying back-up ammunition. Their orders were straightforward: eliminate the terrorists, save the civilians. Use stealth.

Enough light seeped in from the edges of the large slatted windows to avoid the need for flashlights. Now, Vikram strained his ears to pick up sounds from within the building, trying to block out the muted mingling of loudspeakers and public chatter from outside. Thirty seconds passed in absolute stillness. All he could conclude was that the top floor was empty. They still inspected the three rooms with extreme caution, just to make sure, and then moved down another flight.

Even as Vikram and Raj faced the two doors on the landing, the one directly in front – fifteen steps down – opened to reveal a scrawny, bearded man. But it was what he was holding in his hand that all four pairs of trained NSG eyes went to directly – a live grenade.

The insurgent took a moment to survey the positions of the enemy before pitching the bomb with an unsteady underhand toss, squarely in their midst.

2

1030 HOURS

ADITI Shenoy, senior anchor and more recently Deputy Editor-in-Chief of *Capital News*, shifted uncomfortably in her pumps as she watched the footage her cameraperson was reeling in.

The image of the NSG commandos dropping in on the sloping roofs of the house was one remarkably familiar to news viewers – an echo of 26/11. Aditi had been present on that day in '08, after having lost her 'intern' tag and on her first major on-ground assignment. Leading eight-hour shifts on each of the four days, the experience had been epiphanic. She had decided that she liked her job and could remain unaffected and objective without resorting to histrionics, whether counterfeit or genuine. This was mirrored in the viewers' feedback her bosses received and she was fast-tracked to a senior position within months.

She had been the first person her managing editor, Soumik Sen, had turned to when the Kashmir story broke. The sense in the newsroom – hurried movements, indiscreet whispers – was that this was going to be one of the top stories of the year even before the execution clip was spotted on Twitter, piquing global interest.

Three channels had pooled in to charter a King B200 twin-turboprop post the News Broadcasters' meeting and

Aditi and her cameraperson were some of the first reporters to arrive at the spot. Their stringer had met them outside Srinagar airport and driven them to the scene of action, where they managed to secure an excellent vantage from the bridge spanning the listless river. A *Capital News*-owned satellite uplink truck had already left Jammu and was scheduled to reach within the hour.

"There's some graffiti on the wall I think you want to avoid," said her cameraperson, his face emotionless.

Aditi turned and noticed the words 'ISIS' and 'Azad Kashmir' amid paint spatter on the waist-high wall between her and the river below. It was rare for the government to facilitate national news coverage in Kashmir. News channels had paid a heavy price in the 90s for every attempt at challenging the comprehensive censorship that prevailed in the era. Though it was a lot more cursory now, editors had gone on the side of prudence and drawn self-imposed boundaries. A case of once-bitten-twice-shy, political involvement in the management of all media houses further ensured that "national interest" was not compromised. All this meant was that it was the duty of mainstream channels to keep the propaganda alive: that Kashmiris were being browbeaten by foreign elements, and the presence of the army was protection for the citizenry who wanted it. It meant that dissent at the grassroots was never to be witnessed by those outside state boundaries.

She took a couple of steps to her left.

"Frame it out," she said, looking squarely into the camera. The footage they had acquired so far would air an hour later and it frustrated her that social media would disseminate information quicker. Tucking her short hair behind her ear, she delivered words ad-lib, at an even pace with perfect inflections, adding a dash of drama to fashion a gloomy, desperate sentiment. A fan's tweet she had seen when ego-googling herself had stuck in her head: "Hashtags are good, but Shenoy is better."

"It's barely been ten minutes since the commandos went in and already we have witnessed significant action. A minor explosion presumably aiding their entrance into the house was quickly followed by a round of gunfire. There's no way of knowing what's going on inside, but we're hoping that the NSG is making short work of the terrorists and will be able to bring the hostages to safety at the earliest. Local police has been relegated to managing the crowd as it builds, thankfully, mostly across the river.

"The terrorists are demanding that the signing of the historic peace treaty between India and Pakistan be called off. The significance of this treaty is that it will not only be a comprehensive ceasefire, but will also allow for gradual demilitarization along the LoC over the next six months and allow the two countries to take the first steps towards a nuclear-free South Asia. For the first time since 1989, the border will be relatively troop-free. This move will also severely affect Lashkar and other terrorist training camps in PoK and suffocate funding and infrastructure support from their sources, say officials.

"Well, it's now been about ten minutes since we've heard..."

It was then that a thunderous, unexpected explosion behind her ripped off a chunk of the west wall at the top of the building and sent it crashing into the gushing waters of the Jhelum.

3

1038 HOURS

THE grenade arced in a slow, exaggerated loop towards the commandos who reacted in a precise, synchronous manner. For such scenarios, training had evolved into instinct for them. Leading the formation, Vikram and Raj had leapt headfirst, arms outstretched, and both hands firmly gripping their weapons down the fifteen stairs towards where the man had been standing. He had retreated behind the door that had burst open inwards as they crashed through it.

The other two, bringing up the rear, vaulted over the flight they had just come down but lost precious milliseconds in executing the manoeuvre that required turning around and calculating their trajectory to safety. There was no way for Vikram to know if they had made it unharmed once the grenade blasted on contact with the ground. The house shuddered while they were still in flight and the ceilings and walls – well over half-a-century old – threatened to collapse.

Once past the door, Vikram and Raj pitched over behind stray furniture to gain some time to recover from the disorientating, unpleasant ringing in their ears. The terrorist who had thrown the grenade at them lay unmoving, knocked out by the door the commandos had broken through, his nose popped, face a bloody mess. For a second it was quiet, nothing moved. But the hush was short-lived.

Thunderous gunshots reverberated in the room. Raising his CornerShot Glock from behind what he surmised was an antique writing bureau, Vikram sprayed a round of gunfire, while Raj peaked over the table that he had just upturned. He signalled to Vikram that there were two men outside the door. Vikram nodded.

They had little option but to go on the offensive. If there was one aspect that defined NSG training, it was the cliché that attack was the only form of defence. The flimsy wooden units would not hold back bullets and now they had revealed their numbers and location. On a quick count of three, the two jumped up from their positions while simultaneously opening fire.

The bullets slammed into walls. The terrorists had disappeared.

Vikram led Raj, treading past the doorframe into a narrow passage strung across with clotheslines. Some of the sheets on them were still damp. There were two doors at right angles at the opposite end, unlatched, open. Vikram indicated that they should split up. They tiptoed slowly on their respective paths in silence; sticking to the sides so that their outlines would not be immediately visible should a sudden attacker appear from behind.

Positioning himself outside the entrance, Vikram crouched down to his haunches and tried to look through the gap between the shutters. There was no movement on the other side. He tried to pick out any sounds, but Raj's entry into the room drowned everything else.

Still crouching, with one swift move Vikram pried the

door open and darted inside. A huge force struck his hands and his gun went flying. He turned to see a man in camo fatigues swinging an AK-47, using it as a club and taking aim for Vikram's head. He had been by the door, lying in wait. Just before he hit the ground, Vikram moved out of the way of the gun's swerve and aimed a forceful spinning roundhouse kick that connected under his attacker's knee, bringing him down on his back. Vikram scudded to keep him pinned but almost instantly, there was a gunshot. A shooter was taking aim at him.

Vikram realized that there was a second attacker in the room. Using the momentum of the first man's effort to get up, Vikram pitched him up to create enough space to barrel roll and slide under him. Using him as a human shield, and with a tight headlock executed with his right arm, Vikram tried to grapple for the man's gun.

Meanwhile, the second terrorist was trying to find a clean shot with his handgun. Vikram suspected it was a country-made revolver and would probably miss its target anyway. The attacker was thinking along similar lines and tucked away the weapon as he advanced towards the struggling men on the floor.

With four hands on its barrel, the AK was off kilter and Vikram was not anywhere near the trigger yet. His hand tried to squirm its way past the sweaty fingers of the man on top. It did not help that he was doing this blind.

The second man was upon them. Instead of trying to flip them over as he should have, he attempted wrenching the gun from their hands. Sensing relief, the first man let up the pressure for an instant. It was enough for Vikram to take control. His right thumb slid into the guard and pushed the trigger back, as he used his left hand to shove the barrel towards the perpetrator's head. There was a brief look of surprise on his face before it burst open in a riot of red.

As his partner dropped to the side, a rush of adrenalin galvanized the man who had shot at him. He elbowed Vikram in the sides with brutish force and Vikram was forced to ease up on the headlock. This gave the man time to manoeuvre himself out of his grasp and get on his feet.

Staying down, Vikram tackled him using his shoulder that dislodged the AK from his hands. With no weapons, the fight was heavily in favour of Vikram, who was taller, stronger, and much better trained. He grabbed his rival's head and pulled him. Holding the head down, he drove his knee hard into the man's groin. Then pulling him further, he thrust his knee up again and with all his power jammed it into his face. This knocked out the terrorist, Vikram suspected, permanently.

Just as he was about to catch his breath and take stock, he heard Raj scream behind him, "Move!"

Unequivocally trusting the instruction in his partner's voice, Vikram jumped to his right and hit the floor. Shots were exchanged and a couple of seconds later Raj was pulling him up.

He had backtracked towards Vikram on hearing the gunfire. A third terrorist had entered the room from yet another door in this maze-like house and was about to take aim when Raj fired. He had missed and given him the opportunity to fall back.

Behind that door, Raj gestured.

They went up to it. It was bolted from the other side. Vikram held up his gun for cover as Raj employed a perfectly placed kick dead centre, splintering the door.

4

1045 HOURS

PALLID white light from tubes lit the room, barely reaching the expansive, fading traditional Kashmiri carpet that concealed most of the cement floor. Huddled on it at the back of the room were ten people, more than half of them prostrate in prayer. Flanking them were two armed terrorists – recognizable from their ammunition belts – pointing their automatics at the new arrivals.

Even though the commandos were through the door and in full sight, the terrorists did not shoot them instantly. Instead, they swivelled their guns at the hostages. Vikram wondered if this was a slice of sheer luck or by design. Were they expecting a negotiation? Either way, a foolish move when numbers were square. Fidayeen or not, everyone valued their life. However, their hesitation lost them any edge they might've had.

"Weapons down! On the floor! We'll shoot them!" yelled one in Urdu.

Raj and Vikram's CornerShot Glocks remained aimed at their heads. All they had to do was pull the trigger, but their fingers froze mid-squeeze for no sooner had the insurgent barked his bidding than he grabbed the first person he could lay his hands on. It was a young girl, no older than fifteen. A deep red abaya was pulled tightly over her head and created a macabre outline of her expression of total terror flecked with tears. His large fingers hooked around her upper arm and she was, in one rough and swift move, picked up and pushed in front of the barrel of his AK.

The NSG commandos' aim remained rock-steady – each one at a terrorist's head. Vikram had the man with the girl in his sights. *Thump. Thump.* Vikram felt his heart beat twice. That was how long the standoff lasted.

Panicked, the girl tried to free herself. The red abaya unravelled in the terrorist's hand. Everything happened in a blur. Raj fired. His bullet passed clean through the skull of the second fidayeen. Vikram should have pulled his trigger in a coordinated move. But the slightest of lags gave the terrorist a chance to react. Vikram's shot did find its mark, but not before his quarry had the time to pump three rounds into the girl's back.

Six lives had ended in less than a couple of minutes and the entire operation in less than ten since the moment the NSG had taken over the situation.

5

1052 HOURS

VIKRAM and Raj helped carry their colleague wounded in the grenade blast. His right leg was limp and left an alarming trail of blood behind as he was rushed towards the exit. Medical responders, radioed earlier, waited outside. Vikram stopped just short of the main door and put on his balaclava, while the injured serviceman was whisked away in a stretcher. He took a moment for himself, trying to erase the image that was now seared into his mind. *The girl and her unravelling red abaya.* He was grateful for the balaclava that shielded his grief.

Additional NSG troops had secured the perimeter and entered the house with multiple medical personnel to help the hostages and collect corpses. Beyond the perimeter, there were multitudes of people clamouring for a view; media vans like indiscriminate islands in their midst.

"What is this? A terror attack or a circus?" asked Raj, irked at the security threat the crowd posed. They provided the perfect cover for perpetrators and an easy target for mass mayhem. "What is it with people? Why must they gather and grab front row seats to a terror operation? Idiots!"

Vikram was disconcerted too, but there was nothing to be done. He located a cluster of armoured NSG Turs and led Raj towards them.

Aditi sensed the operation had ended when she saw the NSG troops stationed outside close in on the house in a coordinated surge. She quickly wrapped up her shot and started to make her way from the bridge to the epicentre of the action. She instructed her cameraperson to continue to capture footage, in case her assessment was wrong. Then she called her editor as she used her free arm to ruthlessly push through the throng.

"Soumik," she yelled, "do you have a name yet? I'm expecting them to come out any second now."

"I've two names. I don't know who is leading. You'll have to ask."

Moments like these made Aditi wonder about her boss. He had been an award-winning reporter in his day; his field career starting with Indira and ending with Rajiv before he decided to get behind the desk and crunch numbers to start his own news network. On his second innings – armed with spreadsheets and corporate backing and with a first-mover's advantage – his success was unparalleled in the news arena. Deeper pockets had swung by, and international news brands had taken a shot, but *Capital News* survived at the top with Sen becoming a key influencer of public opinion. A studio bully, he would take on politicians without remorse if needed, but could be equally warm in the rare case and for the right reasons. But surely somewhere along the way, he had forgotten what it was like on the field. *Just ask*, thought Aditi.

"Give me the names," she said, fighting the urge to be sarcastic.

"I have a Rajveer Yadav and Vikram Rathore. One of them is a captain and…"

Aditi clicked off the phone. An educated guess increased

the odds well in favour of the fact that Rathore was Captain. Masks on or off, the country's social structure was enough of an identity giveaway. She saw the two men make their way to the temporary base where they had parked their armoured vehicles.

The commandos had almost reached the Turs when they heard the crowd break into a roaring applause. Vikram turned to see the hostages being led out. One of them was probably the girl's mother. Would she have cared for her life to be spared after watching her daughter die in front of her eyes in cold blood? A mortified grunt escaped Vikram's throat.

When he turned back there was a slim, shorthaired figure crouching before him next to the rear tyre, out of sight of everyone but them. She seemed to have ducked the security tape, made her way to their transport, and was evidently waiting for him.

"Vikram Rathore." Aditi tried not to make it sound like a question. Vikram exchanged a look with Raj. For a moment, Aditi thought she had blown her chance. Then one of the masked men responded–

"Yes?"

He knew he had seen her before, but couldn't place where in that instant.

"Could you hold on to this?" She handed him a basic Android. "I'll call you for a quick word if you don't mind."

6

1100 HOURS

THE vehicle was still gathering momentum when Vikram ripped off his balaclava again.

"How did she know it was you?" ribbed Raj.

"How the fuck should I know?" A sudden wave of exhaustion hit Vikram as he pushed back on his seat, his mask limp in his hand. He looked out at the valley as they hurtled towards the outskirts of the capital. *Kashmir.* Would its politics have been any different had it been a low-lying stretch of wasteland?

The phone rang. Instead of a name, '*Please Answer*' flashed on the screen. Vikram showed it to Raj who snorted and suppressed a laugh. Aditi Shenoy. He had remembered that face the moment she had turned and ducked under the perimeter to vanish in the crowd. Might as well…

"Hello?" Vikram tried to sound gruff, businesslike.

"Hello, is that Vikram?" Her voice confirmed her identity.

He chose not to acknowledge.

"Oh, right. No names then. I'm Aditi Shenoy from *Capital News.*"

"I know."

"Right. Just a few questions then, on the record."

"There is no way I'm going on the record."

"I won't name you. As you know, my sources are never disclosed. You will only be filling in the gaps. This is standard. There's nothing to worry about. The operation was a success, so if anything, your words will give the NSG's image a huge boost."

She paused to give him a second to protest. She had him of course; the NSG's image had taken a beating in the media with hundreds of troops relegated to bodyguard duties for politicians and even civilian VIPs. If only the journalists were privy to the level of overhaul that the NSG had undergone post 26/11 and the kind of training their top recruits were receiving in Israel…

Hearing nothing, Aditi went on, "Right, so could you tell me what happened in the ten minutes you were inside from the moment you landed on the roof?"

Vikram felt that he had not given away much. Just the facts that forensics would have unearthed anyway. And *their* reports almost always leaked to the press. He had skipped the part about the girl being shot point-blank in her back. That would have to wait for the debrief. Raj tut-tutted on one occasion and overplayed an expression as if to suggest that Vikram was giving away national secrets to a journalist only because she was pretty.

"That's all I have to say. Nothing more."

"Fair enough."

Surprised that she wasn't pushing for more, Vikram felt compelled to do her a good turn.

"This phone, uh, how do I return it?"

"Don't worry. Trash it. Give it to a nephew."

"No, no. It looks… tell me how I can reach it to you."

He thought he heard her chuckle. "Fine. Post it to PO

Box 1500, New Delhi. Easy enough to remember?"

"1500. Yes."

"Thank you."

The mobile went dead. Vikram looked at it, flipping it in his hand. It was way better than his own worn-out handset that was lying with his gear at the Srinagar Air Force Station.

Pulling into the hangar that the NSG had converted into a makeshift base for forward operations, the armoured Tur rolled to a halt and the door opened. Vikram glanced up at his ride home: the IAF's shiny new toy, the Boeing C-17 Globemaster III, part of a fleet of ten that had recently replaced the ageing Russian Il 76s.

Debrief would take an hour. Operations would wind up in another four. Airborne and in a Hindon followed by an hour-long ride home to Defence Colony. He'd be home in time for dinner if Delhi's traffic allowed him.

The corner of his eye caught a junior running up to him. "Sir!"

"Yes?"

"The chief ..."

"I was just coming in to see him."

"No, sir. The chief minister of J&K has sent you an invitation."

7

1500 HOURS

JAVID leaned on his stick, a dry branch he had picked up in an absentminded gesture, while his goats grazed amid the craggy terrain, to get a better view of the racket emanating from the valley.

The stick almost splintered and sent him tumbling downhill as he gawked at the stunning vista: a convoy of no less than a hundred army trucks – not the usual civilian transport hired on loan, but the ones the army owned, the olive green and heavy kind – were winding their way up the mountainside. Like a python stalking its prey with deliberate movement, only to drown in its own powerful revs and dark exhaust.

What was going on? Javid was no stranger to the Indian army's presence around him. It had been almost three decades since the military had descended onto the valley and his home in the paradisal village that lay practically on the Line of Control, no more than a glorified border outpost and close to the town of Uri. He had been a teenager at the time, but memories before then were hazy. His life had been defined post 1989; the "uniforms" as they called them, were ubiquitous in his life. Even so, he had never seen such a significant contingent in these parts.

He hurried back to his goats and rounded up all ten.

The smallest of them had a brown leather leash around its neck. This was Bholu, the newest addition to Javid's herd, and his twelve-year-old son Khurram's favourite. He picked up the animal and brushed a finger against its nose. Still dry. Still sick. Securing Bholu in the crook of his arm under the pheran – a final layer of protection from winter's wrath – and wielding the stick in his free hand, Javid started to drive the rest of his herd to the safety of his little hut on the other side of the mountain; time to check on his son as well.

It was a long, treacherous walk even for experienced hikers. Javid and his disciplined herd were spry and negotiated the terrain effortlessly. He still had to walk along the river until he reached the path that straddled the hill over to the other side where his house stood. Most of Javid's village had relocated with time, but he and a few others had kept their tenements. Far away from any main roads, it was a harder life with no real connectivity and sporadic electricity; a settlement that was increasingly cut off from the world. An unnecessary bridge, the neighbourhood oddity, traced the shallow valley below. The Jhelum used to pass under it once, before the hydroelectric plant at Uri had shifted its course.

The decades-old cantilevered overpass had been in disrepair ever since Javid could remember; he had been told to never venture on it as a child, the elders hammering warnings into his head about its safety concerns. Now and then, Khurram and other village children would scale its sides on summer nights, their legs dangling above the gaping darkness in the happy belief that no one was aware of their little adventure. Of course, he knew. Much like his father would have too, he realized. The thought revived memories of a time he had long forgotten, of a glorious age he couldn't believe he had lived. Friends smoking shared cigarettes made of unprocessed tobacco on the overpass, the only way to rebel as a teenager when he was growing up. Racing each other from one end of the bridge to the other, nimble as the goats they herded, and just as unmindful of the danger that it afforded with its jagged cracks and gaping holes. It made Javid believe that it was one of the few places that was safer when enveloped in darkness.

Like a sharp U-turn from the past to the present, it dawned on him: maybe Khurram had started to smoke too. That would explain the bouts of coughs that left his son heaving for breath every five minutes. It had been four days now. He made a mental note to mention this to the doctor, the hakim, when he visited later today.

Today.

Everything seemed different today. Following the trail of the river, his gaze fell upon tall floodlights that had been erected across from him, surrounding an area near the town's reservoir. These would bathe it in a kilotonne of light, overwhelming the otherwise impressive, million-star-speckled Kashmir night sky. *Now why would they want to do such a thing?* wondered Javid. He was curious and drawn to it. The dam waters gushing through the hydel plant prevented him from hearing the sound of generators on his approach, but now their sharp chugging stung his ears. There was a buzz of activity: men in uniform bustled – shouting orders from atop rostrums, labouring with jackhammers, and erecting edifices Javid couldn't quite make out.

His agitated herd broke ranks and were starting to scatter. Like a schoolmaster he chased them, rounding the farthest escapee and working his way in an inward spiral.

He wondered if the town was prepping for a full-scale attack from Pakistan.

He reminisced about the first time he had witnessed an exchange of fire between the two sides when he was still young. It was in the early 90s. Short bursts of bullets from the self-loading rifles that both the BSF and the Rangers used had the entire village taking cover in broad daylight, but Javid's curiosity had made him gravitate towards the rat-a-tats. He had hidden behind a short brick wall of an unfinished house and watched through the clefts with great anticipation (though of what, even he wasn't sure). He could barely see any movement on the Indian side, let alone the enemy who was too far to even spot with the naked eye. The action underwhelmed him eventually. Later that night, a Pakistani mortar had fired a shell that exploded on the roof of his house. The fear his family and he had felt in that moment was total. Like many other residents in the village, they too had built a crude bunker behind their house, a cramped underground space with no heating or sustenance, just a cover from such an event. They spent the months of January and February sleeping there, flirting with death every frigid night – a winter that Javid would never forget.

Thinking of it now made him pull his pheran around him tighter and dig his fingers into Bholu, still ensconced at his chest. He had nearly regrouped his herd. There was no sign of the enemy. The army was building, and they were in a hurry.

Suddenly from the shadows stepped out two soldiers and pointed their rifles at Javid.

"Halt!"

Javid did as he was told and stopped in his tracks. Even his herd, sensing the situation, seemed to freeze. He had witnessed such a sight often enough, but a man not wont to confrontation, this was rare for him. His family and friends had suffered enough. But unlike most others instead of being angry, he tried to be indifferent, well aware of the fear psychosis the occupiers employed.

"What have you got there? Under the pheran? Is it a weapon? Show us the item immediately."

Javid lifted the cloak off Bholu's head to reveal the kid. Inadvertently, he touched his nose again. He thought it was marginally moist; perhaps he was recovering.

The soldiers visibly relaxed. They exchanged a quick look and words in a dialect of Hindi that he couldn't understand. He could tell they were new to the area, of a mountainous regiment. But that could mean anywhere from Assam to Ladakh.

"That way, move!" they instructed.

With Javid walking ahead at gunpoint, they made their way to an area where there were even more soldiers and workers resting. Exhausted from their shift, they were sprawled on the ground and warming their hands around a fire lit in a rusty drum. Javid could tell from their uniforms and lack of adequate, appropriate attire that they were of a low rank. While he was still observing them, two men held him by the neck and turned him towards what Javid had mistaken for some sort of shipment container – a large box with a mesh grills and irons bar on opposite sides.

It was a cage.

One of the soldiers opened what turned out to be a small gate and Javid was violently shoved into it. There was not enough room for him to stand up erect and it wasn't wide enough for him to spread his arms. They put on a lock and Javid was terror-stricken. *What was going on? He had done nothing wrong!*

They led the little goat to the group.

"You from the village?" asked a soldier who was warming his hands on the fire. He looked eighteen.

"Yes, sahab."

"How many in your herd?"

"Ten."

"That's a lot. Are you rich?"

"No, sahab," protested Javid.

The soldiers cackled over the din.

"Where were you going?"

"Home, sahab. The village, up the slope and over the mountain."

"Up *that* slope? Then why were you here, facing this way?" probed one of his earlier assailants.

Javid remained silent.

"Speak up when you're being spoken to."

"I… I just wanted to see what was happening."

"Oh, the case of the curious goatherd… what should we do with him?"

"We should let him go," offered the young soldier with a devious smile.

The others seemed to have caught on.

"Oh yes. I guess we should let him go. Should we let you go, goatherd?"

"Yes, sahab. Please."

"But it will cost you."

"I don't have any money, sahab."

"We don't take money from civilians. Do we take money from the ones we protect?"

There were murmurs of 'no', 'never', 'what righteous man does such a thing?'

"No, my dear goatherd. We are your saviours. All we want from you is your assistance."

"Please help us help you!" mocked a soldier who hadn't spoken so far, repeating a line the army used at checkpoints when searching civilians and checking their IDs.

"Tell you what. Why don't you join us for a meal? And then you can go. What do you say?"

"Sahab..."

"Come, come. Now bring that juicy looking piece of mutton here."

The 18-year-old picked up Bholu, who was looking on with his dispassionate eyes, and flung him to the officer. He held down the goat, its head against the ground. In distress, it was bleating at a volume Javid had never heard before. They both knew what his fate was going to be. Another soldier produced a knife. The young boy lifted it up like an axe and brought it down on its neck. But he did little damage. Bholu continued to bleat. He hacked it several times with his unpractised hands until the animal stopped moving.

"Sorry, that was harder than I thought it would be," he mumbled.

"What a bloody mess! Go clean up. You have a long way to go, young man. You, make a spit so that we can cook it over the fire. Who knows how to skin this thing?"

Javid had watched without a hint of protest from behind the mesh. He knew the drill: never disagree with the uniforms. Else, you will be beaten, shot, or worse, made to disappear in hell. He had spared no occasion to reiterate this lesson to his son, who was waiting for Bholu as much as he was for Javid.

One of the men opened the cage and pulled the hesitant victim out.

"Move along then; this is a restricted area."

"Yes, sahab…"

The soldier swung his arm as if to hit him. Even though he was five yards away and unlikely to get to his feet, Javid ducked and staggered backwards. Then, with one last look at the mangled remains of the little goat with the dry nose, he turned around and walked away.

8

1800 HOURS

THE MP took off his toupee and kept it carefully on a cushion beside him. The only person privy to his balding head was his aide. Even his girlfriends never got past or came to know of his state-of-the-art customized hairpiece from Aderans (he had made a trip to Japan on government dime just for this). Neither did his house staff, who were instructed to stay off the second floor of his sprawling Chhatarpur farmhouse when he was in.

He had been watching the news for the last forty minutes in his bedroom. The NSG knocking over the terrorists. Emerging victorious from the house, their emotion – if any – shielded from view. Over and over, the images burned themselves into the 105-inch UHD television. And Aditi Shenoy speaking into the camera, as usual her make-up and hair unaffected, quoting a source from within the NSG with details of the operation. For a moment, he wondered how she had managed.

He realized it didn't matter. This was a minor blip. The prime ministers of the two countries were headstrong about this treaty. It was going to take a lot more than a handful of terrorists storming a civilian house to stop this deal in its tracks. No, the MP's daring plan needed a grander, a more terminal push.

A phone rang. It was his – a devotional ringtone reimagined by a Bollywood film.

His secretary, Ramnath Singh, waddled up to him from behind the plush white leather sofa and held up the handset.

"It's the PMO. They've called an emergency meeting at 7 pm."

This was not entirely unexpected, but it was unprecedented in his tenure as an MP. A cabinet meeting to be convened at this late hour was rare.

He had an hour exactly. Enough time. It would not take more than twenty minutes to the PM's if his convoy switched on their lights and sirens.

As if reading his mind, Singh interjected, "Sir, we have to leave right away."

"What do you mean? Isn't the meeting at 7 RCR?"

"No sir. It's aboard Air India One."

9

1900 HOURS

BOBBY Bhullar poured himself another shot of Lagavulin, his favourite smoky single malt, and looked out at the Thames from his suite at the central London five-star. *So much better than Moscow*, he thought.

In his early days, when he had taken over his father's duties as a middle agent's assistant helping with the paperwork between private arms dealers and governments, he divided his time in the corridors of the defence ministry and Raisina Hill, Delhi's five-star hotel bars, and Moscow's upscale restaurants. Always Moscow. Cold, freezing Moscow and its vodka.

But Bobby kept at it. He was diligent with his paperwork and got his break – something his father never managed – when a Russian rep he had worked closely with decided to deal with him directly and cut out his boss to save costs.

His rise was stratospheric. Soon, he was dealing with multiple NATO nations and directly with their ministers. The bribes came in all forms – hard cash, diamonds, property across three continents, and even the consulship of a small West African nation that gave him official perks. The consulate itself was relegated to a small part of his mansion. Small change for the deals that he was getting through for both parties.

In a reflex gesture, he fixed his turban in the reflection and smoothed his already perfect beard before turning his attention back to the laptop. Karol Zakharov, an agent from the Russian arms manufacturing firm Mikoyan Systems, waited patiently with his offer over secure videoconference.

"Bobby, what are you considering?" said Zakharov, his patience wearing thin, his accent thick. "You're acting like a rookie. You know how much India has spent since the turn of the century buying arms from Russia? 65 billion dollars. That's more than all the rest put together. You know why?"

Zakharov paused as if expecting a reasonable answer. Bobby was in no mood to indulge him though. Instead, he took a sip of his whisky.

"Because we love each other!"

This made Bobby laugh. Who knew Zakharov had a sense of humour.

"Look," said Bobby picking up a fistful of salted peanuts, "You've made your proposition. I just need more time."

Zakharov slapped his hand on the table. "Mikoyan gave you that proposal four months ago, Bobby. There'd be less time spent on red tape if I dealt directly with your government. And what do you need more time for? It's straightforward. No one can better this deal. We've been selling arms to the NATO countries since Berlin fell. The whole world knows we're the cheapest."

"You aren't the cheapest," shot back Bobby, unable to keep his calm.

"What's that?"

"HAL is the cheapest."

Zakharov let out a hearty, bellowing laugh. Bobby knew in that instant he had just handed the Russian more ammunition to insult him.

"HAL? HAL's the laughing stock of the defence world. Your country's LCA, what's it called... ah, Tejas! That aircraft is a joke. How many have you made since you started fifteen years ago? One? Two? And this after giving up trying to produce the engine from scratch and acquiring it from GE? Everyone knows Dassault has been conniving with your top military brass to keep further development from happening. Your colonels and ministers and you, my dear Bobby Bhullar, you men are addicted to your imports and the junkets and perks that come with them. You'll never allow a local agency to prosper in a way that doesn't benefit you."

"The ministry is bringing the program back on track. It will happen sooner than later."

"The day it happens, I'll retire to my farm and grow potatoes, maybe brew my own vodka," said Zakharov.

Bobby fingered the hard copy of the proposal sitting next to the laptop. Fifteen attack and fifteen heavy cargo helicopters for under 10,000 crores. It was a fine deal and yet...

"Please, enough. Let's get back to the real world. Now you tell me," Zakharov went on, "why you are you sitting in a hotel room in London? What are the they bribing you with now? Haven't they learnt their lesson from the Scorpion sting?"

Zakharov was pulling all stops. The Scorpions were an international arms anti-corruption watchdog agency, who had only recently got major convictions in a South African arms deal involving naval frigates that went back to 1999. Sweden was the big culprit, but the Brits had their fair share of fish in the net.

Bobby wondered if this was a veiled threat. He took another swig of the whisky. He had an urge to throw the glass through the window into the midst of the city. The drinking was beginning to affect him again. He knew he had to stop; get back in shape. Some shape. At one-hundred-and-thirty kilos and a borderline alcoholic, he was not doing himself any favours plodding around in expensive all-paid-for suites. He took a long breath and the moment passed. He popped a few more peanuts.

"Karol," Bobby's tone indicated the conversation was over, "one week."

"Your country is signing a treaty with the enemy in one week. You know we should do the deal in time, before…"

"There's always China, Karol. There's always China. Now, goodbye."

"Bobby Bhullar, watch your back."

The screen went blank. It was Bobby who had hit the disconnect button and for a moment he wondered if he'd heard right. Was it a friendly warning? Or a direct threat?

There was a knock on the door.

10

1900 HOURS

THE pilot of AI One checked and rechecked the flight roster before signing off on it. The names were a list of who's who in the highest echelons of the Indian government…

Prime Minister	Jaywant Shirke
Minister for External Affairs	L P Krishnamoorty
Minister for Home Affairs	Ajit Sheth
Defense Minister	Ajinkya Ranade
Communications' Minister	Rajiv Modi
Cabinet Secretary	Usha Narayan
Chairman of Chiefs of Staff	Ravi Bhagwat
Chief of Army Staff	J S Garah
Director General of the IPS	Avinash Sadanand

…and other military commanders. The fifty-eight-minute flight path to Srinagar was going to be the pilot's most illustrious hour. When he was standing by greeting them onto the aircraft, CoAS Garah had made the effort to joke while shaking his hand, "Don't fly too fast. Too many old people aboard this aircraft today!"

Once aboard, the PM only had a few words to say. It would have been fewer still had he not repeated himself. As the plane cruised at a relatively low altitude knifing through the twilight, the leaders accorded him every bit of attention as he struggled to form his thoughts in English in his lilting regional accent.

He still took under twenty minutes to reiterate what he was trying to get across: *this treaty must be signed. This is the first step to making the LoC a permanent border. Kashmir is close to being solved. And for once – through genuine concern or just sheer apathy – public opinion remains unaffected. Today's terror attack is to be countered with as much gusto as can be mustered.*

They were flying to Srinagar to present themselves at ground zero, in the aftermath of the crisis to hold a press conference, where the director of the NSG would take centrestage, to be followed by the PM and the chief minister of J&K, Obaid Sheikh. The last time so many VVIPs were in one place was when the party had won the elections and celebrated at their headquarters.

The PM excused himself and retired to his chambers. His seventieth birthday was behind him. If he managed to sign this treaty, it would go down as one of the most significant political accords since independence. Military budget cuts, economic fillip, a Nobel Peace Prize in all likelihood. In hindsight, it almost seemed foolish for every preceding government not to push for this.

Garah asked the purser to bring around glasses and ice and pulled out a bottle of Black Label from his bag. No one was surprised.

"Drink, anyone?"

Ten of the twelve present had raised their glasses in salutation before long. Cabinet secretary Usha Narayanan, the only female officer on board, and communications' minister Modi abstained. The mood had turned jovial;

this was a close-knit group. The politicians had an absolute majority, and the cabinet members were all of the same party. The IAS officers and military commanders were more than content to work with a stable government.

"We should take al-Bashir to task for this move," said LP Krishnamoorty.

"Call him! Call him right now," suggested Bhagwat, the chairman of the chief of staff.

There was a twittering of agreement from the majority. The only man without a glass, minister Modi, had a look of utter shock on his face. Krishnamoorty winked at him, and referring to the number on his phone, dialled the Pakistani External Affairs Minister – Mohammed al-Bashir – on the aircraft line.

A weak 'hello' interrupted the extended ring.

"Mr al-Bashir!" boomed Krishnamoorty, looking around the room with a smug smile.

"Who's this?"

"Krishnamoorty. Are you asleep?"

"What? No. Wait… why are you calling me on open channels?" al-Bashir was confused. He wasn't used to speaking with Indians on the phone. Phones were ISI-bait. Not that he had much to say to them anyway. Whatever exchange was to be had was usually face-to-face at the odd official meeting on international summit sidelines. Once he had hit it off with his Punjabi brethren, the Indian Defence Minister Ajinkya Ranade, in Kyoto. The next few days (and garrulous nights) were a heady mix of guilt and pleasure; they'd felt like adulterers. However, once he was back in Islamabad, the chapter was closed with neither making any effort to reminisce. Back on Air India One, Ranade squirmed in his seat as he heard his short-term friend's voice on the speaker.

"Don't worry, the more people listening in, more the fun. We're on our way to Srinagar to straighten with the media the mess you created there."

"I..."

"Really, al-Bashir. How long are you going to keep this up? The signing is one bloody week away. Do you really want your PM and all of Pakistan to look foolish?"

"It wasn't us, Krishnamoorty..."

"It wasn't you this time, you mean."

"It's beyond our control. It could be Jamat, Jaish, Lash... you know the troubles the Talibs are creating here."

"The Talibs? You made them. Do you not learn at all?"

"What? From you and your Naxals?"

al-Bashir had seized the moment with the pointed retort. Krishnamoorty backed down at this. He couldn't risk further escalation on speakerphone.

"Sleep well. And say hello to your wife. From all of us."

al-Bashir put the phone away, washed and flushed, and got out of the loo. His heavyset wife, already in bed, moved the Bollywood film magazine she was reading from her face to reveal a cocked eyebrow. al-Bashir mustered all the nonchalance he could.

"Oh, it's just the neighbours. Complaining about Billo again."

"You should have had that dog trained better, Bashu. Always off frolicking in the neighbour's garden."

11

1920 HOURS

BOBBY heaved himself out of his armchair and hobbled to the door. The security cam showed an unclear image of a man in a black suit, and a silver briefcase in his hand. He recognized his host: John Steele, the BMD Plc rep. He opened the door and gestured for the lanky agent of the British arms firm to come in.

Steele, impeccable in his manners, asked if he was being taken care of well and if there was anything more Bhullar needed. He stared at him expectantly.

"Should we head out?"

Bobby shrugged.

Twenty minutes later, Steele and Bhullar stepped out of the former's AMG outside Annabeth's, London's most eminent members-only nightclub, heavily favoured by politicians and nobility and the only one the Queen had ever visited. Before he entered, Bobby took an impulsive peek to ensure his own Range Rover had arrived and parked in the vicinity as well.

"BMD's invested in this spot," said Steele, as they walked past the door without the slightest impediment from the two hulking doormen. They were guarding what looked like an ordinary entrance on an ordinary – if upmarket – residential street. No familiar queues, no enterprising falafel seller on the pavement.

Inside, the space opened up to reveal a long cloakroom where they deposited their phones with an attendant. A steel sign listed the rules. "Your guests and your pet dogs remain your responsibility. Ensure that they behave appropriately," read one. This mildly irked Bhullar. He was no chest-thumping patriot, but he couldn't help drawing an instant parallel to what he had been taught in school. Somehow, his country's colonists had managed to extend a reshaped version of their no-dogs-or-Indians-allowed policy into the 21st century.

They skirted past a lofty dance floor with a simulated starlit ceiling, packed with thirty-somethings thrashing about to keep step with the pulsing electronic music. The DJ stood atop what looked like a volcano's mouth, fluorescent LEDs masquerading as lava.

Now they entered an unoccupied and elegant room, only big enough to house a handful of chesterfield armchairs and foot ottomans. Artwork – no doubt well-renowned, assumed Bobby – lined the Moorish-inspired walls. As they selected a corner, a waiter appeared wheeling a bar with him. Steele motioned for him to leave it there and began fixing the drinks.

"I hope you find this comfortable and conducive for a discussion," said Steele, handing Bobby his Lagavulin. All he got was another shrug in return. Bobby wanted the rep to take the lead; BMD had shown what seemed like desperation to get him to London. He wanted Steele to make him a final offer that would help make up his mind. One thing he was clear about was that he wanted a clean deal. There was enough for him even in that.

Almost as if on cue, four women – in sheer, small, shiny

dresses and make-up meant to impress – entered the room. One of them, a Scarlett Johansson-clone, comfortably slid onto Bhullar's lap and placed his free hand on her thigh before giving him a kiss on the cheek.

"I have a wife, you know," said Bobby turning his head to Steele, his dead serious look holding his gaze. "We got married just six months ago." The air desiccated from the room, the music from the dance floor suddenly filling the silence unimpeded. Steele's manner became all clumsy. Then a smile emerged from the corner of Bobby's lips, as he slipped his stubby fingers under the girl's dress and he took a swig.

"I hope this is not all that you've got, John, and you have to know… your offer is nowhere close to what the Russians have made to me."

"I know."

"So? You brought me to London to have a drink with Natasha?" Natasha was code for prostitutes in these circles.

"No… there will be something in it for you, Bobby."

"Brother, the heat the Scorpions are generating is scalding. My own government is going after Swiss and Panama bank account holders. We need to keep this clean. You can't even better the Americans. I *know* you can't." The Charisse lookalike had unbuttoned the back of her dress and the straps had fallen off her shoulders, Bhullar's hand had inched past her abdomen.

"We need this deal, Bobby."

Bhullar considered this – what was Steele trying to get at? Whatever was worth the chance he was begging him to take?

"Why?"

Steele pushed back his head, closed his eyes, and took a

deep breath. When he opened them again, Bobby retracted his arm. He knew sensitive information was coming his way. Steele indicated for the women to leave. They almost seemed disappointed.

"They'll be waiting in your room."

"Get to the point, brother."

"Okay, here it is. BMD's majority stakeholder is a member of parliament. Undeclared assets, family money. He's an Earl. His estate has gone bankrupt and he's – well, he's up shit creek. If we don't do this deal, he will offload his stake. There are no buyers in this market, the Americans' offensives and the House of Commons voting against any further involvement in the Middle East for now have seen to it. BMD will collapse, and with it UK's largest homegrown arms makers. There are 100,000 jobs on the line."

"All this is worth my tiny deal?"

"It just adds up."

It shouldn't have happened; breaching the middleman protocol. But Bobby's ambitions were limitless. He decided to chance it.

"Then I should be talking to your minister. Who is he?"

Steele calmly took the audaciousness of this question in his stride. "The Marquess of Hertshire, Lord Cecil."

12

2000 HOURS

JAVID had taken well until after sunset to steer his goats and return to his village, exhausted. His neck hurt from the rough treatment from the soldiers. As he entered his modest home, he had known in an instant that the last few hours had not been kind to his son either. Khurram's condition had worsened dramatically since the time he had left. He lay running a high fever and erupted in a dry, rib-cage-shattering cough every few minutes that was painful to watch. Javid knew this was not a smoking-induced ailment as he had earlier suspected.

Now as he sat on the floor in a corner of his house, a hakim examined Khurram in the pallid light of a single source. Standing behind him was Shaukat, his neighbour's son. He was five years older than Khurram and invoking the young boy's reverence by already shaving around his goatee. He had summoned the hakim from Uri for his younger friend on Javid's instructions.

The bespectacled physician of traditional medicine had finished with his check-up. He put his stethoscope back in his bag and covered Khurram with his fraying excuse of a blanket. It had been a straightforward diagnosis.

"He has pneumonia," he informed Javid. And then, taking out his prescription pad, "Send for these medicines.

The dosages are in there too."

Javid and the boys watched, dreading the next exchange as the scratch of the ballpoint riddled the silence.

"Hakim sahab," said Javid reaching a trembling hand to accept the ripped leaf, "I don't think I can pay you right now, but perhaps you will accept a week's supply of goat's milk instead?"

The physician smiled and held his arm, "No need for either right now. Just make sure you get the medicine. If that's trouble for you too, then… well, Shaukat can come around tomorrow, I might have some free allopathic samples that I brought on my last visit to Srinagar. Let's hope they haven't expired yet."

Despite the hakim offering to manage things himself, Javid insisted on carrying his bag and walking back with him to Uri. He took along a generous helping of goat's milk, forcing the hakim to accept it as token payment. After the half-hour-long walk downhill and a flurry of thank yous exchanged on the doorstep, Javid felt an inexorable urge to take a path that looped around to the army campsite. He was still curious about the sudden influx of the uniforms in the area and what they were up to. Shaukat was home with Khurram for company; a small detour wouldn't affect anything.

Trudging along in the dark, the path only lit by the stars, a gibbous moon, the stillness of the night occasionally broken by a passing vehicle, Javid took stock of the situation – Khurram unwell, the milk produce at an all-time low, the army callous to the point of cruelty. He had no money. How long could he keep going? He was failing as a provider.

Khurram's mother had passed away when he was just two

and the child had no memory of her. For years since, the father and son's evening routine played out in the kitchen. The boy would sit on a small wooden stool no higher than three inches off the ground, while Javid prepared dinner – usually a chunky vegetable soup, now and then with bits of boiled mutton. Javid would talk – every day a new topic – and Khurram would listen. This was Javid's way of schooling his boy. There was no curriculum. One evening, he would explain effective homegrown treatments for the goats they herded; the next, Khurram learnt about the world beyond the boundaries of their own state and was quizzed about what he would like to be when he grew up. Another time, Javid explained the concept of Kashmiriyat – the social code that unified the people of Kashmir into a singular composite culture that had been passed from generation to generation, regardless of religion – and didn't stop for the next two evenings, wondering if his son would ever understand its true meaning from the ragged whiffs of the notion that was being increasingly politicized.

Javid walked a path avoiding the pools of light. He had an uncanny ability, a skill for staying in the shadows. He believed it had saved his life on more than one occasion. Using a brick bank for cover, he came upon the overwhelming sight that had evolved since the last time he was here: three structures were erected for the troops and labour. Fences had been marked out around the Trade Facilitation Centre, where trucks from Pakistan would arrive with goods in a symbolic gesture of commerce twice a week. Expecting an exponential increase in volume, the Indian government had designated a massive area for this purpose, complete with immense cargo halls and a cafeteria. But now he could see that a slew of sniper towers were being erected. The area was still bustling at this hour, large lights on tripods spawning faux daylight.

Not wanting to risk another encounter with the uniforms, he crept away.

2050 HOURS

"...did you not hear me? They were feasting on your goat. Lamb curry. It was a treat for them, slaughtering your Bholu. It happened with Shoaib's goat. It had to have happened with yours. They probably struck his head off – not even halal – and put him on a fire to slow-roast him, while the masala cooked on the side. If you don't believe me, you can ransack all of Kashmir to look for him, but the only place you'll find him is in the Indian army's stomachs!"

It was Shaukat's voice, agitated, speaking in rapid Urdu. Javid had had his hand on the latch of his door and he was about to enter when Shaukat's words stopped him.

Khurram's weak voice protested, "How do you know?"

"You know it's true, Khurram. I know you know it's true."

Khurram coughed. It was all he had to react with. Javid's hand stayed in place. He wanted nothing more than to comfort his son, but he sensed the dialogue was leading somewhere and he knew that if he walked in, he would never know where Shaukat was going with this.

"I am furious for what they have done to you, my brother, and I can't even begin to imagine how angry you must be."

"But what can we do? This is how it's always been. We have to do as the uniforms dictate. If only..." Khurram wanted to respond in a manner that Shaukat would approve of but he couldn't shake off his father's constant reminders that he must never create trouble for the soldiers.

"It doesn't have to be that way," said Shaukat, his anger giving way to an equanimous tone. "No true Kashmiri wants this; every day we fight the uniforms. So the uniforms prey upon the weak. Like us. But we can't be seen as weak. It will undermine our brothers' fight. We must be strong."

"Should we join them and pelt stones? You know I want to. The money will help Abba too... It's just–"

"Not stones, little brother. We have to go beyond that. Something else, something bigger."

"Like?"

Shaukat looked unsure about sharing more information. Khurram stared unblinking in anticipation.

"If you want Khurram, only if you want, I can talk to some people and help you get revenge. Would you want that?"

Javid had heard enough. He noisily pushed open the door and appeared in the room. The boys went quiet.

"How are you feeling, son?"

"Better."

"I'm here now Shaukat. Run along; your Ammi must be waiting."

"Yes, chacha."

"See you soon."

Javid did not miss the subtle nod the boys exchanged, but he acted as if nothing had happened.

13

2100 HOURS

WITH summons from the J&K CM, Vikram abandoned the idea of reaching home soon. Instead, he made the most of his time weighing in on tactical advice in the control room until all operations and procedures were wrapped up and every one of his colleagues was accounted for and back at base. His debrief was brisk and he was soon in the makeshift mess – all showered, combed, and in a precision-pressed uniform – watching the news with Raj. The political delegation had arrived in Srinagar and the PM had delivered one of his customary speeches at a press conference, punctuated with his trademark pauses for dramatic effect. With the country's power structure descended upon the CM's residence, Vikram hoped it wouldn't be a long night.

"I need you to keep me updated about the last flight out," he told Raj. Ops was dismantling and clearing out and he wouldn't make it on the Globemaster, but perhaps he could get on one of the AIs deputed to the NSG.

"I will. But you know how these things are. All the stealth training in the world won't help you to avoid their bullshit questions and pseudo-concern for your well-being. Frauds..." For a moment Vikram thought Raj was going to spit on the floor in a show of disgust, but he just scoffed and smiled, "Good luck getting out of that mess alive and in time. Too bad I won't have your back for this round."

Vikram's transport glided through swarms of Z-level security guards outside the orange-pink stone walls that perimetered the CM's residence. He had to pull out his ID and invitation six times before finally being zipped into the garden of the VVIP guesthouse by Uzi-toting guards. He whizzed past the slew of high-end cars in the driveway: customized Range Rovers, Benzes, Bimmers, and even an Aston Martin. All of these belonged to the Sheikh family.

Preoccupied about getting home and with spontaneous visions of the mission that day clouding his mind, Vikram hadn't given much thought to what to expect at the gathering. Because when his eyes met the sight before him, he froze in his tracks.

A cocktail party.

There was raucous chatter emanating from the large, luxurious heated gazebo that dominated the garden. A small group of folk singers was mid-performance on a small platform. Every muscle in his body protested each step that he took towards the centre on the lit path. He recognized the famous faces – each of them glowing with unnatural luminescence. What was it about politicians and the rich and famous, he wondered, that they always seemed in the pink of their health – their skin taut, their cheeks full and rosy – even in their 80s when most of them led, by every account, a sedentary lifestyle? He had a theory that all of this was connected to power.

Reach the centre, shake a hand or two. Leave. That was Vikram's plan. He knew them; they didn't know him. He could afford to be aloof and sneak away.

A tap on his shoulder. Vikram turned around and looked right into the eyes of Avinash Sadanand, the Director General of the IPS, de facto head of the NSG and therefore, his boss. He was smiling.

"Vikram. Congratulations on a stellar job today, son. Where's your drink? Come!"

As the minutes ticked on, the introductions were getting less efficient: ("Here's our saviour from today"; "the man who puts the 'ace' in 'peace'"; "gentlemen, meet Squad Commander Vikram Rathore!"), the responses were continually patronizing and Vikram was growing weary of the backslapping. He was keeping mental score and very few of the senior leaders managed to keep their hands off him. Was it the uniform? What if he had come in civilian clothes? And was it his imagination or did Cabinet Secretary Usha Narayanan have her hand on his butt for a good ten seconds before Vikram squirmed away?

The PM too was no exception. He had hugged him, thanked him, and invited him over to dinner in Delhi, all in a slew of breathless sentences. The oratorial pauses then were just theatrics for the public.

Only Rajiv Modi, Communications, had given him the cold shoulder. Survivor of many controversies, Modi could've easily dodged most of them had he not decided to tweet post his sessions on prime-time news debates, when he was half a bottle down. He was well-spoken, but also outspoken – not the best trait for a self-confessed pacifist whose primary job when he was in the opposition was to question every dubious government act that involved any form of aggression or unneeded militarization. For now, Modi pretended to be engaged in conversation with Bashir Sheikh, the ex-CM of J&K and father of the current CM.

The circuit ended with the Chief of Army Staff, JS Garah and the Defence Minister, Ajinkya Ranade, or – as Sadanand had put it as he steered Vikram to the intimate group – 'our people'; those in charge of securing India, from the inside and the outside. Garah had received the mandatory praise without much enthusiasm. He was more interested in the details of the operation.

"When the grenade went off, when the wall tore from the building – we'd all thought it was over one way or another. But you say there were no casualties at all… Oh, LP, have you met this young man who headed the on-ground NSG operation today? Meet Squad Commander Rathore."

Krishnamoorty, Minister of External Affairs, had sauntered to the periphery of the group, unsure whether to step in or move on. He held a florid cocktail, one the bartender thought seemed to necessitate a mini-umbrella on this chilly Kashmir night.

"Young man…" repeated Krishnamoorty. His handshake was limp.

"So, as I was saying," said Garah, picking up from precisely where he had left off after giving the MEA a generous amount of time to decide, "a grenade explodes in a structure that size and what? Everyone just jumped out of the way?"

"Yes, sir. We did. It was lucky. And less than a minute later, four people were dead," Vikram offered.

"Three fidayeens."

"And one civilian, a child–" The red abaya flashed in front of Vikram's eyes. He said it reflexively.

"Well."

There was an uneasy silence in the group. The lyrics

of a Kashmiri folk song hit its crescendo. Garah stared at Vikram. Had he overstepped a line with his snappy riposte? The DM took a small sip of his drink. Sadanand looked confused; had Garah taken offence? The MEA cleared his throat, "Come, come, the need of the hour is to be euphemistic. Should we call it collateral damage? A small price then, for our nation's integrity?" he said, twirling the umbrella in his drink. "Whoop! Don't tell Modi I said that!" This resulted in a few laughs and glances towards the communications minister, two tables away.

Vikram excused himself and walked purposefully towards what he hoped would be the general direction of the bathroom. His phone rang. It was Raj.

"Forty five minutes to take-off."

Lots of time. "I'll be there."

As he pulled on a door with a universal unisex sign on it, standing before him, washing his face, was the chief minister.

14

2135 HOURS

OBAID Sheikh – the young CM, not a day older than forty – towelled his face for an inordinate amount of time and when he was done, stumbled and almost fell face first on the floor. But Vikram moved liked lightning and caught him under his arms just in time. An awkward curl of the lips and tilt of the head seemed to suggest the CM had no idea who this man in uniform restoring him to balance could be. If it were up to Vikram, he'd let it go. If there was one skill the NSG had taught him, it was to maintain a low profile, to be sans identity. What a hash he was making of it all this evening. Here he was at the CM's behest, with the host in his arms; there was little option now but to mark his attendance with a quick hello. Vikram introduced himself.

"Oh, the man who saved Srinagar. I'm glad you could make it!" The CM was effusive. He used both his hands to shake Vikram's extended hand. Even though he could smell the alcohol on the man's breath, there was a genuineness about his greeting that Vikram hadn't encountered in a long time with strangers. "Come," he said, "let's take a short walk. As you can see I've had one patiala too many. I can clear my head a little, get away from these pesky politicians, and oh… even though it's dark, I'd love to show you my rhododendrons." Vikram thanked his stars that he knew this was a kind of flower. Though he hadn't the slightest idea what they looked like.

"Did you know they are the state flower of Kashmir?"

"No sir, I did not."

The CM lurched on a tangential path away from the party. Vikram's stride involuntarily eased up as he followed him away from the music. The chill in the air jabbed Vikram through his uniform as they entered a part of the garden that was exposed to the mountains. They curved around a giant hedge, and in the fragile light of a single faux colonial lamp post, Vikram was greeted by a host of rhododendron plants almost as high as them and bearing thousands of their amethyst-tinged flowers.

"Caterpillars," said Sheikh, his fingers reaching out in reflex to smoothen out a young branch, "they love these leaves in the winter. You'd think caterpillars wouldn't care what they ate, but it turns out their taste buds and my talent are at odds."

"But come spring, they all become pretty butterflies," offered Vikram. "And they'll cross-pollinate and you'll eventually have more flowers, if not a healthy balance at the very least."

"You understand the long-term view of garden politics, I see. Good man. Now allow me to show you something. This here is my party trick–" He plucked out a chrysalis that Vikram had mistaken for a shrivelled leaf. Suddenly, he could see scores of them.

"Ever cheated and peeked into the process of metamorphosis? What do you expect to see inside?"

"A half-formed butterfly; a caterpillar with wings?" Vikram shrugged.

The CM delicately peeled the pupa with deft fingers. A bright, intense pool of light filled his palm as he held up his iPhone as a torch. Vikram was taken aback at what he saw inside. He didn't know what to expect, but he saw no familiar characteristics of either caterpillar or butterfly. There was only some sort of viscid ooze.

"The caterpillar *dissolves* into this... liquid. And the liquid reconstitutes itself into a butterfly. I don't think science can explain how this happens yet. Even nature must obliterate before creating something beautiful."

The CM shifted his gaze to Vikram who was rapt in this instance of wonderment. His smile faded. His brows furrowed. The glow around his face vanished in a tick as he put away his phone.

"Must we obliterate Kashmir before it is beautiful again?" he wondered aloud in a rueful tone.

Vikram said nothing. Obaid Sheikh was deep in thought.

"Kashmir is an expensive habit for India. I am not talking about the inane costs of the military. You know I read on the internet about the government spending three crore a day maintaining its soldiers atop Siachen for a tactical advantage of very little consequence?"

"I... I'm not certain."

"You should know that figure is a lot *less* than the reality. And for what? Someone should enlighten us. Well, enlighten me at any rate; are we planning to build a suburb in those parts? It's not fit of for any kind of vegetation or human habitation. But it's fit for the nation's ego."

Vikram didn't respond.

"Due to the frostbite up there, four thousand soldiers have lost their lives. Every other day a jawan dies in these parts. Five from the Ladakh Scout last week in an avalanche. It didn't even make the news. I know. I meet their families. It gives the numbers perspective. Isn't a single life enough to ask ourselves one question… is it worth it? What is Siachen but an emblem of patriotic sentiment, feeding a national obligation that services a botched history? They didn't fix it in '49; they didn't fix it in Simla. Maybe, they don't want to do this. Shouldn't we just extend the line on a map and be done with this? But you're a soldier, you've been brainwashed from the time you made your career choice."

The CM didn't wait for an answer.

"I'm sorry, I'm sorry. I don't mean to offend you. I'm dr – I've had a few drinks. Today was a difficult day. I tried to speak up but… but you know, well everyone knows I suppose, my father, he's the one in charge. I'm just warming the chair, while he takes every executive decision and stacks his coffers.

"Ah shit! Did I just confess that he takes bribes? Dear, dear me, I just did. Shh… Not a word. Don't let on, don't let on. It must stay an open secret. Just the other day, a young civil engineer came with a proposal in response to an ad the government put up for upgrading the drainage system or some such. So this young kid comes in, an entrepreneur, the rare Indian Kashmiri business success story… and everybody likes what he has to say. The committee is sold, our family is sold. The next day he comes in to sign an MoU and guess what my father tells him? 'A hundred crore deposit, please. Give it to me and you have the tender.' What the fuck is that? A hundred crore? That's more than what the project costs. There is greed and then there is *greed*. Sometimes, I wonder what's got into me. Born into this wealth and power, into a system profiteering from conflict, and I'm being *sensitive*. Maybe this is because they elected me as their leader, put their faith in me. I felt something in that moment. Scared is the emotion that comes to mind. And somewhere, my morals kicked in. I *want* to lead my people. I know they like me. But my father uses me as a carrot, while he steers the cart."

Sheikh sat on a bench and lit a cigarette. He didn't offer one to Vikram. But, patting the bench, he invited him to sit next to him.

"Sorry, I'm being harsh again. We are the government because of the popular vote. That's right, all fifteen percent of it. That's how many people turned up for the election and an even lesser number voted us in. The others? They're supporting the separatists. You know them – Aslam, Haqqani, the lot. You think my father is not a nice man? You should meet them. If fifteen percent can earn you this power and wealth, can you imagine what the eighty five is doing for the separatists?

"Each of them has Z+ security. That's more than most chief ministers of a bunch of states. You've got to wonder why the central government would allow this. Aren't separatists the threat? No, no, no. They're the ones who maintain the status quo. Dressed in their custom Louis Vuittons, their kids all over the world in New York, London, bulletproof luxury cars… these men keep the public deluded that they're fighting on their behalf, fighting for their azadi. The Pakistanis pay them, hoping this will translate into action someday. The Indians pay them to do nothing and because… well a region in conflict is what keeps the economic machinery running.

"There are 600,000 soldiers posted here. Last year, there

were fifty militants identified. You can do the math. You're probably wondering why *you* are here at all. Weren't half a million men enough to handle the situation on the Jhelum? And with the national media too? This was my father, showboating. There's a demilitarization treaty to be signed on Friday. And he's pissed off. Because it probably means a few thousand crores less for him, one way or another. That's why he called in the NSG. And invited the national media into a state where no real news disseminates within or without..."

Vikram was unruffled and betrayed no surprise at this barrage of accusations. He only felt afraid that someone else, less trustworthy, might hear their conversation. Whether this venting was a one-time alcohol-fuelled episode or the CM's deep-set anger and frustration pouring out because of present circumstances was not important. It just seemed to him that it was wrong for a man in his position to be so unguarded. And the CM was showing no signs of stopping.

"I have put my finger on it, soldier. It's education. The kids of Kashmir are going to decide for themselves someday; they need to be better informed. They *think* they like Pakistan better, that utter failure of a state, but of course they fight for azadi. You know what this fight looks like? Collecting three hundred rupees every Friday from the separatists' offices for throwing stones at soldiers. Rest of the week? Facebook and Instagram. We pay a lot of money to teachers in public schools here. To teach the same shit from the same textbooks to our kids that our fathers were taught. You'd think that those silly lessons would be part of their DNA now. But even so, two dozen schools in the valley returned a zero per cent pass percentage. Oh tuition classes are flourishing. Not because of the extra lessons, but because they're the only place where students of the opposite sex may mix. If you ask me, this is them, experiencing azadi. The only azadi they hanker for.

"Corruption and no real education. This is why we have a problem here. And there is no turning back. The populace picks up stones, the army retaliates, and the cycle goes on. Meanwhile the mongrels – those guys all over my lawn back there – make money."

He stubbed out his cigarette under his foot and stood up, swaying as he did. He turned to Vikram. He had not looked at him once all this while, and it was evident now that the unchecked words had come from the gut, unrehearsed.

"That girl today – the civilian who was shot, it was a major blot on their plans, it might just undo the narrative – say… did you witness it?"

Vikram was caught completely off guard. "Yes sir. The militants were using her as a human shield and did not hesitate to pull the trigger when she did not cooperate."

"She made the brave choice then?"

"She was young. It was instinct."

The CM took a deep breath, "She was fourteen. Her name was Gul. She was in school. Her father was caught in a crossfire last year. A brother has… disappeared. And now her family has been reduced to just her mother."

Vikram felt as if a hole was opening up in his chest. Why had he not found out more about the girl himself? He had nothing. He was hearing out the man, only half attentive, all this while thinking of nothing else but getting home. He wanted to kick himself in the face.

"I'm sorry, sir. Can I help in anyway?" He, a lowly soldier, asking a top-level politician if he could pitch in to help the ill-fated. With what? Money? Guilt elicited the strangest statements.

The CM shook his head. "I've already done what I could."

Sheikh started walking back to his garden, Vikram in tow.

"I think it all comes down to this: if someone could calculate what Kashmir costs India, maybe we could make an informed decision… on whether it's worth it." He stopped and looked Vikram in the eye.

"What do you think? Have you given a thought to these matters?" He meant these words kindly.

Vikram picked his remarks delicately, "I believe, sir, that India's territorial integrity is paramount and non-negotiable. Our neighbours are our foes and we must not allow them their whims."

"Spoken like a soldier. But when you have a moment, ask yourself if you believe what you've said – as you said it – or are you merely the quarry of inevitable indoctrination and instruction like every other stakeholder."

The music flared up in sync with the lights; the party's energy had refused to abate.

"Listen," said Obaid Sheikh smiling now, "do you know this year it didn't snow in Srinagar? It's been decades since such an event last occurred."

"Climate change?" offered Vikram.

"Winds of change, my friend. I see this as winds of change."

Vikram stopped short and watched the CM melt into the crowd. Why had Vikram been singled out for this speech? He had been like an unflinching bodyguard. Standing by unreactive, while his VIP thought out loud.

And then the man had mentioned the girl in the red abaya, turning the conversation on its head, making it personal, making Vikram pause, putting in perspective all that the CM had said before this.

His phone beeped. Raj. Ten minutes until his plane took off.

15

2135 HOURS

RAJ was waiting on the runway, smoking a cigarette, as Vikram's car pulled up. The Airbus A320-AI 866 was idling, its fuselage brimming with NSG personnel.

"Thanks for holding us up," said Raj, as they strode the air stairs, three steps at a time.

"Get used to basking in reflected glory," said Vikram, grinning.

It was suddenly warm inside the aircraft. Vikram took off his layers, took his seat, lodged his earphones in and closed his eyes. Forty minutes to Bani.

There she was. He spotted her in the midst of a hundred sets of eyes that were on the intimidating, impressive-looking commandos. Somebody in the waiting area launched a cheer with a, "Bharat Mata ki…!" and this prompted a dozen voices to echo back a heartfelt 'Jai!' Vikram was never a sentimental patriot, but such impulsive appreciation was always welcome.

Bani's eyes were for him alone. He could read them and the graph of her emotions that left signature marks in the creases of her face: concern transforming to relief, transforming to joy. He gave his wife a bear hug. Her slender arms barely reached the sides of his backpack. Then she pushed him away and punched him on the shoulder.

"It was you, wasn't it?"

"What do you mean?"

"Leading the operation. I watched it on TV."

"Which way to the parking?"

Vikram swung their Thar 4x4 out of IGIA and headed towards South Delhi. "You know I can't talk about these things."

"So it *was* you. You know I know when it's you. Mask or no mask. Why does it always have to be you? I saw at least fifty men in uniform walk out before you did at the airport. Could've given any one of them a chance for a change."

Vikram made a funny face, extorting a chortle from her. Bani would complain, but she knew exactly what she was getting into. They had met in their first year in science college. He'd spotted a girl with dark hair falling down the sides of her unblemished white lab coat, mixing colourful compounds for a chemistry experiment. He had gone up to her, after rehearsing a joke about hypothesizing a reaction if he mixed some coffee and conversation. He told her he wanted to become a commercial pilot. She was opting for a career in chemical engineering like her father. They had it planned out at twenty one. Then, inspired by a Sukhoi's acrobatics at an air show and the testosterone-fuelled idea of flying solo in a super-manoeuvrable aircraft consuming him in the moment, he decided to give the Combined Defence Service Exam. The path to the NSG laid itself out for him after that. He saw greater glory as a Black Cat than as a pilot in the Air Force. Ranks did not interest him, action did. Financially, he was fortified with his family's wealth. The mystery surrounding NSG secret-ops was legendary. Recruits were sent to secret training centres from Israel to the Philippines. This was where the real action was. And even though in the eyes of civilians, the Cats were reduced to bodyguards of those in power with weapons that hadn't been modernized despite long-standing promises, the truth was far from it. Ultra-secret divisions of the NSG were doing work in counter-terrorism that India could not even afford to acknowledge.

He was in that top bracket, the top performer of the decade. Parkour, Pekiti-Tirsia Kali, he was proficient in it all. His juniors had nicknamed him 'superstar', but thankfully, that went out of fashion quickly.

Bani and he were distanced for long periods. Often, he was close but inaccessible behind the ochre and tan walls of the NSG HQ at Manesar.

She had started working in R&D in her father's manufacturing company that produced contact lens solution. They got along well with each other's families. Staying at one home or the other was common. Getting married was a mere convenience so that she could stay with him at base. Commuting to her lab in Gurgaon was now easier than the drive from Greater Kailash-II. It had been over three years since then and Vikram – now involved in almost-routine sorties given the sudden spike in militancy and border skirmishes in the last two years – for the first time was regularly in the line of fire. Bani knew that such scenarios were bound to crop up, but her husband was ever-willing to lead the charge, always putting the lives of others ahead of his, always first on the frontlines. Each deployment made Bani stronger, but it was never easier.

"Yes, I could've given any of them a chance," responded Vikram, "but how many are getting to go home with you?

You win some, you lose some."

"Hah. Sure you're driving home with me, but there are at least twenty people waiting there for you. The folks and some long-lost chacha or mama have dropped in too from Bikaner, with family."

The car screeched to a near halt and then Vikram swerved it around. Gears shifted, he zoomed back towards the airport. Bani laughed.

"I knew you'd do that!"

"Call them right now and tell them the flight's landed, I'm not on it, and will be coming in a couple of hours. That you're going to a friend's place nearby and will be back later to pick me up."

"And where are we actually going?"

"It's Gurgaon. We'll find a dhaba… or a mall."

2300 HOURS

Vikram ate sloppily. Bani watched, allowing the imprudence. Often – when he was hungry or the dish was a favourite – he let go off his table etiquette and finesse, entitling the Neanderthal in him to take over. He sat cross-legged on a cot by the unbalanced plastic table; butter dripping from his naan onto him, his hand clumsily shuttling between the plate and his mouth. She had barely started and he seemed to have finished.

"I need a cigarette," he told the waiter who was setting down a finger bowl for him.

"No, you don't," came a sharp reaction from Bani.

"I thought you knew what my day was like. I believe

I've earned it."

It was common practice for his wife to permit him an indulgent smoke once a week or so. But now, he detected a fierce dissent in her tone. The waiter brought him two Marlboros and a matchbox on a quarter plate. Vikram was still not sure what was going on, so he decided to test waters. He picked up one of the sticks.

"Put that right down, Vikram Rathore. You will not light up."

"Hon, you know in my line of work, it's not about longevity..."

"This time it's not about you."

"What do you mean?"

Bani took his hand in hers. She thought about it for a second: this dhaba, with its trucker-sweat fragrance and greasy plastic tablecloths, was as good a place as any. "I'm pregnant."

TUESDAY

16

0830 HOURS

BOBBY felt irritated at having had to dress to the hilt for the breakfast meeting with Lord Cecil. His Canali suit was suffocating him despite the lack of a tie (it was always cravats and pocket squares for him; he could never count on the top buttons of his shirt not popping open mid-sentence) and he had ridden the two-hour distance with the windows down. Now he felt overdressed and out of place on the lawns of the Marquess' estate sitting with the sweaty, pilous 65-year-old who had just returned from his game of tennis. He was dressed in a white, collared shirt and matching shorts. Bobby couldn't help but notice how fitted they were.

The Marquess had simply wiped himself down and started on his scrambled eggs after a courtesy shake of the hand. Bobby, flush from the heat and cantankerous as a result, had skipped his breakfast so as not to be awkward in front of his host. Usually, he followed a routine that went from regimented in the morning to wildly unfettered in the evenings that involved at least a litre of whisky, late-night greasy Mughlai dinners, and a couple of pills to deal with the ensuing acid reflux. So now when the Marquess proffered Bhullar to partake, sliding a basket of assorted bread towards him, he refused and chose instead to pour himself a cup of tea and pick up a biscuit.

"I know Zakharov," started Lord Cecil in his scrapey voice. "I've been to his home in Moscow. Man's got a tank, a T-34 in fact, in his backyard. Oiled and serviced. As if he's going to drive away in that thing one day. Well, he won't get far with the price of fuel these days."

Bobby put his cup down. This was his host putting his clout on display. There was no reason for him to know that he was dealing with Zakharov. He had even deliberately misled Steele – his BMD rep – the evening before, hinting he might be dealing with the Americans or Israelis. He had no information advantage. What he knew, Lord Cecil knew.

"I understand Mikoyan is giving you a deal that we cannot match. But perhaps, I can offer you something else."

Against his good judgment, Bobby blurted, "Sir, I'm through with BMD's cash-and-candy offers. I simply cannot afford to take a chance on a delivery this size."

Cecil's eyes narrowed and his brows bunched up. He flicked his tongue out and his fork clattered to his plate. He was livid in his own noble way. With measured words, each one reflecting anger, he growled, "Mr Bhullar, the last time I met a government-appointed purchasing agent in my home to conduct business was… never. Understand that I've allowed it and made an exception. Don't think for a moment that I am here to ask for alms from someone like you. This is an exchange, a trade. Do you understand?"

An offer that I can't refuse, thought Bobby, stung at the rebuke, suspicious of his motives, and beside himself with curiosity. All at once.

Lord Cecil made the universal gesture to his valet as if asking to get the cheque, which confused Bhullar. Had the old man lost his mind under all the financial pressure he was in and believed he was in some restaurant? Was he to be taken for his word? But the waiter returned with a leather-bound notepad and pen set on a tray.

"Now," said Lord Cecil, his tone softening, scribbling a number on a page, "take this. Sotheby's is having an auction at 3 pm today in London. Bid for it anonymously. It's not an item that will attract much attention. If there is, make sure you outbid the rest. Because for you, it'll be worth everything."

"You're giving me the incentive even before I've agreed to favour you with the contract. You're taking a great chance, Lord Cecil. What is this item?"

But Lord Cecil was already on his feet and said with a defeated smile, "When you know, you will change your mind."

And with that, he walked in the direction of his mansion, leaving Bobby holding the Marquess' crest-embossed note with a four-digit number on it.

17

0600 HOURS

A mujahideen plodded through the pristine snow. He was carrying some sort of package. Vikram strained to have a better look. The man was still far away. The barrel of a Kalashnikov peeked from behind his shoulder. The details on his faded camouflage pants materialized, the shins flecked with snow; they could've been mistaken for socks. Vikram's gaze shifted to his hands. Red. The package was wrapped in red. It didn't have a distinct shape. It was cloth. Vikram knew it from somewhere. The size, the colour. The blood stains… it was the slain girl's abaya. The enemy's breath clouds obscured his face. But Vikram's eyes were locked onto his actions as he threw back the cover. It was a small, naked baby. It was crying. The mujahideen tossed it into the air. Vikram saw its face. A boy. His own. As it careened towards the sky, the terrorist took aim. Vikram launched towards him. A split-second is all he had. Would he pull the trigger first, or would he be able to tackle him in time? Warning alarms and beeps resounded in the white nothingness.

Vikram woke with a start, his arms outstretched as if in mid-flight, clutching a pillow with sweaty palms. His phone rang shrilly but it only seemed so to him. Bani turned over to the other side, in REM sleep. He pulled her towards him, not knowing what to expect. Her face was serene. She was fine. Instinctively, he looked at her belly, sliding his gaze under the blanket he held up. It looked no different from last night.

He answered the incessant, clamorous phone.

"This is Squad Commander Vikram Rathore."

"Sir, this is Lieutenant Sukhbeer Singh from the Rajputana Rifles. Sir, you need to get to Palam by 0645 hours. There's a car waiting for you outside."

Vikram was fully alert, sitting up in bed ramrod straight. "What's happening?"

"Sir, that's all I know."

With not enough time for a geyser to heat the water, Vikram's cold shower had shocked every pore and muscle into action. In fifteen minutes, his mind throwing up a hundred imaginary scenarios, Vikram was in his fatigues and ready to leave. He still had no idea where he was going or for what. He held up Bani's hand. Her eyes flickered open. He told her he would be back soon. He didn't mention that he was heading to the airport. Or volunteer any more information. She didn't seem to want too many answers either.

Outside, an unfamiliar modified Gypsy stood with its windows misting. It was an army car, not from the NSG. He hopped into it and the driver sped away after a quick salute and introduction. But even he had no information for Vikram. He checked a few news sites on his phone. Nothing. It seemed nothing but a calm, peaceful day.

0645 HOURS

The jeep cruised along on the tarmac and made straight for a heli, one of the newer, solid Dhruvs from the army's aviation division. How long was this trip going to be? And where was he going?

He climbed aboard and grabbed the headset that the pilot was pointing to. They exchanged hellos. Looking over, he saw a motorcade of four vehicles approaching. They came around and stopped, a Mercedes closest to the chopper.

From it stepped out JS Garah.

It took a minute for Vikram to register the Chief of Army Staff, even though it had been less than eight hours since he had seen him at the function at the CM's. What was happening? Most soldiers would count themselves lucky to meet the commander-in-chief of the Indian defence forces – a man in charge of 1.2 million troops – while in service. Here he was sharing a ride, meeting him twice in two days.

Garah's posture had authority written all over it. No sooner had he climbed aboard and shaken Vikram's hand than the Dhruv took off and headed southwest.

"Sorry, I woke you up early. It was a bit of a spur-of-the-moment decision to bring you on the mission."

Vikram had to adjust his headset because Garah was yelling unnecessarily to allow for his voice to carry over the din of the rotor blades.

"What's the mission, sir?" Vikram was calm but curious.

"There was a Bollywood star visiting the troops today.

Turns out he has an upset stomach and won't be coming. The men were eager to see him."

It was not uncommon for the army to organize such meet-and-greets. There was an insatiable craze for Hindi movies in the armed forces. Cantonment screening rooms usually hooked up directly to digital distribution receivers so that jawans (and officers and their families) could watch new releases of films simultaneously or even a day before they were released for civilians. These were the only times the strict lines of hierarchy turned somewhat hazy. A subedar could be sitting next to a colonel and hoot and clap during an item song and get away with it entirely.

"How do you feel about Bollywood movies, young man?"

Vikram was caught off guard, "I'm not sure sir, I never quite got into them."

"Do you think it is fair that a supposed movie star cancels a prefixed appointment that would have made the protectors of this nation happy?"

"I don't think so, sir." The question was rhetorical, so Vikram played it safe.

"I'm glad you feel that way. Which is why I am bringing you to them. They should be inspired by real heroes. I need you to give them a pep talk and talk about your missions. The regiment has many men who've not yet faced an enemy. I'd rather they take some inspiration from you than those who sing and dance and make crores for looking good. Don't worry, it's all informal and I have your boss's permission."

"Thank you, sir."

The rest of the flight they were silent. Vikram watched Garah as he brought out his decorations and methodically put them on. Vikram counted no less than seventeen medals amidst the galaxy of commendations. Garah had certainly seen a lot. Vikram tried to think up what he might say to the jawans, but his thoughts kept going back to his nightmare, still crystal clear in his mind. Ninety minutes later, the sand dunes of the Thar came into view. That's when it hit him, they were headed to the army base at Jaisalmer.

18

0900 HOURS

JAVID had taken a state bus and travelled most of the way staring out the frame of his window at the white vista streaked by shifting patterns of chinar trees. Like a stain, the polluting, overcrowded bus sputtered on through the thin layer of unsullied snow. The Kashmiris, nestled in layers, rode without any sign of remonstrance. Only once were they stopped and made to walk in single file across an army checkpost. They were asked to wait unmoving in the open, as snowflakes collected on their shoulders. The bus was swept for subversive activity. As victimized Javid felt during such episodes of harassment, this journey – with his fellow travellers – was always an odd comfort for him.

The bus wound its way to the town where Javid had a few buyers for his produce. There was rampant construction going on, the air burdened with dust and cement. He sought out his destination, a dairy shop in the main market run by an old, enterprising Punjabi businessman. Gulshan Singh had come on his honeymoon in the seventies, and astonished by the sheer beauty of Kashmir, had stayed back and set up shop in Baramulla. Until the late 1980s, his luck was flourishing – he had a network of stores across Kashmir. But the rise of militancy had decimated his business to a single outlet.

Javid was turning the corner when he spotted his son's older friend, Shaukat, smoking at a tea stall. Their eyes met. Shaukat stood up in a reflex action of respect and threw down his cigarette. Javid smiled and indicated for him to wait, and that he would see him in five minutes. Shaukat nodded and sat down with his two companions, who Javid recognized as teachers from a local madrassa.

Gulshan Singh greeted his goat milk supplier with tired eyes and a raspy voice. The variety of his turbans, one hue of the rainbow for each day of the week in his early years were now restricted to gloomy shades. His shop had remained unchanged for two decades. The stainless steel containers for milk and the large brass trays for curd were as shiny as always, but his walls had decayed at a pace invisible to him and his regular customers, much like his smile that was now stockaded by wrinkles.

"Javid sahab, you've been missing. I haven't seen you since Friday." Forty years and he hadn't lost his accent.

"Khurram, my son, is not well. And..." Javid brought out his produce. He didn't need to vocalize the rest of the thought. It was self-explanatory in the amount he had to proffer.

Gulshan Singh looked up with surprise.

"Is this it?"

"For this week, yes. I need to keep some in stock for Khurram."

"But this will hardly be enough for three, maybe four customers."

The shopkeeper weighed the milk and transferred the contents to his drums. Then he took out his creaking, rusting money box and rummaged in it for some currency and coins. Javid acted as if he trusted the amount he pocketed, but attempted a mental calculation. It was less than a hundred rupees.

"Javid bhai, I hope we can have more next time."

"Yes, yes."

Javid's expression betrayed him. Gulshan Singh regretted his reproach.

At the tea stall – an unpainted brick hole in the wall – Shaukat waited for his friend's father on the only bench available. When he spotted him, he reached over and picked up two steaming cups from the counter. Javid gratefully accepted it and took a seat. He looked around. The stall owner had his nose buried in the Urdu newspaper as a folk programme played on the radio. There were no other patrons.

"How is Khurram, chacha?"

"The fever comes and goes."

"Do you have enough medicines? If you want I can ask the hakim to…"

"No, Shaukat. I'll manage."

"Yes, chacha."

"I want to tell you something."

Once again, Javid scanned for flies on the wall.

"Listen Shaukat, I overheard the conversation last evening."

Without missing a beat, Shaukat nodded. "It was tragic. Army bastards. Making a meal of your goat. Stealing from us like that. I assumed they were the ones who confiscated Bholu. I was sure he wasn't lost…"

"You know that's not what I'm referring to." Javid was stern now, losing patience. "Asking him to 'make himself useful' and what not. Now listen to me, Shaukat, listen carefully. I never, ever want you near my son talking about such things… about taking this path. In fact, it would be best you stayed away from him entirely."

He paused. Shaukat had that look of defiance that he had seen on the faces of so many Kashmiri teens in the last thirty years.

"I want him to have a good education. I want him to make something of his life, get out of that village, go out into the world, become a man with a legacy. You must understand this is my dream, like every other parent. I cannot have him join your cause, a cause he doesn't understand yet. I don't want him to throw stones at an enemy that will crush him with their might."

"We don't want him to throw stones. We are past that point in our fight now. There is glory and money in what was being asked of him. And as for not understanding, with all due respect, chacha, that is on you."

Javid ignored the accusation. He did not need this upstart to explain to him how to raise his son. If Shaukat was looking for intent in the man, he was going to get it.

"Now," said Javid treading with care, "keep Khurram out of this. Tell *me* everything. I want to volunteer for whatever it is you are planning with your friends."

19

1020 HOURS

GENERAL Jaswant Singh Garah had seen it all. Son of a farmer, Sainik School, NDA, 4 Corps, IPKF, Sri Lanka, North East, and J&K. In Sri Lanka alone, he had gunned down forty three of the enemy, most of them in a week. He had shown no signs of PTSD unlike most of his colleagues after direct action missions. He told his counsellors that every time he saw a dead man's face, it'd be replaced by the Indian flag, that his patriotic instinct would overshadow any form of guilt. This was not all true. Sure there was a jingoistic streak in him, but no more or less than the next soldier. What Garah lacked was empathy. He even found it mildly thrilling, eliminating targets without repercussions. He kept this from his counsellors, his family, everyone; lest they think him a psychopath. He regarded others as frail and weak. He genuinely believed this trait – this lack of regret and remorse – made him the best man for the job.

Now in the Officers' Hall at one of India's newest and most strategic army bases in Jaisalmer, he sat on the dais watching Vikram fill in the dainty shoes of the diarrhoeal actor. A row of empty chairs looped around him, the jawans giving him space and clear line of sight in an otherwise packed room. A Q&A session of this kind was rare. This sort of interaction between the NSG and the army was possibly taking place for the first time. Rathore didn't look uncomfortable – his Hindi was fluent and he didn't seem to suffer from any kind of stage fright. But perhaps it was a little unfair, thought Garah, to thrust him into this situation unprepared. As expected, most of the questions were met with the same answer.

"Were you present at 26/11? Where else have you been?"

"Sorry, I can't disclose any of the locations I've been activated in."

"What's the physical training cycle like?"

"Fourteen months. First three, basic. Followed by extensive training for stamina, strength, agility. Towards the end some martial arts. The rest is classified."

"What are the guns you've been using?"

"Mauser, SIG, Beretta, more recently post 26/11, CornerShot Glock. There's a speculative list on Wikipedia which may or may not be true."

A tittering went around the room. The jawans were being good sports. Garah sensed that despite the disappointment of not being able to meet the Bollywood hero they had been promised, the inadequate answers to the questions they asked, and the strange reality of having an NSG SAG soldier addressing them, they were not dispirited. Certainly a lot could be attributed to his presence, but vanity was not a problem Garah ever suffered from. As for Rathore, the more he saw of him, the more Garah was impressed. He had the skills, he had the composure. Garah was convinced Rathore was his man for the job.

1130 HOURS

Garah and Vikram sat across from each other in the Commanding Officer's private office, sipping milky tea. Garah too had given a short, prepared speech and was showered with applause and appreciation. But that was not what he was looking for.

"Good talk, Rathore."

"Thank you, sir."

"You could've been more forthcoming with some of the info they wanted. We're all on the same side."

Vikram considered his response, "If I had my way, I'd tell them everything. But there's a code in place, an oath I've taken. And the powers that be must have thought through their reasons."

"I like your discipline. Let me tell you a small story. In 1965," he said, finishing his tea and settling into his chair, "during the war against Pakistan, an Indian brigadier... along this border, not hundred miles from here, made a deal with a senior Pakistani army chief. For ₹20,000 he sold the country's battle plans to the enemy. And you know why? Why he needed the money?"

Vikram looked up curiously.

"His wife. His crazy wife had a home business that needed seed capital."

"What was it?"

"Selling canned fruits and vegetables."

Vikram smiled, but he quickly realized that this was not some historical army tale that Garah was narrating for fun. There was relevance in it yet.

"20,000! The war cost India so much more!"

"Money?" asked Vikram, tentative.

"Lives, Rathore, lives. It is the same story with every war. Compromises lead to lost lives."

"Surely this sort of thing doesn't happen anymore."

"No, you're right. We may not be selling plans for money, but politicians can be a fickle lot. Half-baked diplomacy leads to fucked-up decisions. Who knows how much influence their wives have over these lunatics?"

Vikram found Garah's rancour for the same people he was idling with at the cocktail party only last night rather jarring.

"Our jawans at the battlefront, on Siachen, in Thar," continued Garah, his anger intensifying. "Civilians, never helping. Would Kargil have happened if the civilians spoke up? We lost double the numbers compared to Pakistan. Double! A hollow victory, only completed by international pressure. We had options. We could've wreaked havoc in enemy territory, decimated it, reclaimed PoK. It was there for the taking! We chose not to. Nuclear threat, they said. All a bluff. They had nothing! We should have called it."

While it was no secret that soldiers had nothing but disdain for a country's foes, for a man in his position to be spewing such venom… he would be skewered if his ideas were made public.

"But finally. Finally, our policy makers are willing to take a risk like they haven't since Pokhran in '98. To bring back glory."

Vikram didn't doubt that given his momentum, Garah would have no hesitation spilling what was now beginning to sound like a state secret. But he also sensed that his Jaisalmer sortie wasn't a mere friendly appearance. And that Garah had grander, more sinister plans for him.

"It starts with one small step and will culminate in what will be a pushback for the ages. So tell me Rathore, are you ready to serve the country? To stand up for all that you believe in, to take the glorious path?"

The moment had arrived. Vikram went with his instinct and stood up from his chair, and whipped his hand up to his forehead, saluting his superior.

"Sir, yes, sir!"

"You are to leave for Pakistan immediately. You will be travelling undercover, as a member of the press delegation going to Islamabad to cover the summit in Uri from the Pakistani perspective. Mission details and relevant papers you will find in here."

Garah put a Pelican case on the table and pushed it towards Vikram.

"And the mission, sir?"

"Assassinate the Pakistani Minister of Foreign Affairs."

20

1010 HOURS

BOBBY Bhullar hadn't waited to get back to his hotel. While still in his car, he opened up his laptop and fired up Tor, the anonymous browser he used often to track illegal weapons sales trends across the globe. He searched for the lot number on the Sotheby's website, locating it easily. The item was a framed painting mounted on canvas, a creative representation of flora and fauna in the Sunderbans by an obscure Bengali artist of whom Bobby had never heard. He googled the artist as well, but couldn't find a significant connection. The painting itself – bundled under the day's auction of 'Asian Masters' and in the company of the likes of FN Souza and Yayoi Kusama – was one of the least expensive. Still at a range of $100,000-$200,000 it was steep by any standard and when Bobby realized he would have to pay for it with his own dime he grunted in annoyance; Cecil had made no mention of any reimbursement and Steele would be at sea.

Back in his hotel room, he logged on to the site and set up a bank account. He called his secretary, Bhushan (the balding ex-IAS officer inherited from Bhullar Sr, a man who still preferred to wear Safari suits like his earlier boss) in Delhi to transfer $300,000 to the new temporary account that was to be cleared and terminated by 3 pm.

At noon, with his curiosity peaking, Bobby was in front of his computer live-streaming the auction. The hypnotizing voice of the auctioneer had him hooked as the hammer was brought down on paintings sold one after the other. Bobby noted that there was no media present. When the canvas of interest was brought out, the auctioneer carried on with level enthusiasm, talking more about the painting and its subject than the artist ("The Sunderbans in the early twentieth century, a rare sight captured in the manner of the great post-impressionists…")

Bobby waited after the suggested opening bid was announced to spot any interest. It took half a minute, but a paddle shot up. Mildly panicking, Bobby moved fast and clicked to up the amount by $5,000, the minimum. After some deliberation – the auctioneer frozen in mid-air as if in the midst of a B-boy step – then the only other bidder raised it again. Bhullar, more coolly now, realizing there were only the two of them in the fray, clicked to bring the amount to $115,000.

"Everyone done in the room? Last chance." Pause. "I'm going to sell it." Very long pause, arms raised, the tiny hammer held delicately in his fingers. "For $115,000 to the anonymous bidder online… Sold!"

21

1430 HOURS

WHY had Vikram agreed to this mission? Could he have said no and walked away? Retracing the exchange, he marvelled at how Garah had spelled out what the assignment was, *after* he had gotten Vikram to sympathize with that patriotic outpouring. It all seemed a well-rehearsed sales pitch. And Vikram had gone along. He had no doubt that the order had come from the top and that this was a political manoeuvre, as all assassinations were. And then there was the matter of the treaty. Weren't the two countries burning the midnight oil to broker a demilitarization deal? Wouldn't this move be counterproductive and set back the process possibly by years, if not reverse it all the way? Or was the MFA getting in the way of peace and this sacrifice was imperative for the greater good? Certainly there was no indication in the media of such opposition.

Also, why pick an NSG commando? There were never any NSG deputations on foreign soil. This was a pursuit for the RAW. Vikram had an inkling, a theory. He was amongst the best trained soldiers in the country. And because of his recent success in Srinagar, and the subsequent meeting with the top brass at the CM's residence, he had become a natural candidate. It didn't matter what agency he worked for. And the Chief of Army Staff had complete discretion in such matters. He had special powers; it would take him a minute to have the RAW commission Vikram. If he couldn't do it, the prime minister could step in. And who refuses the CoAS? This man was next in line to be the supreme commander of the Indian Armed Forces when he took over as Chairman of the Chiefs of Staff Committee. The rigidity of order simply did not permit turndowns.

Sales pitch or not, Vikram never had a choice.

And so he now found himself in the business lounge at the Indira Gandhi International Airport once again, waiting for what would be his sixth flight in slightly over a day, if you counted the helicopter sortie from Srinagar airport to ground zero. He was fast-roping through the air in full combat gear then. But this time, he had a boarding pass and a duffel as he waited for his PIA flight. The case he had been handed over by Garah included an Indian passport – it had a picture of him, but under the name of Amit Sharma – a burner phone, some currency, and documents that validated his credentials as a reporter. The actual press delegation had left last evening, which was a blessing. An unfamiliar face amidst them would have raised eyebrows.

The flight to Islamabad, despite it being under 700 km away from Delhi, was over five hours with a layover and change of plane in Karachi. Vikram tried to relax; his earphones delivering a medley of classic rock to soothe his mind.

Back from Jaisalmer, he had returned home. Bani was out, running errands. He had put on the plainest full-sleeve shirt he could find and packed two changes of clothes. He emptied the contents of the Pelican case into his nondescript duffel bag and left all his other personal effects – wallet, phone – behind. The waiting army car dropped him off at the airport. Vikram was almost relieved he didn't have to explain this departure to his wife. He knew he wouldn't be able to clarify any of this to her. He'd call her from the airport, he told himself. He'd tell her he was out on a mission and would be back soon (*How soon?* he groped for an answer.) and they'd take a long break together, maybe celebrate a babymoon. He walked up to the payphone. But he never picked it up. Vikram just couldn't get himself to talk to his partner.

1605 HOURS

At Karachi's Jinnah International Airport, after much internal debate, Vikram bought a packet of cigarettes from the duty-free store and retreated to the cramped smoking lounge, standing in a far corner, one eye alert. He lit a stick and took a tentative drag. Bani would have thoroughly disapproved. But this one was easy to justify.

Outside the window, he studied the airport's structure, familiar to him from the Taliban attack in June 2014. Pakistani news agencies had scrambled initially to blame India and the RAW. But the Pakistani government had been exemplary in not giving any credence to unconfirmed reports. Soon, Uzbek militants and the Taliban claimed it. Vikram considered the media eyewash – just how susceptible were common folk to propaganda? How much of it were they subject to in India? And the RAW suicide-bombing the Karachi airport? He scoffed at the idea. And yet – a wall of pragmatic reality enveloped him – here he was on a mission that would change the course of history between the two nations.

Why him? His recruitment for the mission was most unorthodox. From stand-in for a film star to a covert mission operative in a matter of minutes – why did Garah spring this ruse? Why the trip to Jaisalmer? His documents had already been readied; they could've been handed over in Delhi. Why a counter-terrorism commando for the job? This was clearly RAW's realm. He would solve this once he was back; he would ask Garah himself.

1945 HOURS

Touchdown at Benazir Bhutto Islamabad International Airport. Vikram's turn at passport control was three people away. For the first time he felt nervous. Would they stop him? He had his backstory memorized, but an Indian passport holder in Pakistan was certainly going to be under close scrutiny. He looked around, trying to spot other Indians in the many queues. There was no way to tell.

Vikram handed over his documents to the moustachioed man in uniform at the counter. He reached for it lazily, but was jolted into an alert state when he looked at the blue cover. Suddenly, his movements were purposeful. He looked at Vikram squarely in the face, longer than was comfortable. Next, he held the booklet under a UV light. His eyebrows arched, he shook his head. He picked up a phone and had a quick whispered conversation that Vikram couldn't overhear. He put down the receiver and went over the passport, page by page. Vikram was about to interrupt and ask if everything was in order, when a man in civilian clothes showed up, took the passport from the moustachioed man and walked away, disappearing behind a door.

"Come with me," said the officer in throaty Urdu. He put a 'closed' sign on his counter. The large family behind Vikram let out a huge groan. Pushing his chair back into place – a sign that indicated that he wasn't going to be back in a hurry – he gestured to Vikram to follow him. A man from airport security discreetly brought up the rear.

He was ushered into a featureless, tiny room with a table and a single chair that the immigration officer appropriated and then proceeded to light a cigarette. Vikram was trying to work out what could have gone wrong. Was the passport a rushed job? A tacky forgery? Did the government assign someone incompetent who compromised this most basic task? This was not supposed to happen.

"Who are you?"

"Amit Sharma. I am a journalist."

"I'll ask you again. Who are you?"

"Sir, is this necessary? I am part of the press delegation covering the summit meeting."

"Why are you not travelling with the other members of this delegation, especially when there was a designated flight arranged for this delegation? We have not got any forward information of a straggler."

"Sir, I was on an assignment and reached Delhi only this morning. If you'll check my papers, I have the necessary permissions from the ministry. They should've forwarded it to you."

The officer took a long drag from his cigarette and let out the smoke, clouding the unventilated room. All part of the play. Unnerving the suspect. Muslims all over the world were humiliated at airports. This was his personal payback. Vikram hoped he was right and there was nothing more to it.

A knock on the door. It was the man in civilian clothes. The moustachioed officer crushed the cigarette on the floor and walked out. "Stay here," he said.

A minute, two minutes. The door flew open. The two men trooped in.

"Fine. Go."

Vikram was handed his papers back. He picked up his duffel bag and with calm, measured steps, proceeded out of the room, past immigration, and through the sliding doors of the airport into the cool, cacophonous Islamabad evening.

22

1500 HOURS

BOBBY had been pacing his room not knowing what to do. His mind was scrambling to make sense of what was happening, of what secret a painting might hold that would affect a multi-million-dollar international arms bid. He had finished half a bottle of whisky in between all this thinking and walking around the suite.

The package finally arrived – via the auction house's discreet courier service – exactly two hours later. Bobby ripped open the box and propped up the frame on his desk. He switched on every light in the room and stared at it. What on earth was its significance? He poured himself another glass of Scotch.

Fifteen minutes passed and Bobby was beginning to believe this was some kind of joke. He had examined every square inch of the artwork, looked for patterns, codes. He had nothing. He considered booking a ticket to Moscow right away. What a bloody waste of time.

His phone beeped. Text message. Truecaller identified the contact as 'Yorky', Lord Cecil's well-known nickname.

Open it.

Bobby flung the phone on the bed. He held up the painting gingerly, turning it in various angles. Despite the instruction, he didn't want to rip apart something he had spent a small fortune on only a couple of hours ago. It went against everything he had been taught as a child growing up in a middle-class Sikh home.

He went to work on the frame instead. It was thick enough for him to try to wedge a blade from his Swiss knife into it and work it top down till it began to split. He held it apart and shook the canvas. Out popped a manila envelope that fell on the carpet.

Bobby picked it up, broke open the seal and scanned its contents. He had barely got past the first few words when his hands began to tremble.

23

2050 HOURS

VIKRAM checked into what was the fanciest hotel in the city, the Serena, on the Khayaban-e-Suhrawardy. The media delegation had split up on the basis of the budgets they had; only a handful of the big names lodged there. His ride from the airport had been an eye-opener. By every account, Islamabad looked like a beautiful, well-planned city. Not that it was shorn of crime or poverty, but any eyesore had been pushed to the fringes. The morning would bring the alluring Margalla Hills of the north into view.

In the reception, Vikram watched carefully as he was handed over his key card. He got a sense that his room had been pre-assigned and this thought gnawed at him. The moment he was ushered in by the bellboy, he shut the door of the second floor room behind him and got to work right away, checking to see if there were any recording devices present.

He scanned the room – every crevice, every corner – with his eyes and then walked with his ears tuned to pick out any noise – any whirr, click, or buzz – that a motion-detecting camera might make. Next, he switched off the lights and looked for any LED source that a bugging device might have. Still nothing. He fished out a torch from his bag and shone the light into every square inch of every mirror to check for a one-way-glass. Satisfied and certain there were no bugs in the room, he switched on the TV for some ambient noise and sat down. Geo News was reporting intelligence on a Taliban threat to the police and military establishments. Vikram paid no attention to it.

It had been months since he had participated in any field action when he had awakened on Sunday and kissed his wife good morning; a day like any other. And then the summons to Srinagar, and now – not sixty hours later – he was in the very heart of enemy territory, disguised as a civilian and sitting on a very comfortable couch.

Vikram's stomach growled. The prudent move would be to pick up the phone, dial room service, and order in. He had to meet Jamal, the RAW contact, at 2230.

But there was an easy argument to be made for stepping out; understanding the lay of the land, getting a sense of the conditions, and to sample the much-talked-about Pakistani cuisine. Could they better his butter chicken? He had to find out.

A quick shower and change; Vikram wore a grey shirt and jeans. He stood in front of the mirror considering what to do with his face to help him stay unrecognizable. Inspiration came to him from the classic superhero trick. He changed the parting of his hair to the right. Studies had shown that the way you parted your hair was enough to change your personality and the way people perceived you entirely. Clark Kent did it. JFK did it. It had worked for both of them.

The hallway was empty. The lush carpet allowed him to walk up to the elevator without making a sound. A single button to summon all the available cars. He pressed it.

The closest one was a few floors above. He watched the number count down to 2; the ding of the doors opening; the presence of people inside.

Two heavyset men with walkie-talkies and a dour demeanour scrutinized Vikram as he stepped inside. Bodyguards, he inferred. The Serena was the capital's premier hotel, so it wasn't an unexpected sight. They rode the elevator in silence.

Downstairs, he asked the concierge to organize a taxi.

"It'll be five minutes. Do you want to wait in the lobby?"

"Where can I smoke?"

"You'll have to step outside, sir; the hotel has a strict no-smoking policy in all areas. You could smoke while you wait for your cab."

"Okay."

Vikram walked past the high, grand arches of the lobby and stepped out into the driveway. The air was crisp and cold, the temperature having fallen sharply since he had arrived. He spotted a floor ashtray on the side, where a couple of men stood enveloped in their own personal fogs.

He walked up to them, pulling out his pack from his pocket. Then as he got closer and the faces of the smokers became more discernible, Vikram's blood turned to ice. Right in the centre, nonchalantly scrolling his phone, flanked by unmistakeable ISI agents, was the Pakistani MFA, Mohammed al-Bashir, his assassination target.

24

1715 HOURS

BOBBY had a few phonecalls to make.

First, he dialled Steele. "Let's meet at 10 am in my hotel room." He hung up, not waiting for a reply.

It was the next call that he had to make that was bothering him.

Zakharov.

As he dialled him on video conference, he took a breath to steady his nerves. All this has to be, he told himself, is mere courtesy. There was no obligation, no moral imperative. And yet he felt apprehensive turning down the Russians.

"Karol. I'm sorry, we cannot go ahead with this deal right now."

"Motherfucker. How much did they bribe you?"

"It's just a better deal..."

"Liar... liar!"

"I'll call you, Karol, for the next round. This one is closed."

Rage shadowed Zakharov's features. "I'll sic the Scorpions on you!"

"Listen..."

"Fuck this, you fuckin' towelhead. You're not getting away–"

The audio and visual went off, replaced by the app's icon. Bobby figured he must have slammed his screen shut.

"Fuck!" Fuck him, thought Bobby. The mechanics of making the deal seemed legit and convincing was routine for Bhullar. No arms company worked in all-white cash. The Scorpions would have no angle if *both* governments were party to this.

He realized he was shaking after the call. An inner voice told him that the envelope and its contents weren't safe with him. He could have junked the painting, but he picked up the hotel phone and dialled the concierge, telling her he needed to ship a valuable canvas to his office in Delhi. Thirty minutes later, he had signed documents and paid in cash to the logistics company specializing in high-value and fine art shipments.

He made one more call to his secretary Bhushan: Expect a package. Keep it safe. Book me a flight out of Heathrow tomorrow evening.

He was covered in sweat. The winter sun had arced behind the London skyline. He retreated to the bar, but couldn't find the last bottle he had uncorked and the decanter was empty. He picked out a new single malt and struggled to open it. When he finally managed, he didn't bother with a glass. The room shrank with every gulp. He felt claustrophobic. He stood looking out the window and had a sudden craving for the chill on his face. Not used to such breakneck action, the events of the last few hours had him spent. He needed to get out. Yes, a meal at that trendy new Indian restaurant that his colleagues in Delhi had been on about would settle his nerves. He texted Bhushan to make a reservation and send him the coordinates. Putting on his sneakers and a heavy jacket,

Bobby left his room.

Exiting the hotel's monumental revolving doors and stepping on to the street, he felt better straightaway. But no sooner had he taken a few steps, than he was tempted to take a taxi. He had forgotten how much he hated walking. Or any physical activity, really. But there weren't any cabs around, so he ambled along the route flashing on his GPS.

Ten minutes later, the path cut across a park. Running out of breath, his back aching, Bobby veered towards a bench to take a break. He had barely leaned back and looked around when he spotted two mountainous men on the same isolated track. He was surprised that he hadn't heard them.

The two walked up to the bench and sat on either side. Bhullar was palpitating. He could smell their proximity. It was a squeeze, their shoulders rubbing against his. Their short-cropped hair and tight army-issue jackets focusing attention on their menacing, muscular bodies. One of them said a word in Russian and in that moment Bobby knew exactly who they were: Zakharov's contacts, members of the Russia's London mafia. He made as if to get up, but was pushed back down. An indistinct scream left his lips.

"BMD bribe… Where?"

Bobby Bhullar, whose pain-threshold gave way at the mere sight of blood; whose sense of adventure was mislaid; whose hero quotient was zero, would not have hesitated to volunteer everything he knew. But the Russians did not know this. One of them had pulled out an AF-1 pistol from his pocket and placed the barrel on Bobby's head.

His eyes glazed over. His body went limp.

Talking to each other in rapid Russian, one of them slapped him a few times across his face to wake him up. The other, observing no reaction, held up his hand to stop the assault. He looked at his partner with disgust.

"He's dead," said the man, holding up Bobby's wrist.

25

2130 HOURS

THOUGH his heart was pounding, Vikram recovered quickly. Walking a couple of steps past the MFA and his men, he claimed a position on the opposite side of the ashtray. As he lit his cigarette and turned away, he stole a glance at the minister. There was no acknowledgement necessary since his future target wasn't looking up from his mobile screen. The politician's over-sprayed cologne saturated his senses.

Then he felt the hairs on the back of his neck rise. The MFA had suddenly lost interest in his phone and was now studying him. A low rumble of a voice broke the desperate silence.

"You are Indian, no?" asked al-Bashir.

Vikram gave it a second before turning around, as if to give the impression that he had only realized a little late that he was the addressee. He looked him squarely in the eyes and nodded with what he hoped was a perplexed expression.

"I can smell Indians a mile off. What are you doing here?"

"I am a journalist."

"Ah, to cover the summit?"

"Yes, sir."

"First time in Pakistan?"

"Yes."

"Funny. First time I've met an Indian journalist and I'm the one asking all the questions."

"Sorry sir, didn't recognize you there for a minute."

"You're not a very good journalist then."

Vikram smiled at the irony of it.

"Take care," said Mohammed al-Bashir stubbing out his cigarette. The minister and his security detail swiftly turned and walked back into the hotel. Vikram stood for a second, watching him and making mental notes about the MFA's physical attributes, before realizing his taxi had arrived.

26

1840 HOURS

ADITI stepped outside the Bull and Boar pub in Shepherd's Bush. She took a long drag on her friend's e-cigarette and watched it crystallize like a cloud over her head. Her plane had touched down at Heathrow only four hours ago, and Kirti, her best friend since high school, was waiting to pick her up. On Aditi's insistence, they had headed straight to the local pub next to Kirti's house, bags still in the car.

Two pints of Guinness and several rapid-fire exchanges later, Kirti, who had been trying to give up smoking (since college, Aditi reminded her), brought out her gadgety USB-charged e-cigarette and asked Aditi if she would like to give vaping a try.

The sun had long set. As she buttoned up her coat, Aditi's phone buzzed.

"Who is it?" asked Kirti.

"Soumik."

"Ignore him."

"I don't think he remembers I've left. He's probably calling out of habit. Hello? Soumik, I'm in London."

At this point, Aditi realized it must be well past 10 pm in Delhi and Soumik rarely called this late. He was a family man now, and his kids were a big priority.

"Wait," she was concerned now, "is everything okay?"

"Yes, yes. It's just that there is serendipitous – er – news."

"What happened?"

"A major Indian arms dealer has been found dead in London. There's all sorts of conspiracy theories coming out of Raisina. You know what would be great?"

"Don't even suggest it, Soumik… I just got here…"

"There's a stringer waiting at–"

27

1440 HOURS

JAVID promised Khurram he would return within the hour.

"Try to sleep," he said. "I'll be back before you wake up."

As he closed the door behind him, Javid heard his son erupt into a ferocious cough. He considered abandoning his little foray and staying with Khurram, but given the tight time frame, another opportunity would be unlikely. So Javid walked away from the wheezing boy with a leaden heart.

He strode down the main road and cut across a sterile piece of land that once was a saffron field. Every time he passed through it, he imagined he could smell a lingering redolence of the maroon and purple flowers in bloom, despite the fact that it had been over a decade since anything had grown here.

He caught a narrow path that was the shortest route to the next village and soldiered on at a rapid pace, belaying his tormented thoughts.

Shaukat had not revealed much, but it was enough to convince Javid that Khurram's future was no longer viable in the village. When Javid volunteered, Shaukat was nonplussed at first. But after a few calls he seemed pleased to have him take Khurram's place. Javid was convinced they'd be back for Khurram later. The boy was still impressionable. And there would always be reasons for young men to be angry. If not now, they would recruit him eventually; maybe a month, maybe a year later. Insurgency or freedom struggle, however you looked at it, both needed cannon fodder.

No, Kashmir could no longer be Khurram's home. It distressed him to do what he was about to, but it was also surprising for him how quick and natural the process of making up his mind had been. As of this moment, he knew his son would resent, even hate him for it.

Javid retracted his arms under his worn pheran and folded them as a wind kicked up. The afternoon sun was now veiled by an endless blanket of clouds. The path joined the main road once more and snaked through the small village. Small groups of people sat outside open shops, smoking and chatting.

Javid soon reached his destination.

Lotus Cyber Café was a cubby hole of a set-up, with all of two ageing computers. It was one of the few places in Uri district that offered Internet access, popular amongst teenagers living in nearby settlements. They also had a private phone booth with STD, in which Javid now enclosed himself.

He fished out his weather-beaten pocket diary that he had carried with him from home and turned its pages, looking for the Delhi number noted down in it over a decade ago. He punched in the digits and braced himself as the phone rang.

"Hello," a young boy's voice answered.

"Salaam aleikum, son. Is your father home?"

"Who are you?"

It took Javid a couple of seconds to recall what his relationship with this child could be.

"I'm… your petir." He wondered if the boy's Kashmiri was poor, given his Delhi education, so he gave him a Hindi alternative, "Tell him it's Javid chacha. Your uncle from the village."

He heard the boy shout his name, followed by scuffling footsteps.

"Hello… who's this?" The grown-up voice now.

"Shamsherbhai, this is Javid. From Kashmir… from the village." Javid replied with hesitation, unsure how to introduce himself.

A pause. It had been years since they'd even heard each other's voices. Their fathers had been partners in a timber business, and their families had been very close growing up in the valley together. Shamsher's father had moved to Delhi after '89, he had seen the future, not the mess that Kashmir would find itself in, but simply a future that was unfavourable for business. They'd met at a wedding in the valley after that, but the friendship had not lasted the distance. Still, he was the only contact Javid had in a big city.

"Oh, Javid. How are you?" he inquired, his tone formal.

"I'm fine. It's Khurram. My boy. I need your help."

"Oh… I see. I'm actually a little busy right now, so maybe you can call later and we can talk–"

Before he could continue, Javid quickly interrupted, "I'm sorry Shamsherbhai, but I don't have time. I am sending Khurram to Delhi in a few days' time with your address. Please take him in. Your father has always been kind to me and my family, and I am requesting your help now for Khurram."

"What do you mean? Is he coming for a holiday? How long is he going to stay?"

"No brother, not a holiday. I want you… to take him in."

"What? I don't understand! You can't just send your son here. How can you expect me…"

Javid cut him off again, entirely prepared for this agitated reaction. Pulling out his trump, he said, "He will have ten lakhs with him. I request you to keep the money, as it will be of no use to me. Whatever you give him in your house will be sufficient. I am sure you will take good care of him."

Silence. Then, his tone softening, Shamsher asked, "What is the meaning of all this? Why are you sending him away? Are you okay?"

"I'm fine. I have urgent work and I have to be away for some time. I can't take Khurram with me, and I can't leave him in the village. The money…" he emphasized the amount once more, "ten lakhs, I think will be enough to put him in a good school. I would like him to grow up in the city. Just like your father decided with you. He was a wise man. I want the same for Khurram. I hope you understand that."

Silence again. Javid knew Shamsher was weighing the pros and cons.

"But when will you be back? What should I tell him if–"

That was all the confirmation Javid needed as he cut him off one last time, hanging up the phone.

It wasn't the best of plans, but there was no one else he could turn to for getting Khurram out of Kashmir. He didn't know when he was coming back. It's not as if he had volunteered for a desk job. He needed a guardian for the boy, even if it meant spending every last rupee he was getting in return.

He tried to ignore the growing darkness in his heart that seemed to be getting heavier with every footstep. He couldn't shake off the thought that had been eating him up ever since his conversation with Shaukat: in trying to protect his son's future, he was abdicating all responsibility towards it.

Forgive me and my helplessness, Khurram, he thought to himself, as he made his way back home, hoping that one day when he grew up, the boy would understand and forgive him. Perhaps, even thank him.

28

1935 HOURS

PADDINGTON Station was adjacent to St Mary's Hospital. Aditi got off with her borrowed Oyster pass and was about to call the stringer's number when she spotted him at the Praed Street exit, fiddling with his camera.

"Riaz?"

The young, gawky Pakistani looked up somewhat in awe.

"Yes, ma'am."

"Lead the way."

The Victorian building housing the famous hospital was visible as they turned the corner and they wasted no time in locating the entrance of the trauma centre. Predictably, a policeman was posted outside. Riaz watched Aditi as she confidently walked up to him and had a quick word. All he did was nod and she gestured for Riaz to start rolling and come in closer.

"Bobby Bhullar was found on a bench in Green Park. The likely cause of death is severe cardiac arrest. He was dead upon arrival. We are waiting for formalities to be completed. His family has been informed."

"Is this case closed or is there a possibility of foul play that Scotland Yard would like to look into?" She turned to the policeman as Riaz stepped back to frame him in.

"This case is closed, ma'am. Scotland Yard does not believe there is any foul play involved. Mr Bhullar's family has confirmed cardiac episodes in the past."

Aditi had no chance to check her sources on the conspiracy theories Soumik had been talking about while on the underground. There were no leading questions she could ask. But the way Soumik had said the words 'found dead' had stuck. Not for a moment had Aditi thought of anything but murder. The image her mind had conjured up refused to acknowledge what the police were saying, a heart attack. Soumik would be content with the provident opportunity that *Capital* would be the first to break the news with his star reporter anchoring. But Aditi decided to dig deeper.

She had already completed her piece-to-camera when two more reporters – harried and clueless – showed up. However reluctant she had been when she acquiesced to her editor's request, now that she had a head start, she was going to make the most of it.

Aditi instructed Riaz to upload the clips to the *Capital News* server and told him they were done here. She called Soumik and told him as much.

She needed to know more, why he was here, what he was doing. She got on Facebook and looked for Bobby Bhullar. Many of his posts were open to the public (*so much for security, and to think he was an arms dealer*, she thought.) And though most of them were benign status updates on nationalist opinions (cricket! Down with vulgar videos!), there was a picture captioned 'view from hotel in london', from six months ago. It wasn't the most dramatic view, not from very high up and yet overlooking a park and some hotels. Like most affluent people, he would've developed a preference over time and there was every chance he stayed at the same hotel during every visit.

It took her all of five minutes: image search, reverse image search, putting it in the vicinity of the park Bhullar was traversing at the time to realize it was 'The Lanesborough'. She broke into a jog across Hyde Park (she was still in her favourite travel shoes) and this workout washed away the last of the tipsiness before she reached the hotel.

No cops, no media. She heaved a sigh of relief as she caught her breath. She put on Kirti's baseball cap that she had borrowed before leaving.

Then she casually walked up to the reception.

"I'm waiting for a Mr Bhullar, he hasn't shown up yet. Is there any way you can call and check?"

She hoped the news hadn't reached the receptionists.

"Sure. Who did you say?"

"B-H-U-L-L-A-R."

The young woman in her spotless clothes looked up the number and made the call.

"Sorry, no answer. He must be on his way."

"No problem, I'll wait outside."

Aditi had noted the room number and she confidently walked away, but veered towards the elevators.

The fourth-floor corridor was empty. Aditi walked past twenty doors, noticing only one CCTV camera at the far end. The cap should take care of things, if it came to that. She turned a right angle and spotted what she was looking for: an open room and a housekeeping cart. There was little chance of stealing the master key from the cleaning lady. So she had to fall back on an old trick she hated: acting drunk.

She tapped the stout housekeeper who was vacuuming

the room with her headphones on. As she turned around and her sour face came into view, Aditi flashed her widest bacchanalian smile.

The housekeeper asked what she wanted. Aditi assumed this is what she said, as she couldn't put a finger on the East European language she was being addressed in. And just to make it even more confusing, she responded in Hindi saying she had lost her key and needed her door open.

"Lobby, key. Lobby," said the housekeeper, trying to meet her halfway in broken English and pointing down the floor.

Aditi frowned, and swayed as if about to lose balance any second. She had the option to beg, but she decided to go with the spoilt-rich-kid play. She course-corrected her body language accordingly and introduced an icy edge to her words.

"Come, now." She waved her hand, beckoning, turned and stomped towards Bhullar's door. She crossed her fingers, hoping the housekeeper was following. She was on bonus time until the police arrived. And she had to get into Bhullar's room before that.

29

2225 HOURS

WHEN Vikram reached the rendezvous point, it struck him as a counterintuitive choice for a clandestine meeting with a RAW agent. He had called the number at 10 o'clock from a payphone – as Garah had instructed. And once he had said who he was, there was a terse reply asking him to meet here: a massive, bustling sheesha bar named Sultan, not very far from his hotel, in the heart of the diplomatic area.

"Amit Sharma?" Vikram turned around and faced a tall, wiry man in an oversized shirt and glasses. His skin was taut all around his face, eyes deep in their sockets, veins trying to break through skin. Vikram nodded.

"Jamal." He shook his hand and smiled, "You got cash for this joint?"

A strange question, thought Vikram, nodding again. Jamal cocked his head towards the entrance and led the way with long, spasmodic strides. Once inside, it became apparent to Vikram why Sultan was a good place for a clandestine conversation.

It was designed to resemble an underground cave network. What an anthill might look like from the inside. Alcoves carved out in varied sizes accommodated groups of people on colourful mattresses and large cushions, as they pulled on gurgling sheesha and enjoyed kabab skewers in relative seclusion.

Jamal went up a winding staircase and found them a cavity carved into the wall, spacious enough for a private two-person seating area. A waiter arrived promptly.

"Vegetarian?" Jamal asked Vikram.

"No."

"Praise the lord."

He ordered a sheesha and some food, speaking only once the waiter had left.

"Sorry, I hope this is not coming across as bizarre and hollow. I don't get a decent meal too often. It's only when there are visitors like you and they are few and far in between."

"What's your cover?" Vikram prodded in the best Urdu that he could muster to match Jamal's fluency; he still didn't have a measure of the man.

"I run a small electronics store," he said, and then laughed. "Well, a really small one, yes. The roadside variety. My top seller is a beard trimmer. Made in China, like everything else."

"Are you running any undercover ops? You don't have to give me any details…" said Vikram, lowering his voice.

"What's that? I can't hear you. You can speak up, it's safe. Only expat kids and yuppies here, the type who get their news about Pakistan from CNN and BBC."

"I asked if you're running any ops, and that you don't have to tell me if you don't want to."

"Are you crazy? There are no ops on in Pakistan." He thought about this for a second. "At least as far I know. If you really care, I got here in '95 as part of CIT-X…" Jamal let that sink in.

Counter Intelligence Team-X was a RAW programme

started in the sixties with deep undercover units comprising not only spies but primarily saboteurs who undertook retaliatory strikes within Pakistan, stirring insurgency in the country to keep their cost of involvement in Indian matters high. The programme was most active under Indira and Rajiv and peaked with Khalistan. The risks were directly proportional to how desperate the agents were – usually villagers from border areas – to take on the job. Training involved everything from learning how to use small explosives to getting circumcised to crown the forged persona.

"Fucking Gujral. Wrapped up all RAW ops. Over seven hundred people incarcerated or dead in prison. Sarabjit hanged. Everyone a destitute. I was lucky. Never got caught. There are others I think. I don't know. There is no apparatus, no Pakistan desk of the RAW, no way to know. It was bleak for a while. I was on the streets. I tried to get a job at the consulate. They didn't even let me get past security. Bastards. I *am* their security. The government had washed its hands off the lot of us. Then of all people, JS Garah, supreme commander, reaches out to me. Now and then he sends money. But it's the recognition; that's important. India has turned its back way too often on its heroes."

"How did you survive?"

"Well, to start with, I'm Muslim. That helped. I was smarter than most of the others, who were basically villagers – either stealing things, mostly inconsequential; or attempting to blow things up… buses, theatres. My job was significantly more high-profile; keeping an eye on – and sabotaging – Pakistan's nuclear interests. I did manage a big coup. They covered it up astonishingly well."

What was it about him of late, Vikram wondered, that made people trust him with sensitive information the moment they met him. He wasn't sure how to proceed, but was saved the awkwardness by the arrival of the appetizers and sheesha. Jamal got busy starting the pipe, fiddling with the shaft and valve, and pulling on it like an expert. When he had it all set up and looked satisfied, he offered the hose to Vikram.

"No, thanks."

"Your turn, Amit Sharma. Who are you? Why are you here? And what can I do for you?"

"What did Garah tell you?"

"The usual. Gave me your arrival details. Said you'd need some sourcing."

"Okay, listen Jamal, come close."

Jamal hastily blew out all the smoke that he had just taken in and leaned forward.

"That is how it's going to be. You are not going to get any details from me. We're going to stick with our instructions and that's that. Now," Vikram pulled out a small folded sheet of paper from his pocket and handed it to Jamal, "memorize this."

Jamal whistled, looking at the list. Vikram took it back after giving him half a minute. Jamal was still impressed. "So you going to tell me what you need all this for or do I have to hear it directly on the news? I've seen similar lists. Stake-out equipment and a long shot? You are here to kill someone important is my guess. Who?"

Vikram shrugged, smiled, and picked up a kabab.

30

1900 HOURS

DESPITE the carpeted floor, Aditi was acutely aware of the housekeeper's footsteps behind her. The woman had decided to follow her in after all.

At the door Aditi pirouetted, feigning to keep balance and startling the woman. She gestured her to open the door with the master key; instructing, not asking. The housekeeper stood still, deliberating. After a long moment in which Aditi stared her down, the woman opened the door reluctantly. A curt nod, a half-smile, and Aditi slipped in.

Aditi's first object of interest was Bhullar's laptop, plonked on the table, still on. She swiped her finger on the trackpad. A password prompt showed up on the screen.

She dialled a number on her phone. She counted ten rings before it was answered.

"Anmol?"

"Aditi, it's past midnight."

"Are you up?"

"No."

"Get to your computer right now. I'm connecting my phone to a laptop. I'm in London. I need all that you can get out of it. It's password-protected. I don't have much time. Maybe five minutes."

"Five minutes? I told you these things could take up to hours."

"That's ten seconds gone. Move!"

"Okay, okay. Windows or Mac?"

"Mac."

"Okay. Make sure your data connection is on."

"Call me when it's done."

She plugged in her charging cable into the USB port and stared at the screen. After about half a minute, the phone rebooted into shell mode and a host of commands that looked like gibberish to her started to play themselves out. Anmol was a twenty-year-old hacker that she had kept on call at a small retainership for exactly such situations. The instances were rare; this being the third time the occasion had presented itself in a couple of years, but the first with such a small window.

They had gone over the MO a few times, and Anmol had mod'd her work phone to act as a backdoor entry into machines it was plugged into. Her phone security was compromised – she was sure he could listen in on all her conversations if he wanted to, but she in turn had info on Anmol in the event of blackmail, enough to scare a just-out-of-his-teens boy. And in any case she had a separate, personal number. So far this arrangement had worked without hiccups.

She gave the room a once-over and found nothing else of interest; no papers, no clues of any kind. Just a bunch of empty whisky bottles. Then she heard a siren. She looked out the window and sure enough there was a police car pulling up at the entrance. The officers didn't seem in any rush, but she knew she had to be out quick.

She checked the screens and all she saw were quick

flashes of different windows popping on and off. There was no progress bar of any sort. There was never any progress bar when a hack was taking place. Plus she knew if she dialled Anmol, it would break the connection. If she opened the door to check, she would risk being spotted. *Enough*, she thought. Maybe the obese man did die of cardiovascular complications. It wasn't worth getting caught for. She knew she had to pull the plug. But how much information had been transferred?

Aditi yanked the USB cord out.

She had been careful not to touch anything but the computer and she wiped it down to remove her fingerprints. Then in one swift move, she snuck out of the room. As the elevator opened onto the lobby, Aditi found two cops standing just outside, looking straight at her.

31

2230 HOURS

THE MP held a full-house. The nut game too. With the river yet to come, six other players were still in the fray in this variation of Texas Hold 'em poker. Now all he had to do was to draw out the bets, his guests – nine-figure millionaires at the very least – were inebriated to the point of pyrrhic bravado. His face remained impassive. The amount he would make with this hand was enough to fund the Rolls-Royce that he was planning to gift his son on his eighteenth. No, he rebuked himself in his head; never equate gambling with the cost of luxury. That was a sure-fire way to lose your grip on the value and power of money. He was upset with himself. The phone rang. It was JS Garah.

The MP looked up. One of the players – a guest of a guest – was dilly-dallying, trying to spot a tell. Slurring, figuring the odds.

"Fold," said the MP. *That should teach me*, he thought. His son was going to get the Rolls all right, just not out of his gambling fund.

"But you're pot-committed!"

"Rubbish cards. Okay, I have to take this."

He stepped out on the deck of his Chhatarpur farmhouse and answered the vibrating phone.

"Done?"

"Yes." Garah's voice felt distant.

"Who did you send finally?"

"Vikram Rathore."

"He didn't question it?"

"No, that's what works for me, what helped me pick him. He's got blinkers on. Sticks with the rules. It makes him a good soldier and the best candidate for the job."

"Okay," a pause as if he was going to say something, but then – "Okay."

32

2200 HOURS

THE cops returned Aditi's smile, making space between themselves to allow her to exit the elevator. She was out in the street and in a taxi in seconds.

Back in Kirti's apartment, Aditi reflected on her actions while taking a shower. Not only was her conduct ethically dubious, she had probably broken a stream of laws on foreign soil. She didn't know what to make of it. In India, journalists had low standards when it came to maximizing a chance at exclusivity. A shallow interview with the terrorists of 26/11 *during* the attack was the nadir of Indian reportage. It had gone unaired after the world reacted to news channels giving away strategic plans to the fidayeens by broadcasting them while the action unfolded, along with speculative commentary, allowing the terrorists to be a step ahead.

Aditi herself had crossed this blurry divide many times – only yesterday she was trying to corner an NSG commando into sharing details of an operation – but this was different somehow; she felt uncomfortable. *You know how Indians are wary of littering when they're travelling abroad – this is that guilt,* she told herself.

And then there was her intuition. What if she was right?

What if there was foul play involved in Bobby Bhullar's death?

A knock on the bathroom door startled her.

"How long are you planning to be in there? Your phone's been buzzing," yelled Kirti, trying to be heard over the shower.

Aditi snapped out of her thoughts. She could barely see anything in the steamy cubicle. She turned off the water and grabbed her towel.

From the missed calls list, she dialled the number that mattered most: Anmol, her hacker ally.

"Tell me."

"It's an empty laptop and he doesn't seem to be hooked up to any cloud storage either. Some password-protected porn. Card games. He's using it like a glorified iPad. Mainly for surfing. I can tell you some of what he did all day… you didn't give me enough time."

Aditi could sense he had something substantial and he was only building up to it. Casually mentioning the porn, alluding to her poor job of not managing time well. Miserable attempts at power play. She let him have his moment.

"Go on."

"However, his phone browser is synced. Which is crazy because he used Tor all afternoon. Why would you use Tor on your laptop and Chrome on your phone…?"

"Anmol…"

"Yeah, sorry. So I can tell you he was on the Sotheby's website in the afternoon. There is a particular item he looked up. A painting. This is the only website he visited on his phone today. And only that one item. After that he logged on to Tor. You know what Tor is, right? The anonymous browser that leaves no trace… so I only know that he used it, but have no idea why. Oh and there are some secure videoconferencing tools as well. I can't trace the IP or the name. But I know it was to someone somewhere in Russia. A couple of calls in fact."

"Send me the link to the painting. Is there any banking website he accessed?"

"Yeah, I think he has tabs opened at all times – a bunch of netbanking links. All timed out, of course, no saved passwords."

"Anything else, towards the end of the day?"

"Last Google search was… for… oh yes, 'high-end courier', which I guess yielded nothing, followed by 'art packing and shipping'."

"So it's safe to presume he bought the painting anonymously online and shipped it somewhere?"

"Yes, that's what it looks like."

"Was there an online form that he filled out for the destination?"

"No. But the company website he had visited seems to be the most expensive, and… secure."

"Text me the name. Okay, thank you, let me know if something comes up."

"Will do."

She checked her email. Anmol had already sent the link to Sotheby's painting. She had never even heard of the artist. She wondered if Bobby was an art connoisseur; the kind who would take the trouble of anonymously bidding astronomical sums for obscure paintings. Could it be a gift for someone? Even then, what was the hurry? The shipping firm was – what was that term Anmol had used – secure?

She dialled the firm's customer service. It was late; they would be closed; no reason for them to answer, she thought. But five rings later, there was a crisp male voice speaking into the receiver.

"Hi, I need some help. I had a package picked up today and I was wondering if I could change the address on it."

"Sure. If it hasn't been shipped already, you sure can. Can I have your docket number?"

"Well, here's the thing, I've lost the number. Can I give you my name? Will that help you look for it?"

He hesitated. Aditi seized the moment. "Please," a soft, almost sensuous please.

"What is your name, ma'am?"

"Bhullar. B-H-U-L-L-A-R."

"I'll check the status. Hold on." A minute later. "Well, it's already been shipped to India. You'd opted for 'instant'... there's little I can do right now."

"Thank you for trying."

Aditi hung up. She knew she couldn't ask where it had been shipped to without raising an instant alarm.

Her phone rang. It was Anmol.

"You found something more?"

"Oh yes, I did."

Her heart skipped a beat on hearing his tone.

"With the help of the Google sync, I have dug out a shitload of juicy info."

"Like?"

"Like his locations since he landed in London."

"Go on."

"Okay. He has mostly been in his hotel, which is The Lanesborough. He went out last night to a club. It's called... hang on... ah yes, Annabeth's. Then this morning he took a longish drive to Hertshire. To a specific estate."

"As in? Someone's house?"

"I Google Earth-ed it. It looks like a fucking mansion of some sort."

"Whose place?"

"Hang on... looking up... ah, the Marquess of Hertshire. Mar-kess? Mar-kees? How do you pronounce it?"

"Markwis," said Aditi, while googling her own info as Anmol continued to feed her details.

"Anmol, what can you tell me about this man that's not already on Wikipedia?"

"I'm going to need some time."

"Okay."

"Could be a couple of days."

"By morning."

"Aditi..."

"Bye. Don't sleep. Get this done."

She hung up, her eyes scanning the multiple tabs open on her laptop, her brain working the jigsaw that was Bhullar's last forty eight hours. Why was he meeting British nobility? Ah, he was an MP. This would mean his record would be public. Business assets reports from Wealth-X show him to be a stakeholder with BMD Plc, the arms company! It was coming together now...

Kirti came in.

"You done? Think we can go get some dinner now?"

"Maybe on the way to the airport. Sorry K, I have to go back."

0220 HOURS

It had been gnawing at her conscience. While Aditi waited in the business lounge for her British Airways flight, she made a decision. She exited and walked a fair distance on the concourse and reached a payphone. She dialled a number she knew well enough.

999.

"Metropolitan Police, what kind of emergency is this?"

"Man named Bobby Bhullar. Dead today. You were investigating. It was murder."

"Could you please give us your details, ma'am?"

"It was the…" Aditi was only taking a wild stab now, "…Russians."

She hung up the phone. Russians or not, at least they wouldn't close the case right away.

33

2230 HOURS

JOHN Steele was distraught as he watched the almost unnoticeable scroll on BBC News make repeated appearances after short intervals. "Sikh Indian citizen found dead in London park identified as Bobby Bhullar."

It had barely been a few hours since Bhullar had called to fix a meeting with him the next day, presumably to sign vital papers and complete the transaction. Steele thought that he had sounded somewhat flustered on the phone, far from the confident, blustering Bobby he knew. Now there was no Bhullar and no transaction. Barring a miracle – which would involve the Indian government appointing a new agent who would then have to be swayed to go with the UK-based firm as opposed to the cut-priced Russians and all before Friday – BMD would be filing for bankruptcy.

Even as he was contemplating his next move, his mobile rang. *Yorky.*

"Steele?"

"Yes, sir."

"I presume you've heard the news about our friend."

"Yes, sir."

"Okay, so circumstances now compel me to tell you what has transpired in the hours preceding the Sikh's untimely passing… in his possession was a painting. It is what had secured us the agreement–"

"A painting?" Steele cut in, confused.

"Yes, the painting was a cover. There was a document inside. My contacts in Scotland Yard have given me a complete list of personal items belonging to Bhullar that were found on him and in his hotel room. Turns out there is no painting or document. The conclusion one can reach is that he's shipped it to India. Now I don't know anyone influential in Delhi. But you do. You've dealt with the brass. It is imperative that the price we're paying reaches the right hands. It is the only way to save BMD…"

…even though it may jeopardize the future of the subcontinent, he finished the thought in his head.

"I… I think I know whom to call," said Steele.

34

2230 HOURS

KHURRAM had been watching his father acting strangely ever since he had returned from the market. He'd tried to talk to him, but Javid was too busy to respond with anything but monosyllabic grunts; busy putting the house in order in a manner he had never bothered with before. He'd explained the dosages of the medicines to Khurram at least thrice and had brought all supplies that were out of the boy's reach down to the floor. Then he had brought out his woollen shoulder bag. That's when Khurram had begun to panic.

There was nothing more to hide: Javid packed two pairs of pyjama-kurtas, an extra pheran, a container of nuts, some toiletries.

"Where are you going?" Khurram yelled, unable to contain himself. He was sitting up, attempting to get on his feet.

Javid shook the bag, and secured the mouth once the contents had settled. Then he took Khurram's hand, guiding him back to the bed. He knew he had handled his departure badly: putting off telling the kid and sweeping his actions under the carpet even though they were painfully obvious to anyone.

"I've to go on some work, son," he said, caressing

Khurram's hair. His son flicked his hand away in a rage.

"I'm sick. How can you just… leave?"

"You don't understand son; I'm doing this for you."

"The only thing you have to do for me is stay here. Why would you… where are you going?" Khurram was crying now. Javid was shaking. His problems had compounded in a matter of hours. A single event – his son's affliction – had mushroomed into a situation that called for extraordinary measures. He could sell his goats, make some money for now, but then he would have nothing for later. They had no other family, no one else who could support them. It was nearly impossible to get a job. He had to take matters into his own hands, especially before Khurram did. He had to save his son.

He picked up his bag and stormed out the door, without looking back. Khurram was too weak to react quickly enough and by the time he had stood up, Javid had bolted the door from the outside. The boy banged on it, kicking it, calling him names; words that neither imagined he would utter let alone use to address his father.

"Listen to me, Khurram. Listen carefully. Take the goats to Shaukat's ammi. She will take care of the herd. Somebody will come for you. Go with them. A journey by bus to Jammu. From there a train to Delhi. Then you will be taken to your uncle's house. He's expecting you. Think of it as a long holiday, an adventure. It'll be okay. I'll come back. Don't worry, son, I'll come back."

And with that he turned away, Khurram's sobs still echoing in his ears.

35

2300 HOURS

THE cloud cover ensured that not a single star was visible. Even moonlight couldn't make it through. Now and again the wind prodded the gentle snowfall. Shaukat and Javid had walked for an hour after meeting outside the village, with only a small torch to show the way. This too they kept switched off most of the time. Even though there wasn't a curfew, they were cautious to avoid any check posts or indeed, running into anyone at all. If they saw a light on the road ahead, they either laid low or circumvented it by taking a route deep through the woods before emerging in the distance.

The Indian side had completed fencing the border in 2004. There were two rows of electrified, floodlit, thermal imaging-equipped fences that stretched over hundreds of kilometres from Gujarat to Kashmir, a feat that made for an intriguing sight from space. The fences constructed of concertina wires also had been recently upgraded with surveillance-dependent alarms. And in the narrow area in between the fences were thousands of deadly landmines.

What the constructors of this formidable engineering effort had not entirely taken into account were avalanches and heavy snowfall that damaged or washed away or rendered useless sections of the fencing. Every summer, scores of kilometres of wires would need repairs and it became difficult to account for any infiltrators in the winter. And while they did slow down and often stop unwelcome elements, the fences were never meant to be hundred per cent effective.

The harsh winters were the best time. And the worst as well. The improbability of an Indian bullet finding its mark in this season was offset by the odds of nature martyring the intruders. The lull in activity with the ceasefire in place had only heightened their chances. Plus there was always the small detail – for now – of getting out, rather than getting in.

0315 HOURS

Though he hadn't exchanged a word with his companion, Javid knew they were almost there when he saw the large gap in the distant unbroken streak of light that was the fence. As they approached, the chain broke up with individual lights forming its links. He had a sense of scale now. The gap – perhaps a quarter-kilometre long – had probably suffered some sort of power outage. The concertina wires, he could just about make out, were very much there.

Suddenly, Shaukat stopped and hooted. It wasn't the worst impression of an owl. Perhaps, he had been practising. Before long, there was a reply. Shaukat hooted once more and from the shadows of trees, stepped out a giant figure.

It was so dark, Javid couldn't make out any features on the man even though he could smell his breath.

"The volunteer, is he with you?" asked a gruff voice,

producing plumes of breath.

"Yes, here. His name is Javid."

"I am Aziz."

"Salaam alaikum," greeted Javid.

"We must make up for lost time. I cut across last night and was hiding all day. There has been no BSF patrol since then, thank Allah. The power is off, the cameras ineffective, the fence is benign, and there is much snow between our feet and the landmines. But we must make it across before sunrise. Come, follow me."

Javid hesitated and Aziz sensed this immediately. He turned around.

"What happened?"

"I just want to clarify the terms. Your organization will take care of my son – you will send him to Delhi with the money. This should happen in no later than a week. I will do the necessary work for you and return when my service is complete, which could be a few months by your reckoning. Is that correct?"

Javid could hear and see Aziz's breath crystallize into vapour against his silhouette. Shaukat, who had been panting earlier, was all but inconspicuous.

After a very long silence, "Yes, that is the agreement. You have our word."

They moved along, Aziz with some speed. Shaukat ran ahead and caught up with him. He knew there was trouble brewing.

When they assumed they were out of Javid's earshot, Aziz murmured, livid.

"*Return?*"

"All in good time, brother Aziz. In good time," said Shaukat in a feeble attempt to pacify him.

WEDNESDAY

35

0630 HOURS

JAMAL was half-sitting, half-lying in his bed and staring, when Vikram emerged from the bathroom. Technically it wasn't a bathroom, just a squat-toilet with a waist-high tap that doubled up as a shower. They were in Jamal's apartment: a grimy, narrow one-room makeshift block of bricks in the illegal settlement of Miskeen Colony. A ghetto with a view of the upscale Centaurus Towers, amongst the tallest buildings in Pakistan.

Jamal had left an hour before dawn to source the weapons on Vikram's list. The soldier-turned-assassin had given him a wad of USDs and seen him off. He thought about going back to his hotel, but decided not to be overly conspicuous and invite unnecessary scrutiny in the midst of a midnight entry. So he had decided to wait. But sleep eluded him and he paced up and down the small apartment, watching the slum come to life from the small sliding window. Just when he'd finished using the bathroom, Jamal had returned.

"Sorry about the facilities, I'm afraid they're not quite five-star," said Jamal.

Vikram shrugged. Being a soldier meant he had been through much grimier situations. Sometimes, it was just easier to pop a couple of antidiarrheals and clamp down on all bowel movement for a few days. Showers were a luxury;

a *hot* shower, almost unheard of.

"I hope you succeed in your mission, whatever it is," continued Jamal, "because then maybe supreme commander Garah throws in a bonus as he does when he's not feeling crotchety every leap year. And who knows, I could have a showerhead, maybe even a bathtub to lounge in like they do on TV."

"Have you got it?" asked Vikram, scanning the room.

"Right, back to business." Jamal heaved himself up and uncovered the bed with a flourish. In the centre, framed by ammo, a night-vision pocket monocular, and two Tokarev handguns was a new if slightly battered Dragunov SVD, the Soviet Union's mainstay sniper rifle in production since 1963.

Reliable, but far from the best, thought Vikram picking it up and looking through its telescopic sight. From its magnification, he estimated that he could hit a target two hundred metres away with it. Anything more, and the scope couldn't be relied upon. Cutting-edge scopes and the right gun in the hands of an expert could make a target one thousand metres away. No sound suppressors either; he would have to test the gun out of earshot. Jamal seemed mesmerized by Vikram's virtuoso-like fluidity as he examined the ammo and pulled triggers on the handguns, loading and emptying their chambers to assess their balance and speed.

Save for strangling with bare hands, elimination by firearms was the *least* reliable method for an assassination. Drowning, poison, and – most effective of all – contriving an accident were preferred methods and statistically proven to have a much better chance of success. The public perception – and Hollywood – was all about guns because of the ensuing drama. The truly immaculate assassin never left evidence behind or incriminated himself in any way. He was a ghost.

But with little time to plan any of the more effective tacks, and instructions from Garah to use a rifle in the interest of time, Vikram had little choice in the matter. He picked up and cocked the Dragunov smoothly once more.

Satisfied, he nodded at Jamal, still sitting and watching, a smile plastered across his face.

"Breakfast?" he asked.

0730 HOURS

The city's workforce was not quite yet in gear. The air was clear and the mercury was struggling to keep up with the sun. Vikram and Jamal sat on a bench on the promenade by Rawal Lake, each of them holding a kabab-stuffed paratha roll. Vikram was formulating scenarios in his mind and when he needed clarification, he asked guarded questions to Jamal.

He already knew the location of the MFA's office – the Pakistan Foreign Office – on Constitution Avenue. It was a couple of minutes' walk from his hotel. But it was probably well-protected as were most buildings on the street including The Serena, outside which paramilitary troops were stationed with heavy guns at the ready. He would have to recon the area and see for himself. It was tedious work.

He wavered for a moment, wondering whether he should share information with Jamal, get him in on the loop; it'd make intelligence gathering twice as quick on specifics. Right now, he could only ask vague or misleading questions that would in no way reveal his target. Jamal for his part, he could see, was keen to know, perhaps even help. He was effusive in his explanations and had the mouth of a tourist guide who had been promised a hefty baksheesh. He did not hesitate to volunteer information about his own past or any information that he thought might come in handy for Vikram – however half-baked – in his jovial manner. And he still thought of him as Amit Sharma.

"I hope you know," said Jamal, taking a stab in the dark, "that a couple of the big government offices have been emptied on account of… are you ready for this? Rats."

"What's that again?"

"There's a rat infestation in some buildings on Constitution Avenue. The officers have moved out too."

Vikram put on a face to act as if this information amused him.

"Rats, huh? They must feel right at home in these politicians' offices," Vikram's feeble attempt at generic humour was enough to induce a hearty laugh from Jamal.

"Just an excuse for the pols to check themselves into fancy hotels."

Vikram's mind was racing. Was that how he happened to bump into his target outside his hotel lobby? Had the MFA set up his temp office at The Serena? Could this outrageous piece of luck hold out?

He had to find out immediately. A quick recon of Constitution Avenue to confirm that Jamal's information was in order.

"Okay Jamal, thanks for breakfast. Now I need you to go home and dismantle the Dragunov carefully. Then organize a car. A decent sedan so that it doesn't look out of place in the neighbourhood. I can't be walking or in public transport with guns. I'll come by soon."

"Got it."

Jamal upped and left. Vikram waited, watching him get swallowed by a passing auto-rickshaw, then made his way on foot to the Foreign Office.

0810 HOURS

A lone gunman was smoking behind his sandbag fortification. Vikram paced around the block. No cars in the parking lot, only two pick-up trucks that belonged to a fumigation service. The building was empty; just the one window with tube lights switched on inside. Vikram veered towards the guard on duty at a small pedestrian gate at the back of the building. Without stopping, and putting on an air of nonchalance, he hailed the man with a *salaam alaikum*. He kept his words to a minimum in an attempt to not give away his accent.

"How long until we have this peace and quiet, brother?"

The guard shrugged. "The first day they caught hundreds. A week later, they're still notching up a score or two. Inshallah, the officers will be back next week. It feels wrong guarding a building full of vermin."

Vikram waved and moved on. He intended to double back to Jamal's and collect the guns and then head back to the hotel. He had a plan for sneaking the guns in, but he wondered if he needed to do that at all, given the access to The Serena's campus from various sides. Still, any of the refuge areas on every floor would make perfect vantage points.

As Vikram continued evaluating his options, he was altogether unaware that he was being tailed and that a set of eyes had been on him, charting his every move all morning.

36

0830 HOURS

ADITI'S direct redeye from London wasn't as rough as she had thought it would be. There was no time to go home, so she took a taxi from Delhi's IGI airport straight to the Bhullar residence. All the way she had considered speaking with Soumik, and at the very least, inform him of her return if not reveal her suspicions (without giving away her transgressions). But in the end, she decided against it. If she was chasing a wild goose then she risked embarrassment and if she was right and managed to stumble onto a bigger plot, then she would be hailed a hero. Plus, she was technically on vacation, and if her boss knew she was in town and available, he would probably pile some other assignment on her.

The Bhullars' South Delhi address was easy to locate, but Aditi looked up with dismay when she spotted a slew of news OB vans parked outside. Bhullar was no celebrity, so this was entirely unexpected. She thought she'd be the only journalist there. Had she missed something while she was in the air? Her heart pounding, she scrolled through her Twitter timeline. There it was: **Arms dealer Bobby Bhullar dead. Leaves govt in 5,000 crore debt.** She scanned through the story. In a deal from last year, he had approved advance shipments from an American firm on a small advance and now the company had panicked (presumably he was their single point contact) and leaked the story about being owed. It was the amount that had caught the media's interest; big figures always made prominent headlines. Aditi cursed her luck as she got off her taxi and walked into the gate, startling a guard who didn't know how to react to her confident entry.

Mrs Bhullar looked like a model with her striking blue eyes and tall, graceful frame. Of course, thought Aditi, why wouldn't she? She guessed she was in her late twenties. Behind her was her son, about six months old, in his nanny's arms. Mrs Bhullar wore her widowhood well, as she addressed a barrage of questions from the gaggle of reporters with a quiet confidence.

"Mrs Bhullar, why was your husband in London?"

"He was on a business trip. He goes… went there often."

"When did you last speak to him?"

"We spoke on Tuesday morning, like any other day."

"What did you speak about?"

"The usual. How he was. Had he eaten. He asked about his son."

"Did he tell you who he was meeting?"

"No. I guess I never asked."

"Are you aware that his company is responsible for debts worth thousands of crores to the MoD?"

"No, I wasn't. I found out from you."

There was nervous laughter from the group who didn't know how they were to take this light comment on this solemn occasion. Aditi was impressed by her composure. There was no way Mrs Bhullar was going to give any *real* information to this gathering. She would have to find another way to get her answers.

They were gathered in the estate gardens in front of the bungalow. Behind Mrs Bhullar stood her palatial white house framed in grey stone walls, French windows and red asphalt shingle roofs; a huge, opulent estate. Aditi stepped away from the entourage and traced her steps back along the driveway to the gate. She looped around the house, trying to peek through windows and saw no signs of expensive art, confirming her suspicions that Bobby was a philistine in these matters.

Sunlight was breaking through the early morning haze. She took out her phone and started to text. Pretending to wait for a reply, she looked at the guard who was trying not to stare at her. She smiled at him.

"I am sure it's been a rough morning for you," Aditi said to him. "This must be very difficult for her… alone at this age and to have to manage this big house by herself…"

The guard was somewhat startled by this amiable conversation initiated by a famous television personality.

"Memsaab doesn't have to worry. Bhushanji is there. He will take care of it."

"He's a friend?"

"He's Bhullar sahab's man. He knows everything about the estate… about the business… everything. Bhullar sahab spent more time with him than his wife. Or anyone else."

"Oh, I see. Then I'm sure he would've been here first thing in the morning."

As if in response, the watchman stood up and saluted. Aditi turned to look in the direction of his glance.

Bhushan Pratap Singh exuded confidence. He was physically unimposing; short, stocky and almost bald. But his gait had the purpose of a man who knew his place in the world. He was talking in rapid whispers on his phone as he approached the gates, and did not seem to notice Aditi as he walked past her towards the house.

She instinctively sized him up. Even as she turned around to follow him inside, a plan was already formulating in her head. She tried not to think of what she was going to do, as she started to walk back. But she had one item of business to attend to before she rejoined the group.

She called Anmol.

"Aditi..." the boy sounded sleepy.

"Quick, tell me if you've got something."

"Look, I haven't really got much on Cecil. I've been compiling stuff into a file that I've shared with you, but it's all from the public record."

"What? That's it?"

"I'm... Well, there's this one thing, but I don't know..."

"Quick, quick!" She was on the fringes of the people lining up around the funeral car, trying to keep Bhushan in sight.

"Well, because this Cecil fellow stays in a rather remote place, there aren't too many mobile phone signals. I've identified his phone's CDR... and using cell tower triangulation–"

"Can you tell me where he's been in the last forty eight hours?"

"Yes. He's only stepped out thrice – twice to a complex of tennis courts and on one occasion he's driven to Milton Keynes."

"Milton Keynes," repeated Aditi without reason.

"Yes."

"Anything more specific?"

"I have rough coordinates."

"What's showing up there, on the map?"

"Tiny village called Hanslope Park. It's owned by the government. And there is a 'Her Majesty's Government Cent–'"

"Back up, back up!"

"What? What?"

"Hanslope Park?"

"Yes."

"Okay. Anything else? I got to go."

"No. That's all I got."

"Okay, get some sleep. This is good for now."

The words Hanslope Park dinged a bell in Aditi's memory. One quick look at the Wikipedia entry and she knew precisely why she had felt excited on hearing the words. Hanslope Park housed the Foreign and Commonwealth Office's archives. This was a highly secure and secret storage facility that held millions of documents and Imperial records from every British colony, including India. It had only recently come under public scrutiny when a few Kenyans had taken the UK government to court for compensation. It had brought to light the existence of colonial secrets warehoused in the facility and now they were being declassified – deliberately slowed down by red tape – one document at a time.

Is this where Lord Cecil had gone? And what connection did pre-independence records have with the arms dealer?

Now she was more determined than ever to find out. And the answer, she knew, lay in that elusive painting.

37

0900 HOURS

IT occurred to Javid that the heated discussion between the small group of militants was at once all about Kashmir and taking place in the heart of it, but also utterly oblivious of and discordant to the majestic vista that girdled them. Would the inheritance they were fighting for in the name of Allah stay intact until the fight was won?

Javid, Shaukat, and their handler Aziz had arrived in the early hours of the day. Javid had given up trying to follow and analyze the route that the ISI man was charting out for them with his expertise. Even if he had persevered, the exercise would've been futile; later, he was informed that the location was *ilaqa-e-ghair*, the most secret level of terror camps, off the map and literally 'forbidden territory' and in the final two hours of their trek, they had been asked to put on blindfolds. Javid – already limping and stopping to catch his breath – had slowed the company down considerably. Now they had been reduced to a crawl with the blindfold and each hesitant step.

When the cloth was removed from his eyes, the first light unveiled the camp. Javid thought it much smaller than he had expected. He saw fewer than thirty people and only a handful of structures: three long trapezoid barracks, a communication building with a radio tower of some sort, and another featureless construction presumably for storage and supplies. It looked like a hard life, but the impassive expressions on the faces of those he encountered gave nothing away.

Javid was positioned on the camp's periphery on some rocks and asked to wait. He sat down on a smooth stone and even though he would've loved dearly to lie on his back and fall asleep, his arrival had sparked a curiosity across the camp that he couldn't steer clear of. It wasn't long before a young, aspiring jihadi sauntered up to him. The lanky youth was no more than fifteen, his pants hitched high, and a thick unibrow that made his thin face distinctive. Javid wondered if he could get some information out of him. He wanted to know where they were and the sort of missions run from this base.

"Salaam alaikum," he greeted the boy.

"Wa-alaikum salaam," the boy's response was halted and high-pitched as he waved his hand in a childish manner. In that instant, Javid knew that there was a discrepancy in his age and mental development.

The lad – Afzal – had only just arrived from another training camp near Pallandri two days ago. This particular camp, the one they were at now, the one with no name, was notably smaller. Javid assumed it was a launching pad for various missions given its proximity to the border. When Afzal learned of Javid's status, that he had no prior experience and had come from India-occupied Kashmir, his unibrow arched into a straight line with interest. Javid tried to be gentle with the boy and fend him off, telling him that he was tired and even speaking was an effort. Could they continue this conversation later? Afzal had reluctantly agreed and moved away, hunting for another distraction.

From his corner, Javid watched the council of camp commanders consulting with Shaukat and Aziz. There were three of them; all dressed in pathanis, camouflage jackets, and traditional Afghan pakuls for headgear. Their arms were flailing and from the occasional coordinated glances of spite coming his way, he knew he was the sole topic of discussion. Clearly, it wasn't going very well. They seemed upset. Looking in another direction, Javid strained his ears and picked up bits of the conversation.

"We were expecting a teenager and you've towed his grandfather!" said the oldest man.

"Father," corrected Shaukat sheepishly, adding, "he just looks old."

"I said as much to Shaukat when I first saw him. It's my mistake. I should have aborted the journey back right there and then," interjected Aziz.

The structuring of extremist jihad only allowed for impressionable young minds. A consensus was beginning to form that this man was too old for the job.

"Look at him, he can barely sit! The wind could blow him off his feet. How is he going to wield a weapon?"

"Just don't ask me to take him back," protested Aziz.

"Sirs," interrupted Shaukat. He was less than half their age, but his manner and fierce green eyes gave him an air of wisdom beyond his years. "I know this man. He already understands the word of Allah. What you have taught us over the years, this man needn't learn. All he wants from you is the money for his son. For this, his life is yours."

The men looked at this young boy, who hadn't even reached his adult height.

"I already told you he won't be able to wield a weapon."

The moment he uttered the words, the leader of the

camp council knew he had walked into Shaukat's well-laid trap.

"What if we give him the new weapon, the one that Ahmedbhai has imported from Saudi?"

A maulvi's call for prayer rang out in the camp. Heads turned and bodies lumbered towards the middle barracks. Javid followed them.

He took his position in the last of the four long rows and waited for namaz to start. At the front of the rows, a man from the group was whispering into the maulvi's ear.

After the prayer had concluded, the maulvi called out, "Come forward, brother Javid. I welcome you on everyone's behalf. Tell us, are you ready to serve the will of Allah?"

38

0930 HOURS

WHEN Vikram arrived at Jamal's, over an hour had passed. To cover his tracks, he had had to change rickshaws midway in addition to getting off a couple of kilometres away from his destination. Unfamiliar with the labyrinthine layout of the slum, he found himself wandering – a little lost – until he stumbled upon signs that led to Jamal's house.

The RAW man was waiting. As instructed, he had neatly dismantled the weapons and laid them out on the bed. Vikram sensed that the some of his ebullience was gone. Perhaps, the lack of sleep had finally caught up.

"All okay?"

There was no answer.

Vikram stopped mid-movement while putting the parts in his backpack and turned to him. Jamal was sweating.

"What is it?"

"Amit. Sir. Please listen to me. I don't mean any harm. But…"

"What do you mean?" Vikram had inadvertently reached for a Tokarev that he'd put in a side pocket. His fingers clasped the grip and the trigger guard, but he didn't pull it out yet.

"I just…" Jamal hesitated at first, but then blurted out. "Is the Minister of Foreign Affairs your target?"

Now Vikram whipped the gun out in a single fluid move and held it not two inches away from Jamal's forehead.

"What's going on, Jamal?"

Jamal's hands shot up in the air, his eyes fixed on the barrel, and his voice sounding panicked. "I'm sorry. I followed you. I saw you survey the Foreign Office. I just want to help. But you won't give me any information. You won't let me in on your plan!"

"You followed me?" Vikram cocked the gun. *He was tailed and he didn't even realize.*

"Sir, you have to understand. I want to serve the country. This is what I signed up for, not the life that plays out for me every day. Let me be a part of this; we can get this done."

Jamal had barely completed his sentence when in a flash Vikram gripped his arm and twisted it in a way that forced Jamal to swivel around and bend over. Vikram slammed him against the wall, pressing his face against it while bringing up the gun to Jamal's temple, which was now glistening with sweat. He detected no resistance. Jamal was breathing heavily. With an assured vice-like grip on his wrist, Vikram began to angle the arm in a slow, deliberate arc. Jamal let out a yelp.

"Please, hear me out! I mean no harm."

Vikram was buying none of it. "What do you really want, Jamal?"

Jamal was quivering in pain. Any more pressure and he was certain the arm would snap at the shoulder. The gun took up most of his field of vision. One wrong thought expressed, and Vikram would not hesitate.

"I'm hoping I can help. That's all there is. That's my play. You don't understand. I'm here only because there's no way out. I know there's nothing for me in India; no one waiting, no recognition. But this life here, I cannot manage. Only you… you can help me get out."

Vikram looked Jamal in the eye, seeking signs of conviction. Could he be trusted? He decided to test him some more.

"I don't believe you," he said and flipped Jamal around. Grabbing his collar, he rocked his body in a whiplash and head-butted him, bringing the crown of his head to land a thud on Jamal's nose. Then, without giving him even a moment to recover, and using all the power of his shoulder, Vikram slammed his fist into the right side of his jaw.

Again, there was no anger, no sign of a counterattack, Jamal just lay in a heap on the floor, clutching his bleeding nose, sputtering.

"Sir. Get me out of here. Please. Get me out of here…"

Vikram put the gun at the back of his head; it was bait, he was well aware that Jamal could easily reach out and grab it. But he didn't.

The RAW man could well be an asset that could prove useful to the mission. There was enough evidence of his ability: sourcing weapons, shadowing Vikram without his knowledge, surviving undercover since 1995 without detection…

And could a man with ill intention be so inert in the face of physical humiliation?

Vikram brought the gun down.

"Okay," he said with caution, "okay. You can be in on the plan. But I cannot guarantee extraction."

Still on the floor, Jamal turned to face Vikram. "I understand. I'm sure even your extraction is far from guaranteed."

Vikram winced. These were not the kind of words exchanged in the NSG. Of course, their lives were at risk, of course, death lurked at every corner and in every second of a live operation. But you never spoke of not returning home. Jamal grasped Vikram's extended arm and got to his feet and sat on the bed, still nursing his injuries.

"So how do you think you can help?"

"You need to kill the MFA?"

Vikram dithered.

"Please. Trust me, Amit."

He nodded. You can know my target, but not my name, thought Vikram.

"Good. So my work hasn't gone to waste. I've already found out where he's going to be in the next few hours. And he's going to make for an easy shot."

39

1015 HOURS

THE slow procession of family, friends, and reporters wound its way to the gurudwara.

It had taken the better part of two hours before other relatives had finally begun to show up at Bhullar's house, well after the press was in full attendance. Bhushan had resumed taking over proceedings as soon as he had arrived. He had organized a homemade breakfast for the reporters, complete with tables and seating on the lawns, before turning his attention to the more demanding task of preparing for the arriving guests.

By 10 am, a number of politicians, corporate bigwigs, and a bevy of major and minor socialites of the Delhi swish set flit down to Bhullar's bungalow, outnumbering Bhullar's relatives. They all seemed to know Bhushan. He met them individually and accepted their condolences with a humble joining of hands as if he were a family member.

Aditi knew a good performance when she saw one. She understood that it would not do to try and flatter or deceive him. A direct approach was her best bet to get some answers. She would have to bide her time.

Finally, when it seemed that even this large house could no longer accommodate more people, Bhushan announced that they would head to the gurudwara for a short service, after which they would proceed for the cremation.

Bangla Sahib, in the heart of Delhi, with its distinctive gilded dome and edges against its white framework, was a fitting final destination. Bhullar's body was freshly dressed in full attire; the five holy articles of faith – the kakars – were all on him, including a sapphire-studded short sword. The body was placed in the main prayer hall, in front of the *Guru Granth Sahib* and surrounded by attendees. The chamber was soon packed to capacity.

The hour-long service was the opportunity Aditi was hoping for. As the shabads and kirtans reverberated across the hall, she slipped out and walked across the vast compound of the gurudwara to the steps that marked the entrance of the building. There was no way Bhushan was going to be separated from his cell phone and his calls for a complete hour, and sure enough, she spotted him standing near the visitors' footwear storage counter.

She thought she heard the word 'Moscow' before he hung up and looked inquisitively at her as she approached him.

"Bhushanji, my name is Aditi Shenoy. Can I speak to you for a few minutes?" Of course, he would know who she was.

"But I've already addressed the press and told them all there is to know."

She stayed silent, as if giving him another opportunity to pick a different response. As more time elapsed, he got all the more uncomfortable, the less choice he had in the matter: "Why would you want to talk to me?"

Aditi gambled. "The questions I had to ask you were

not for public discussion. That's why I wanted to speak to you in private."

He gave her a once-over and then looking past her, said, "Well, there's no one else here. What did you want to speak about?"

"I was in London when your boss was murdered. I dug around a bit, asked some questions. And even though he did die of a heart attack…" He was stoical, so she continued, "Bhushanji, what was in the package that he had sent to you? Where is it now?"

It worked. She could tell he was aware of it.

"I don't know what you're talking about. I don't know of any pai – uh, package."

Aditi knew she had struck home.

"Were you going to say painting?"

Her eyes bore into his. Bhushan let out a grunt and smiled, a gold tooth catching the light.

"I need to see it," she pressed on.

He tried to gauge her desperation.

"What's in it for me?"

40

1020 HOURS

"SHOULD we do it?" asked Jamal.

Vikram stared at Jamal, while a million pieces of information ricocheted in his head in an effort to align themselves into a decisive picture that spelled either 'Yes' or 'No'.

Jamal had told him that the MFA was going wild boar hunting in the Margalla Hills National Park this evening. And this was his best shot.

The park was thousands of acres of forest-covered hills and renowned for its hundreds of multifarious species of birds and mammals. A constant tussle between the Capital Development Authority and the Tourism Board had caused several projects to make the park more tourist-friendly to be abandoned or delayed.

With the fauna unchecked, the population of fast-breeding wild boar flourished. They now numbered over a million. Many of them often spilled out on to the streets of Islamabad, roaming brazenly in its upmarket neighbourhoods; rummaging in their garbage bins. Until 2009, they could be openly hunted in any suburb or neighbourhood of the city at any time of day. But the administration, realizing the absurdity of legitimizing armed hunters to take a shot at every street corner, especially in the wake of increasing terror attacks, banned the culling. Now and then the odd Christian poacher snuck into the forest for sustenance, but rarely for sport.

There was nothing legal about the MFA's jaunt either, but if a top-level politician decided to hunt boar, obviously no one was stopping him. As it is the citizenry wanted the administration to address the menace, and if he were caught in the act, it would bother no one.

Vikram instinctively disliked the idea of being rushed into action that he had not planned or prepared for. He did not know the lay of the land and his escape would need improvization. If the hunting party was small, he could potentially clear all targets and traipse home. If the number was beyond his capability to clear in a fell swoop, he could make the kill, find a hiding place and survive until dark. A lot of his combat training had been in hills with forest cover, not unlike Margalla. Though the experience could come in handy, it was no substitute for a bona fide mission.

Meanwhile, his own plan was labouring to take shape. One viable option was to take out the MFA at the Serena, where they were both hotel guests. And while the location was a convenient cover, sneaking the guns in and out was always going to be a challenge with the beefed up security. There was high risk of being identified in his window of escape: from the time he made the kill until he made it back to his room after ditching the guns. There was no leaving the building and all his escape routes would always be compromised in this part of town, even if he maxed the distance between him and the target, which he would have to do before there was a serious investigation. The forest was safer on this count because it left fewer traces of him.

His option was the the minister's residence. Again, he presumed round-the-clock security but with an added disadvantage – when he passed by the area on the way to Jamal's the night before, he had noted that there were no high vantage points. He would have to tail the minister and wait for an opportune moment.

CCTVs at the Serena. Losing the guns. Tailing without being ID'd. Vikram had forty eight hours.

The 'opportune moment' could take a month.

Margalla, he could sneak up from any direction. They would never know. One shot. It would be over. It would be imprudent to trust his only source of this intel, but the only way to find out would be to go in with a plan. If the target showed and if he had a shot, he would take it. If not, he would return and revert to plan A. The pieces snapped into place.

Yes, he nodded.

41

1330 HOURS

THE morning prayers were followed by a hearty breakfast and a much-needed nap. Javid woke with the sun high above him, allowing the mix of delicious warmth and cold air wash over his body. He let it seep through his consciousness, being in no hurry to wake up.

About a half click from the camp ran a stream down the mountain slopes, one of the reasons the camp had been set up here. A wash in the cold water seemed like a good idea and Javid made his way down the path that led to the stony water bank. He was no stranger to functioning on less sleep, but the long trek through the night had tired him. His knees and back hurt; his own body betrayed him and echoed the doubts the camp's leader had expressed about his viability for the mission, whatever it was. He entered the freezing water and sat half-submerged and trembling against a large rock.

Javid had tried not to think of the mission that the jihadis were going to put him up to. But it was now near certain – from what he had gathered about the camp and the morning sermon – that the impact of the violence planned was high and would involve killing and perhaps... getting martyred himself. He realized that when he offered his services to Shaukat he was really offering his life.

Bribe for a word, road toll for walking, life for freedom; he remembered the adage so fervently whispered amongst the elders of his village. That was life in Kashmir. Javid had heard it and repeated it and forgotten about it. Today, he understood the final part. That freedom was not Kashmir's azadi; it was freedom for his son from a life of persecution.

How he had found the strength to leave Khurram, he did not know. How would Khurram survive while he was away? Who would give him milk twice a day? Would he heed all the instructions he'd left him? Who would answer his innocent, intelligent questions that only a twelve-year-old could ask? Would he ever be able to return to his son?

A scampering of footsteps distracted him. It was the kid, Afzal.

"Here you are," said the agitated boy, his bony arms flapping erratically. "They're calling you up for lunch."

"In a minute. Let me wash my face."

Afzal waited while Javid completed his ablutions. Then they walked back and assembled at one of the larger, flat clearings for lunch.

Over skewered lamb and rice, Javid learnt more from a loquacious Afzal, who seemed happy to have found a willing ear. Afzal had spent about a month in training together in the company of other teenagers, all 'rescued' from villages across the border.

"What did you do there?" asked Javid.

"Mostly study," Afzal managed to reply between mouthfuls of food. "There were two dozens of us. We read the Quran every day. We had to get up very early in the mornings. They made us exercise a lot, it was tiring! But the food was yummy, so I didn't mind. And then they gave us guns to play with. That was the best part!"

"Guns, huh?"

"Yeah, do you know how to use one? I can teach you. They told us that we should be prepared when we meet the uniforms. I even know how to use a knife to kill them."

Afzal picked up a stick from the ground and demonstrated as he spoke, "You have to slash, not stab. Slash as hard as possible so you catch an artery. That way a soldier dies quicker. If you stab, stab them with the knife horizontal and not vertical like they show in movies. And then you twist the knife so that even if he gets to a hospital, it will be hard to fix him."

Afzal stuttered a lot as he delivered his high-strung speech. But Javid did not react. An image of Khurram speaking these words flashed before his eyes. He tried to blink away the likeness between the boys.

"You mean the Indian uniforms? Why do you want to kill them?"

"I was told they killed my father. He's been gone for years now. And then, they said to me, they will come and rape my mother. That if I want to stop that from happening, I must go with them. Ahmedbhai brought me here. He explained to us how the occupiers have tortured our Muslim brothers and sisters and thrown their bodies together in graves all over Kashmir."

Javid watched Afzal relishing his food. Hatred was no acquired taste, he thought; it was easy to feed off. The young boy's narrative had been moulded for life. There was no turning back for him.

A shadow loomed over them. Shaukat interrupted their conversation.

"Javidbhai, after your lunch is over, Ahmedbhai would like to meet you."

42

1620 HOURS

THEY parked the car off the edge of the highway on the far side, green-topped hills between them and the city. Vikram and Jamal were dressed in camo but wore loose pathanis over them so as to not arouse suspicion. They had broken into a slow run to cover the five odd kilometres to get to the staging area in the heart of the forest. Vikram's backpack housed the Dragunov and the side arms; Jamal's contained supplies for a day. Once they located the hunting party, Vikram would track them until the three factors aligned for him to pull the trigger on the target between his crosshairs:

A clear shot.

Good cover from all sides of the target within three hundred metres.

An escape plan.

The cover would help conceal his location. The idea was that once the target went down, the remainder of the hunting party would have to fan out in a 360-degree radius, and that would lessen the odds of someone discovering Vikram. And if someone did run into him, it would probably be an individual. He would take care of that. As for the escape, there wasn't much to think through. Luck had a huge part to play, as he decided on an ad-hoc route to get back to his car without detection. If he managed, the mission would be entirely successful.

Twice they had to circumvent wild hogs; looking menacing in their natural habitat, unmoved and defiant at the sight of the two humans. Myriad birds kept up the tempo of their cacophony. In an hour they had reached the top of one of the hills, away from the tourist camps, wildlife lookout spots, and the five major hiking trails that crisscrossed the park. Jamal hypothesized that the MFA and his party would avoid these areas and this hill was a preferred spot amongst poachers. He knew, he said, because he had been there a few times before in their company.

"This is as high as we go without risk. Good spot to assemble the gun, get ready. I'll go have a look in that direction and circle back to you," said Jamal, pointing to the side across from where they had climbed.

Vikram considered this for a moment and nodded. "Be careful. Even if you spot a party but can't confirm the presence of the minister, come back and we'll go together."

Jamal flashed a thumbs-up and a smile and walked away with his long, spidery strides. Vikram moved the backpacks behind a large tree and got to work with the gun. He had practised putting the Dragunov together a few times before leaving. He could piece together the barrel, sight, and magazine in seconds. But just to be safe he had disassembled it into many more components so he could carry it in an unsuspicious regular-sized backpack.

Seven minutes later when he was all prepared, he heard a rustle and a whisper of his alias. Jamal was back. Slowly sticking his head and arm from behind the tree, he gestured for him to come over.

"They're half a click out that way. Moving slow."

"Are you certain?"

"You can tell the bodyguards apart from the hunters with ease."

"How many?"

"I counted eight. He's with a friend. Rest all staff."

"You saw him?"

"I think so. Can't be certain. I came back quick to get you because it's them alright."

"Let's go."

They moved at a brisk pace through the copse. Jamal raised his hand indicating for them to slow down and then stop. They had reached some sort of a low stone wall that ran on until it disappeared out of sight. An embankment, surmised Vikram; he could hear a stream babble some way beyond.

Jamal offered his binoculars to his colleague. Vikram pushed it away, and brought the gun up to his shoulder. Through the foliage he could spot a few men in pathanis with guns. One of them was walking in a crouch, his rifle held up as if he was tracking a target. The others watched expectantly. They were still too far for him to make out their faces. He couldn't possibly aim for the head in a clean manner. Why did Jamal ask them to settle here? Maybe the party was closer when he was here earlier. He took his eyes off the sight and, putting the gun down, turned to look at Jamal when the RAW agent – with all his might – clubbed him across his face with a rock, sending him sprawling. Vikram lay on the ground, out cold.

43

1400 HOURS

JAVID, Shaukat, Aziz, and one of the seniors from the day before were gathered in a barracks that revealed itself as the armoury. Here, a man Javid hadn't seen at the camp until now was examining the ammunition reserves. When he turned around, Shaukat introduced him.

"Javidbhai, this is the camp's commander, Ahmed al-Hashem. I have told him how keen you are to help our cause. He wanted to speak to you."

Ahmed was a burly man with a well-groomed beard that reached the bottom of his chest. It was hard to guess his age. His weathered face was marked with the telltale signs of an onerous life: pockmarks crossed swords with the disfigurements of battle: a glass eye, a maimed nose.

He did not say anything for a while, staring at Javid intently, making him uncomfortable and forcing him to lower his gaze and acknowledge his superiority.

"I see you have already found a friend in our young warrior Afzal," Ahmed said finally, speaking in fractured Urdu with a thick accent that Javid assumed was from the Middle East. "It's not surprising. He must be but a little older than your son."

Javid did not reply. He eyes still lowered, he gave a

slight nod.

"Shaukat says you volunteered without being asked. What I'd like to know is what do you think you've volunteered for," Ahmed's words, though sardonic, were delivered in a cajoling tone.

"Shaukat said that you are fighting the Indian Army in Kashmir. I am here to help... with... your mission."

"And what is it that you've presumed about our mission?"

"I... don't know. I didn't ask."

"And yet you're willing to help. While this is admirable, it is also so rare that I can't help but think that your reasons go beyond just our cause."

Silence again. Ahmed glanced at Shaukat who seemed to be waiting for some sort of instruction, then back at Javid.

"Your son... Khurram. We promised to take care of him for you. Send him to Delhi with money. Is this what you're after? This is what makes you happy?"

Javid looked up. He wasn't sure what Ahmed meant. He was amicable, but could he be trusted? "I would be happy if Khurram lives a long, healthy and prosperous life, yes," Javid said finally.

"And if you had two sons, I'm sure you'd want this for both."

"Yes."

"I want that too. For Khurram, for Afzal... for all the sons of Kashmir. You think we are here to fight Indian soldiers. But I don't care for them. I am only interested in protecting our people, mostly our children, so that they may have the Kashmir they deserve."

Javid did not say anything, but his eyes betrayed the

lack of conviction in what he had just heard. Ahmed read the look and smiled with benevolence.

"I know you don't believe me. You think we're terrorists – jihadists thirsty for blood, for warfare, for battle. Ready to sacrifice our own for what seems – given all indicators – a losing battle. You see yourself as a victim of circumstance, forced to join hands with criminals, yes?

"You don't have to answer. I know that's how you feel. It doesn't bother me. It does make me wonder why I should carry on, but I'll come to that. For now, I want to say this: I will not bore you with passages from the Quran. I won't tell you that you are Allah's soldier, that His cause is your cause and you have been chosen by His will. You are a learned man. You know better. You've made hard choices and gained life experiences out of that. You've learnt the true ways of the world. That we are humans. That we are not here for some higher purpose. I'll go so far as to say the evolutionists are right. After all, aren't we all simply fighting for our survival?"

Ahmed paused for breath.

Javid's mind was racing. He had come prepared to hear a sermon of jingoistic theology, and he was ready to ignore it. But an endorsement that went against creationism? This bordered on blasphemy even for him.

Ahmed didn't wait for a response, and carried on.

"What is stopping you from giving your son the life he deserves?"

Javid had spent a great deal of time, years in fact, thinking about this; not in a philosophical way, but in a pragmatic sense. His deep-rooted aversion to violence as a means of struggle started with a protectiveness for his boy, his own brother's unlawful incarceration, and watching helplessly as his young neighbours gave up their lives for so little in exchange. Ahmed was right of course, about being a victim to his circumstances. And unfortunately there was only one agent of change for these circumstances – money. In the end it had always come down to money. And he realized then that the moment he had been offered it, he had grabbed the opportunity at the cost of his principles and his own well-being.

What the devil was Ahmed al-Hashem up to? Javid had not expected a discussion, in all seriousness, on the single most consequential issue of his life – the fortunes of his son.

"I will tell you what is holding you back from giving Khurram what he is entitled to–" Ahmed continued, "politics and politicians, Javid. Let me explain, and tell me if I am wrong."

Javid looked straight at Ahmed, acknowledging for the first time in the last fifteen minutes that he was participating in a conversation.

"For decades now, India's politicians have ordered the occupation of Kashmir, making it a battleground by stationing an army amidst a land of civilians. Yes?"

A fleeting image of Bholu lying in his blood, butchered, as Javid watched from behind the bars of the cage, flashed through his mind. He nodded.

"The army is a destructive tool used to systemically disintegrate the state of Kashmir. You know how it is. Hundreds of thousands of uniforms in our towns, on our streets, and in our homes. Storming our land, women, and children. Oppression by curfews, the show of power by rape. This is an occupation of a people by a country that deludes itself into thinking it is civilized. And the propaganda the politicians belt out to their countrymen and the unsuspecting world, the muzzling of our stories, the asphyxiation of our collective voice, it's… it's…"

Ahmed's talk had been building up to a crescendo. He paused, clenching and unclenching his fist to relieve the stress. The room remained silent. The anger in him was palpable. He resumed, restrained.

"Who are the terrorists here? Just because they wear a uniform, do they have a licence to do as they please? Will not 700,000 uniforms create a terror much worse than a handful of those in the cause of jihad? The army is the aggressor, we are but mere responders, a faint resistance in its tyrannical face. They say we brainwash our young cadre. But who're the ones that are really brainwashed? We tell our children that we dream a destiny of fulfilment for them in a land that's theirs to begin with and for that they must resist occupation. But look at the other side: soldiers are blinded by the brass on their uniform. Transformed into engines of hate, they're merciless in their inquisition and treatment of the common people. They are the true aggressors in the valley, having killed over eighty thousand of us! I don't know if you have been able to take time out from your hard life to find out what is happening in the rest of the world, but I assure you that it is the same story everywhere. In Palestine, in Iraq, in Afghanistan.

"No state's citizen can stand and watch this persecution. All we want is for them to leave. No army, no jihad, no need to take up arms. No conflict, no fear. *Fear*. It is what prevents society from flourishing. They leave and you will have land, animals, schools, jobs. You would be *happy,* and Kashmir, the paradise it was meant to be."

Ahmed was sharp and eloquent and the effect on Javid

was evident. He was conscious these were a distortion of facts, but they weren't untruths either. Every word al-Hashem spoke resonated with Javid. He knew this man would have an answer to all his apprehensions. Still, he wanted to pluck holes, find a reason to disagree, because an extreme violence was where this conversation was headed. So he gambled.

"But Kashmir… is it for Muslims alone? You say with the army gone… but wasn't it us who drove an entire population out in the first place?"

He didn't need to spell it out. Everyone in the room knew precisely what he was referring to. Time had brushed the topic under the carpet.

"Kashmir is for Kashmiris, my friend. Kashmiriyat is what runs in Kashmiri blood. You talk of the ousted Pandits. Well, the same blood runs in the Pandits too. They are Kashmiri, Kashmir is them. We will welcome them with open arms in a free Kashmir. Indian politics was to blame then, as it is to blame now. And let me tell you what happens next…

"We go after Pakistan. They call it Azad Kashmir. No citizen in Azad Kashmir has an inkling of what azadi means. We will win them their freedom too."

"But isn't Pakistan making all this… possible?"

"An enemy of the enemy is the friend. Or so they think. Yes, they arm us to fight India. But we are not fighting against India. We are fighting for Kashmir. And that includes the Kashmir Pakistan administers too. They don't know what's going to hit them. Time and again, we have witnessed this in history. Those who arm freedom fighters, do so at their own risk. There is no payoff. You should know this. The people who built the Twin Towers gave

Osama Bin Laden his means. This is the truth. So you tell me if I am wrong."

The hollow whistling of the gusty wind outside the barracks filled the sudden silence. No one said a word to interrupt the uneasy quiet that surrounded them. With no rebuttal from Javid, Ahmed decided to wrap up the discussion.

"The fact is, Javid, at the end of it all, it's you and I who are left behind to fend for our sons and fight for a better future. I believe that we can have a world where our children can play in our apple orchards and pick the ripening fruit without fear of being butchered or shot. Where they grow up knowing that their future does not hold being a masked stone-thrower constantly battling the police who were meant to protect them in the first place. Where they can hope to leave a legacy behind, and not just an unmarked grave."

He looked towards Shaukat. The teenager produced a phone from his pocket, punched a few buttons and gave it to Javid.

On the screen was a picture of Khurram. He was in the foreground, looking straight into the lens, not unhappy. There were several people in the frame going about their business. There was a large yellow signboard in the distance. Javid brought the phone closer. The board said 'New Delhi'.

"It's from this morning. You son has reached safely. We are ready to hand him over to his uncle. With the ten lakhs we promised. I just need to know… are you going to help me reclaim our destiny? It is going to cost you your life."

Javid didn't dither for a second. Still looking at the screen, he said, "I am ready."

44

1700 HOURS

AN abrupt, breath-stopping splash of water on his face snapped Vikram back into consciousness. He whimpered from the sudden onslaught of pain. As he came to, he saw that he was naked, tied to a tree with a thick rope that allowed no movement. A small towel was stuffed deep into his mouth. The discomfort was extreme: the cold jabbed his innards; his limbs were numb from the lack of circulation; his back chafed against the scraggy bark, and – worst of all – a throbbing headache consumed him.

He looked up and saw Jamal screwing the lid on the water bottle.

"Want a sip?"

His voice sounded odd to Vikram. He was still struggling to comprehend what was happening. Yes, he wanted a sip. No, he wasn't going to beg for it.

"Suit yourself."

It was coming back slowly. They were close to the hunting party. Close to his target. He had turned around and Jamal had clubbed him, a manic look on his face. Jamal. The man he had chosen to trust – not on instinct but after much deliberate evaluation – was the enemy after all.

"ISI," said Jamal, as if riding Vikram's train of thought.

"Turned ten years ago. They caught me. Took a long time for me to convince them that I could be more useful to them outside of solitary confinement. Had to prove it the hard way. Poor Dilip. We were from the same village. Grew up there. Recruited by RAW as a team. One sultry night we crossed the line together. To convince my jailers, I had to shoot my friend in the head. Still don't regret it."

If this story were true, it spoke volumes about the agent's tenacity for survival. *What an asset for the ISI*, marvelled Vikram.

Jamal pulled out a small wire-cutter from his knapsack.

"Now," he said, prying the towel out of Vikram's mouth with care, "I want to keep this simple. I need you to tell me everything. Who you are, who sent you, and whatever you know about this mission; especially the origin of the order."

"I know nothing more than you. Whatever Garah told you, he told me."

"Bullshit. What's your name?"

"Amit Sharma."

Jamal sighed. "I've spied for two governments involved in a region that the world considers the most dangerous nuclear flashpoint on earth, convinced both in turn that I'm their man. I've continued to mislead the Indians for a decade, shot my best friend dead for the job, and have got India's best candidate for a high-profile assassination tied to a tree in his birthday suit… you still want me to believe that's your name? Do you have the slightest idea of the kind of things I can do with this simple instrument?" He held the wire-cutter inches away from his captive's face.

Vikram had endured a lot of physical pain during training. But torture-assisted interrogations were a different beast. If an enemy decided to torture you, there was little hope. Only in the movies did a hero clench his teeth and not sing. At the academy, they were instructed in an implicit manner that resisting torture was futile. If you had a secret, it was better to kill yourself before you got yourself into a situation like this one. Vikram realized that he had very little to give away. He hadn't questioned his orders, and no details had been proffered. But Jamal didn't know that. And he certainly wouldn't believe Vikram. Not right away anyway.

"Here's how this is going to work. I am going to ask you a question. If your answer doesn't satisfy me, I will chop off your toes, one at a time. Next will be your fingers. And if twenty tries later I am still not happy, I'll just plunge these into your eyes."

Vikram's headache and other aches went on the wane as his mind scrambled to invent truths that would buy him time. He wasn't even sure why Jamal had isolated him. If he worked with the ISI, protocol would demand that he hand Vikram over.

"What are you hoping for, Jamal? That you will get two bits of information out of me and sell it to ISI?"

"Sell? Oh, no no no. That's not how we look at it. It'll be a gift. And in exchange they will give *me* a gift. A better position perhaps, maybe a better life. It'll be all very civil."

"And what about me?"

"Oh, they know you're with me. Even your target – the minister – knows. The hunting party were all ISI, a decoy keeping a watch on us. How should one put it? The hunters became the hunted only to become the hunters again?" He cackled with laughter. And then suddenly he was on his haunches, holding the wire-cutter over a couple of Vikram's toes.

"Name?"

"Amit Shastry."

Jamal looked up. He wasn't expecting a different name. Vikram knew he had bought enough time to wedge in an argument, an offer, anything that would give him some room for a literal or figurative manoeuvre.

"Listen," said Vikram, "I don't know much, but I can tell you a few things. You don't need to spill blood for that."

"Oh, but I do. They asked me to bring you dead or alive. I like the halfway option. Pakistani brass likes that too."

And with that, Jamal savagely shoved the towel back into his mouth and applied a pressure so sudden that Vikram didn't even realize until he looked at the spray of blood puddling on the ground, mixing with the soil. When he lifted his head in a scream, he saw Jamal holding onto two of his toes from his left foot.

A new wave of pain coursed through his body, radiating from the bottom left. It helped that he was tied up, with no way to physically react to the agony; he watched the blood gush out as if his foot were disembodied.

"Sorry, I've been waiting for a long time for a moment like this. What were you saying?"

Vikram looked up in horror at his smiling captor who was swaying with glee. He took out the towel.

"Jamal," his voice came out hoarse, it was getting difficult to breathe, "I didn't question my orders. I work for the NSG, I was assigned in an hour's notice by Garah. You should know, this is how it works."

Jamal disappeared around the tree. Vikram felt the cold metal of the wire cutter at his fingertips.

"Keep talking," said Jamal. He jabbed the instrument beneath the fingernail. Vikram howled in agony. This was one of the most simple yet brutal forms of torture. The sound must've carried far, but Jamal wasn't bothered. This whole ruse had been set up in the hills, far from urban centres, for good reason.

"There's nothing more. I promise..."

Jamal jabbed deep this time. His body unable to cope with the blood loss from his foot coupled with Jamal's probing under his nails, Vikram lost consciousness.

45

1930 HOURS

"WHAT'S in it for me?"

The answer to Bhushan's question was something Aditi was trying hard to forget. It did not help that his gold tooth glinted now and again in the dim light of his bedroom, and Aditi couldn't help but stare at it every time it came into view.

She took cold comfort in the fact that she had judged him right. He was a dealmaker, a trader, a barterer of information. He didn't care about loyalty, certainly not after Bhullar was dead. Whatever the situation, he only cared for one thing – his uptake. If he had something that someone else wanted, he was only interested in finding out what was the best he could get out of it.

Aditi knew that sleeping with a reporter he had seen on TV, a proper celebrity, was not a deal anyone else could give him. She had told him that they should discuss it with discretion; perhaps she could meet him at his house? He took her number. He had immediately understood what she was implying. *I'll text you my address.* That's all he had said and walked off before his glee reflected on his face.

His house was in a redeveloped apartment block about

fifteen minutes from Bhullar's bungalow. The security guard was distracted and had not shown signs of recognizing her. Upstairs, she had accepted his offer of a Scotch.

"A little more please," she had instructed after he'd poured her a large one. She needed all the help she could get. As she downed it in a couple of gulps, she asked him to show her the painting, as proof. He led her to his bedroom where the painting leaned innocuously against the wall. It had been opened and repackaged in an untidy manner, the shipping label indicating that the contents were still intact. The date was from two days ago and the sender's name was Bhullar. Aditi instinctively knew it was authentic the moment she set her eyes on it. She looked over to Bhushan; he was standing by the bed.

For all his bravado, Bhushan had never slept with someone like her. He had seated her on the bed and fallen on her hungrily, pushing her flat on her back. She fought the urge to resist, and let him grope her. She needed this to be over as quickly as possible. He didn't even try to kiss her, and she recognized it as the first sign of his own lack of confidence. He pulled open the buttons of her thin woollen jacket, tugged up her shirt, and ripped down her bra, yanking it roughly from her shoulders. She shuddered, and it wasn't only because of the cold fingers that crudely crushed her breasts. She flicked his hands off her, signalling the end of foreplay, but he stayed a few moments in defiance. He was panting now, like a dog left in the cold too long. He must have thought she was shivering with excitement, and this aroused him to the fullest. He disengaged to undo her belt and pull down her jeans. She could see his bald pate glimmering with beads of sweat that were starting to roll down the side of his face as he unbuttoned his shirt in imprecise, hurried movements. He wasn't looking at Aditi, but she saw the same expression on his face the first time he had spoken to her, at the funeral. She felt disgusted.

Bhushan was ready, more than ready. He clawed at her lacy underwear, digging his stubby fingers on the inside of her thighs prying them apart. He groaned and wedged himself in between, mounting her. It was perhaps the sheer unexpectedness of her response that registered as shock on his face, as she pushed him back and out. He tried again, and again, she pushed him. This time harder, so that he toppled over and fell awkwardly next to her. Before he had a chance to protest or remind her of their deal, she was on top of him. There was no way she was letting him control the proceedings. She was going to take charge. Of all the things he would have fantasized about tonight, this was not one of them. She steered him with her inner thighs as she rode him without letting him enter her. He was in raptures now, and too far down the road to sense what was really happening. It was over within minutes. This wasn't the first time she was thankful for a man coming before her, but it was the most she had ever wanted any instance to get over as soon as possible. His chest heaved and he sighed in short bursts as he closed his eyes, twitching and shuddering his way down to normalcy. She got off him, picked up her clothes, and went to the bathroom.

She emerged to be greeted by a sight that, despite herself, amused her. Bhushan was still in bed, a sheet covering him all the way to the chest, a leg sticking out. He stared at her as smoke curled from a cigarette he had lit.

"Hope you don't mind."

"I don't mind. Look, I have to leave, okay?"

She proceeded to pick up the package. It was lighter

than she had expected.

"Anything you want to tell me about this?"

"It was bought at an auction. Bhullar sahab asked me to open a temporary account to pay for it. He was bidding anonymously."

It was clear that the painting had no value for Bhushan. But his interest was enormous now.

"Why are you after this?"

Aditi scoffed at this unexpected display of naiveté; as if she would have told him if she knew.

"I don't know… yet. I think it's connected to what led to your boss's death."

"He was an alcoholic and a compulsive consumer of all things unhealthy. This day has come later than what many had anticipated."

"Still. It doesn't seem in his character, does it, purchasing this painting?"

"No, I have to admit it is not."

"Then we'll see."

"I could sell it and make some money off it, you know."

The man's greed knew no bounds, thought Aditi.

"Well, it's not yours to sell anymore, is it?"

"But I am the one who gave it to you. I was thinking it may be helpful, now that I am transitioning between jobs."

"Bhushan," said Aditi, dropping the suffixed *-ji* once and for all, "you can't just sell a famous painting off like a used car. And I don't think you know any better about black markets in the art world. Anyway. I'll be going now. I'd suggest you better keep quiet about all that has transpired in this room tonight. For your own safety. Try not to gloat about it to your friends."

She knew he would. She also knew they would never

believe him.

Aditi shuddered and tried to shake off the lingering glance that followed her as she exited, some of her disgust wearing thin as she stepped out into the windy Delhi night. She flung the canvas into the passenger seat of her car, resisting the urge to tear it open and give a good, hard examination. No, she would wait until she got home.

46

1930 HOURS

THE sound of the drilling machine seemed distant, but it was creeping up on Vikram. He was blind to its origin. And then at once it was upon him and inside his head. His eyes shot open. He held back a gasp.

He was lying on the hard, grimy floor of a large vehicle. Its diesel engine sputtered with even dissonance. As his head bounced up and down on the floor, Vikram began to understand what his short, distressing dream was about. He heard a man's voice fade in mid-conversation, but it wasn't addressing him.

He narrowed his eyes into slits and tried to get a sense of what was going on without giving away the fact that he had regained consciousness. He was in the back of some sort of van or a covered pick-up truck; hands tied, but in the front where he could see them. His legs were free and his feet were bare, facing the direction they were travelling in. His clothes were back on. The driver was up ahead in a cab, separated by a small grill. In the compartment, he could see the legs of a man. And a hand balancing a rifle on them. Though he couldn't turn and look, it would be a fair assumption that there was at least one more person in the section. He looked down and saw his foot that was missing two toes bandaged with a black cloth. It took him a moment to realize that the cloth was, in fact, not black, but was soaking with his blood. He tried to wiggle the foot slightly and braced for pain, but there was only a dull sensation. Not a bad sign for now.

The voice was speaking in Urdu again.

"What are you waiting for, Hamid?"

"Relax. I'm just trying to pick the right words in my head. How many times will I get a chance to speak with him?"

Vikram caught his breath on hearing the voice of his torturer.

"Dial the number. He was expecting your call five minutes ago."

"Yes, yes."

There were two punches of a mobile phone's buttons.

"Salaam alaikum. This is Hamid. Can I speak with Minister al-Bashir please?"

So Jamal was Hamid, and he wasn't exaggerating when he said the minister was aware of the plan.

"Hello sir. I have the Indian agent… yes, alive… NSG, not RAW. Says Garah instructed him an hour before sending him over… yes sir, you were the sole target… I can only speculate… yes, debrief post the handover, the moment we get there. But… when can I meet you, sir?… No problem. Thank you."

"So is he meeting you?" asked the other voice.

"Next week he says."

The other party stifled a laugh.

Vikram was contemplating his options when there was an ear-shattering blast outside. The driver pulled hard on the steering and the van careened, suspended on its two left wheels for what seemed like a long time. Vikram grabbed on to a leg of the bench that was welded to the floor, while the man flew into Jamal. With the rising centre of gravity, the van eventually turned and fell on to its side and glided along the road and barrier. The jolt dislodged one of the rusting doors and it came loose at the hinges. Finding sudden strength in his legs, Vikram leaped headlong out of the van. There was smoke everywhere and the air was getting thick by the second. Vikram was still flat on the ground when he saw that the vehicle in front of them had snapped into two and was on fire. Just like on his own van, there were Pakistani police markings on it. Shrapnel of all shapes and sizes was strewn around. The few cars in the vicinity were scurrying away. They were on a main road, approaching city limits. Even as he wondered what had caused the mayhem he saw a streak of fire whoosh in from behind him and explode the moment it hit the van out of which he had just jumped. He turned around and followed the smoke trail of the RPG missile. It had come from underneath an overpass on the parallel road. He could vaguely make out a group of figures, but could guess who they were.

Only the Taliban would have the audacity to ambush a police motorcade. He remembered the threats they had made. It was on the news Vikram had put on when he'd checked into the hotel. By all accounts, this sort of an operation was usually outside the city, where they had territorial advantage of aiming at sitting duck targets – usually American – operating on single lane roads on mountainsides. So this was adventurous even by their standards. Fed up of Pakistani authorities toeing the American line and with the Bin Laden fiasco – an operation now proven to have been carried with the blessings from the highest government levels – being the last straw, the Talibs had decided that the enemy within had to be taught a lesson. In a systematic way they had targeted the military and the police, and this was another attack in a series that was getting increasingly brazen.

Vikram got to his feet tentatively, testing his legs, relieved he could handle the pain if he hobbled. He moved away from the heat of the burning metal. In the distance the Talibs were dispersing. The road to escape lay before him. He had barely taken a step when a stifled groan behind him made him stop. Someone was still alive inside. He peered, keeping a safe distance from the blaze, but the darkness in between devoured all detail. Instead of walking away, he took a small run up and jumped in.

Seconds later, he had dragged out Jamal's limp body. He rolled him on the ground to douse the last of the flames. Jamal was convulsing. His eyes opened intermittently. Emergency services would be here any moment. All Vikram had to do was leave. But he picked up a gnarled fragment of a fender; corrugated, rusted and sharp-edged. He held it above Jamal's flickering eyes and drove it deep into his chest.

"Traitor."

Grabbing a bunch of keys from the dead man's pocket, Vikram lopped off towards the countryside.

47

2040 HOURS

THE helicopter landed on the freshly cemented helipad at Prime Minister Inayat Nur Khan's residence, waking the estate's peacocks and sending them panicking for cover in the meticulously manicured lawns. Mohammed al-Bashir, Pakistan's Minister of Foreign Affairs, stepped out with a scowl on his face that would last the evening. Leading his aides, he made his way through the main entrance of the single-storied palatial accommodation and through the long hallways lined with lion and tiger taxidermy mounts. The meeting chamber was carpeted with the finest Persians and four ivory-lined sofa sets were placed in a square. al-Bashir nodded his head to those seated on the left – the usual suspects, the mousy Defence Minister Mirza and the DG of the ISI, Liaqat Hussain. He was, however, surprised to see the Army Chief Maqsood Malik and the Director of Military Intelligence sitting opposite them. The last time men representing the office were at a PM's official residence, there had been a coup.

"Take a seat, al-Bashir," said Nur Khan as he followed in right after the MFA and shut the door behind them. "Would you like something? Tea? Hookah?"

al-Bashir kept standing. No one else moved as heads

turned towards him. Since that phone call from the turned RAW agent, his thoughts had been boiling as if in a pressure cooker. Now he blew his lid.

"Sir, there is no time for a hookah. You realize I almost got assassinated? The Indians have gone mad. They are not to be trusted! We should be readying for war."

The PM was taken aback. "A bit of an overreaction, don't you think? If I had a rupee for every assassination attempt on the people present in this room, we'd be rather well off. Please. Take a seat for heaven's sake."

al-Bashir moved towards a large singe sofa, but still didn't sit. Instead, he mounted the offensive, "Getting targeted by the Taliban and getting targeted by India are two very different things. Sir, I have had my reservations against this treaty you're going to sign from the very beginning."

"And you have not failed to remind me every single time that we have met since the idea came up. There's always trouble before any talks or treaties, you know that. Usually, it's us. So this time someone came along from the other side, it doesn't necessarily mean–"

Much to everyone's consternation in the room, al-Bashir interrupted the PM mid-sentence.

"This is RAW we are talking about, not some halfwit from the saffron brigade. My agent tells me that it was an operation directly handled by Garah."

"You're acting as if the Pakistan government has been a silent spectator in our proxy war on India. At least learn to separate your own propaganda from the truth." The prime minister knew this statement wouldn't go down with the brass, especially the ISI's DG.

"We should not sign the treaty. Who else here thinks we should not sign the treaty?" said al-Bashir, trying to seize the moment, despite his earlier recklessness.

Inayat Nur Khan held his breath in anger. When he had come to power on a platform of rebuilding the country and a promise of progress, Kashmir was the first issue he tried to get a grip on. What he realized was that there was no 'solution to the K-problem'; it was not a problem you solved. It was a problem you got rid of. His predecessors and their Indian equivalents in collusion with separatist leaders had maintained status quo in Kashmir because it suited their personal needs. On the face of it, for both countries, nuclearization and high military expenditure – $50 billion for India, $8 billion for Pakistan – kept their economies engaged and the national morale boosted. But what Nur Khan unearthed was that a significant portion of this amount was mislaid to corruption by those administering the state, at a political as well as at a military level. As he dug deeper, it wasn't long before he got feelers that there were millions for the taking even for himself.

But Nur Khan was a patriot. And this meant putting his country's interests first.

Immediately, he engineered a meeting with the Indian Prime Minister, Jaywant Shirke, on the sidelines of a climate change summit in Berlin and seeded the idea.

Nur Khan wanted India at the table for an open discussion about Kashmir. In principle, he was willing to reach an agreement to make the LoC permanent with a few concessions. This would mean Pakistan would be the overall loser in this game of one-upmanship that had been on since independence; after all, the very founding principles, the very reason of Pakistan's existence, was at stake here if Kashmir – even a smidgen of it – be left behind with India. But the need of hour was to resurrect themselves as a nation by revitalizing the economy, not emptying the government coffers into government servants' pockets. And this necessitated all the help the nation could get, even if it meant gains for India. Stability would bring the world's nations to its door, not least of all its prospering neighbour. Over the years Pakistan had quickly gone from being equated with India to the likes of failed states such as Somalia, Sudan, and Afghanistan. India was no longer Pakistan's problem. Pakistan was Pakistan's problem. Getting targeted by the Taliban or India didn't matter. The fact was that Pakistan was drowning, and Kashmir was the ballast it had to let go off to stand a chance to resurface. Shirke was cognizant of Nur Khan's earnestness.

Continuing to work tirelessly with Shirke, the talks had gathered momentum with more meetings at summits around the world, backchannel discussions, and one bilateral exchange in New Delhi where they had concluded their negotiations and decided to tell the world about the treaty. It had taken half their cabinets by surprise. The other half were shaking their heads in dismay.

It was in every way a good plan, a firm plan – the cost of Kashmir was weighing their coffers and their very countries down, and they were going to snip the cord at the base.

And even though this plan had taken sentiment into consideration, they were not ready for the volume of nationalist backlash. The two leaders tried hard to play up the demilitarization angle. They could not be seen as going soft on their neighbour. But peace can never be a well-kept secret. At its core, this was about Pakistan reining in their home-grown terror outfits, cutting all funding to separatists, and closing the chapter of militancy. Nur Khan knew that once he pulled the plug, he would bleed the separatists in IoK. If India followed through as well on this front, they would be livid and would attempt to change the narrative to a pro-Azadi anti-India *and* anti-Pak stance. But they would not have the means and the movement would be short-lived. Nur Khan did not know if he was entirely correct in wanting to quell the Kashmiri dream of azadi, but he suspected that Kashmir as a nation-state would fail in the twenty-first century and its people would be much worse off than if they had India's economic support. Maybe some time in the future – aided by a robust economy, education programme, and development – the populace would mature and the countries would be sagacious to allow a vote, not unlike the Scottish independence referendum of 2014.

But if he were to be honest with himself, he didn't care. IoK was India's brunt to bear. If there was a confrontation, it would be a civil war and none of Pakistan's business.

As expected, the greatest opposition to this agreement came from the army. The army had always dictated Pakistan's India policy and this announcement came without the majority of the top brass being in the know. Ex-Pakistani PMs had paid with exile and worse for much less. But Nur Khan had anticipated this and had started work on the Chief well in advance, reasoning with him, sometimes for days at a stretch, convincing him that the budget saved could be used to shore up the Services and the ISI and the investment was better utilized in intelligence. And why worry when there was China; the dragon had their back in case anything went south. "Look at the Chinese incursions into India, we can always piggyback with them rather than Lashkar and Jaish," Nur Khan had offered Malik in desperate half-jest. The Chief was not amused. And so far, he had remained stolid.

Nur Khan shot Malik a glance. In asking for a vote, had al-Bashir inadvertently provided Malik with a platform here? The PM did not want to wait to find out.

"Thank you for your democratic take on whether we should pull out of a historic stepping stone towards peace and bring out the nukes because your life has been threatened. We need to ascertain the facts first. That is why we are all here. We are taking this seriously."

"Are you saying it's not India?"

"I did not say that."

It most definitely was an Indian agency, if not India. Counter-insurgency activities were on the rise from their end, but at this juncture, the PM was doubtful if it were his opposite number who was responsible or even apprised.

Nur Khan let out an audible breath as al-Bashir finally sat down and kept quiet. But relief didn't last. The Army Chief had something to say in his gruff Punjabi accent.

"If you make this news public, it will serve two purposes. First, it will eclipse and drown the noise the Talibs have been making with their effort to stoke civil war and unite, as it always has in the past, the populace against a common enemy and second, we will get a sense of what they want. I don't think I see any signs of the public warming up to the idea of cosying up to India. You have tried to convince me otherwise; this can be the litmus test."

Defence Minister Mirza, the prime minister's close friend, had a problem with this: "Bad idea. Mohammed's alleged assassin–"

"Alleged?" al-Bashir almost choked on the cashews he'd picked up from the centre table. He quickly coughed it out and let it lie on the floor where he had expunged it.

"Fine, your *assassin* has escaped, thanks to our friends. What are we going to show the public?"

"We can produce any tonsured, ponytailed Hindu and parade him. We've done this before."

"No!" interjected the PM. "Give more credit to the public. They will not buy it, and it could snowball into a huge scandal if any information is leaked or if new intelligence comes to light. No, it's better we locate the perpetrator first."

"Dead or alive," snarled al-Bashir.

The director of Military Intelligence weighed in. "We are already on the job. His escape routes are limited. He's probably keeping low somewhere between Islamabad and Lahore. Maybe, he's still in Pindi or Gujranwala. I have no doubt he will stay here for now." The confidence in his words spread a sense of calm in the room. "But let's be honest, if we put out his face in public, there is a much better chance of catching him. Until then, surely sir, you must call off or at the very least delay the treaty-signing. The Indians are answerable."

Khan stared long and hard at the carpet. From the corner of his eye, he caught the Army Chief lean back in his seat, the silence indicative of his smugness. al-Bashir's poll had had an impact after all. He needed to curb the sentiment. But then again, could he really ignore this incident? There was little doubt that an Indian agent had made an attempt on a cabinet minister's life.

He tried to think of what would have happened if the tables were turned, if India was the target, how would their administration handle the situation?

For decades Pakistan had denied involvement in any terror activity that India had pegged on them. They had even denied that Ajmal Kasab was a Pakistani citizen. Nobody believed them, certainly not in international circles. The lip service had gotten tiresome, and even his own citizens – despite the swell of anti-India sentiment – were losing faith in their government's abilities to take on India at an international level and tiring of the misinformation. When it came to terror attacks, of late India had been on the offensive, always taking the moral high ground, sparring via media and international forums and not taking the bait for tit-for-tat showdowns. But if a historic treaty were in the offing, would they say it like it was? Or could in this instance a terror outfit and a nation be dehyphenated for a greater cause? *Yes*, thought the PM, *India would calibrate their response*. Could he pull off a similar feat here? What if he were to expose this assassination plot through the media, suggesting the perpetrator to be Indian, but not an agent of the state? This compromise could work for everyone. al-Bashir would get his sympathy, the treaty could still be signed and the windfall of international goodwill would brighten the mood of the nation. For him? A Nobel Prize perhaps, as he had joked with Shirke once.

Nur Khan afforded himself a small smile. The first step was clear. In every eventuality they would have to produce proof. For the public, for India. They needed to catch the fugitive.

He turned to the ISI chief.

"Call the RAW chief. See what he has to say."

"What do think he'll say, sir? He'll deny everything," protested al-Bashir.

"Go to the comms room and make the call."

The ISI chief returned in less than five minutes.

"I did all the talking. He says he has no clue and if you

ask me, he seemed genuinely surprised."

Judging from a response over the phone; the PM hoped this wasn't a case of confirmation bias.

"I told you," said al-Bashir, "they're all a bunch of devious crooks. Actually, you might be right. Maybe he is surprised. We all know this RAW idiot. He doesn't know what's happening on his wife's side of the bed, let alone anything of this importance and scale."

Everyone turned to the PM for his call. His decision was going to set off a chain of events from which there was no turning back now.

"Let's find him."

48

2110 HOURS

VIKRAM skulked about, hiding in plain sight in Rawalpindi's teeming and chaotic Saddar Bazaar. He had managed to steal a shawl and pakul from a sleeping old man with unusable, deformed legs. He almost did not take it, until he spotted him clutching a shiny new mobile phone, undoubtedly stolen. All is fair on these streets, he thought as he proceeded to spirit away bananas and a money box from a vendor who was in the midst of a hectic bargain war.

This basic disguise on, Vikram's plan was to keep moving. Pindi was still a mid-sized city and it would not be impossible to spot him if someone was on the lookout. The idea was to not get holed up in one spot, but to remain a moving target.

The bazaar was in the north-west quadrant of the city and he figured he'd take a winding route towards the south-east and eventually out. To where, he did not know yet.

That he was going to attempt re-entering India was never in question. But it was the worst-case scenario as there was no plan B for extraction in place, something that had rankled him from the start. If he did not manage to hold on to his cover and return via official channels, Garah had warned, then he was on his own. Vikram was calm yet – he had his options – and none of them were insurmountable for a man of his talents. Whether from Gujarat, Rajasthan, Punjab, or Kashmir, the fence was vulnerable and porous in enough places. Militants with the most elementary training could make it across, even though they often had the support and cover of the Pakistani Rangers and the advantage of long-term gambits such as tunnelling under the border. But Vikram believed it would be short work for him, especially considering he was walking into India and all he had to do was engage in conversation with the army, while avoiding being shot first by friendly fire.

The big question was the time frame. Vikram was confident that with enough planning, he could choose his path. But he quickly discarded Gujarat and Kashmir. The terrain in both places was treacherous; barren and unconcealed in the Rann of Kutch and unforgiving and heavily guarded in the valley. Gujarat was still fenceless in parts, but it was too remote. The farther he'd have to travel, the more time it would take and create more chances of his identity being revealed. Kashmir was too restrictive, besides Vikram was not geared for the terrain.

That left Rajasthan and Punjab. The last incursion along this stretch was when terrorists lay siege in Pathankot. The militants were all taken down, but not until they were all well within Indian territory. If they had maintained a low profile, they could have made their way anywhere they wanted. More importantly, he was only five hours away from the border.

Vikram paused for breath. A whiff of coal-fired kababs on a grill from a roadside shop made his stomach grumble. He thought of the last time he had had a tension-free meal. The dhaba with Bani. *He was going to be a father.* An inner prompt was compelling him to make the safe choice.

Just then, through the window of the two-storied neon facade of the KFC outlet in the bazaar, Vikram saw himself on television. A picture of his bloody face, eyes closed, looking as if he were dead; taken during his capture. *Shit*, he thought, *the Pakistanis had gone public with his identity and mission.*

He needed to hear what was being said, but stepping into a brightly lit high-end fast food restaurant in his present attire with his face on TV was not the best idea. He quickly turned around, desperately seeking another source. He was in luck. Not ten feet away was a small restaurant with a TV blaring on the cashier's counter. He strode over, focusing his ears to pick out the volume. He stood outside, nonchalantly eating a banana, but his senses sharp and tuned in, his heart pumping hard. The report talked of an Indian Black Cat operative, who had tried to assassinate a leading politician; lost in the Taliban attack; now wanted dead or alive.

Vikram had vanished from the bazaar before the news item had concluded. He was moving fast now despite the agony caused by the wound on his foot. Banking on the odd street sign, he hoofed it to the closest intercity bus station, which was two kilometres away. He bought himself a ticket, operating with monosyllables during the interaction and keeping his movements unhurried. The coach was in good condition and he settled into a window seat and turned away, pretending to be asleep. But his mind was churning – the implication of this announcement would be far-reaching. From past instances, he could infer that even the peace process could be in jeopardy – at the very least postponed – with such a public revelation.

It was true that his link to the NSG would take some uncovering by the media; as a Black Cat commando, his public face was unknown. But the Pakistanis had his picture plastered all over, making him identifiable to his colleagues and the authorities in the services. He needed to get out ASAP. So he picked the shortest, albeit most deadly route in: via the Wagah border.

49

2220 HOURS

THE MP was livid in the backseat of his Innova, as it smoothly coasted across Delhi's streets in a convoy of eight cars, heading from Lutyens' to his Chhatarpur residence. The emergency meeting with the PM and cabinet had barely lasted twenty minutes, but months of his elaborate planning had unravelled in that time. He had almost lost his cool and brought suspicion upon himself in the assembly. The memory of the moment annoyed him. He downed his Scotch and threw his glass on the floor. He replayed the events from the last hour in his mind.

From the time he had entered the PMO, Vikram's bloody face had followed him on multiple cacophonous news channels and televisions, as he wound his way to the designated conference room. Through the glass partition he could see the PM pacing up and down, while his cabinet sat around the coffin-shaped table. There wasn't even the slightest acknowledgment as more people entered. Once everyone had taken their seats, the PM had looked each one of them in the eye and asked – slow and deliberate – if they knew anything about this incident: a man, an Indian, a commando, an elite member of the NSG, who they'd just interacted with, had gone to Pakistan to assassinate one of their politicians. Acting as a lone wolf was most improbable, he said, implying it was one of them.

Of course, everyone had denied it. The MP had tried his best to look surprised.

"We had all expected some sort of response from the hardliners when we announced the treaty," said the PM. "There's always some form of violent opposition from terror groups when any resumption of talks has been announced. From Kargil to Pathankot, it's been a certainty. We knew it was coming. A minor infiltration at best, another 26/11 at worst. All cities and forces have been on full alert. The Intelligence Bureau is working overtime. *But we always fucking assumed it would be them, not us!*"

This was serious. The soft-spoken PM had never quite had an outburst, let alone one where he had used an expletive. He quickly regained some of his composure, but was still seething.

"How could this happen? We are on the cusp of a historic agreement! We need this! Are you not tired of Pakistan, of terrorists, the shit up to our necks in Kashmir? Our jawans, their funerals every day, their retribution… unmarked graves… parasitic NGOs and their human rights… heaven forbid if what they're blaming us for is even half-true. Haven't we had enough? Our crown is haemorrhaging. And don't for a moment think I'm some bleeding heart here. I know how this works – I am the one who authorizes the funds from the PMO – and I know which pockets how much lands up in, and I am telling you now, I am done. And we are moving on. Or should we stay here in this status quo of backslapping sycophancy forever, this nonsensical nationalist cover for our corruption?"

"We are with you, sir," said the MP, breaking the loaded

silence, much to everyone's relief.

"But did they have to make the news public?" added the Cabinet Secretary, Usha Narayanan.

"I have spoken to Inayat Nur Khan. He said that if they were to catch the perpetrator, putting his picture out there was their only option. He hopes this will not affect the treaty. He does want to go ahead with it and I have assured him that we are all on the same page. I trust we are now," the PM eyed them all for a beat. "If this man is in India, we need to find him."

The convoy pulled up outside the MP's house. He stepped out of the Toyota and walked past his Rolls and Aston Martins. As with every government officer, he too always opted for the modest car when on duty. In fact his reputation was that of one of the more frugal politicians of the city.

The MP's aide informed him that his guest was waiting in the first floor study.

JS Garah was seated in the lavish room that at first glance seemed more of a bar than a study. Bottles of wine and whisky outnumbered books by a wide margin. *Just another corrupt politician*, he thought, angry at himself that he had gotten himself into this mess. Befriending Pakistan – the enemy he had trained his whole life and all his juniors to target, the binder that kept the Indian Armed Services united – was neither part of his job nor written in his destiny, and to stop this crazy idea of fellowship, it had meant a necessary tie-up with the MP. And now, it had all gone to hell and this buffoon would blame him one way or the other. He promised himself that he would be calm. He was about a pull a bottle from the shelf when his host walked in.

"Go on, help yourself, Garah."

"I was just checking the label."

"Sure you don't want some?" the MP pulled out the bottle Garah was eyeing and poured him a glass. Then another for himself.

"Okay. So this has not been a good day," said the MP.

Garah marvelled at this underplaying.

"The PM will not be convinced it's a lone wolf episode."

"Does he suspect you?"

"Less than others I think."

"Do we have a plan?"

"First, distance yourself from Vikram. Put him on the wanted list. To discredit him, we need to create a backstory with the NSG to present to the media. There is going to be a press conference first thing in the morning and you're going to be speaking. This much I wrangled at the meeting. You're going to tell them that the civilian casualties during the Kashmir ops were all him. Including the little girl. Vikram was going to be court-martialled and when he heard the news he disappeared, only to resurface in Pakistan, targeting one of their leaders. This is all we need to put out there."

"Those bastard activists came in handy after all."

"The court order for tapping his phone has come in. You need to get in touch with the IB and ensure that any communication from him is shared with me. Put his house under watch. Any other place he might go. Be thorough. We – you and I – need to get to him before anyone else does and put a bullet in his head."

"Oh, believe me, I want to personally do that for failing his mission."

"We simply cannot have him talking to anyone. He is

the only link to us. Should someone else get to him first, I will try to intervene and we'll have to stage an encounter. The PM wants him alive. This won't be easy. But I'm sure you will think of something when the time comes."

"What if we don't get him in time?"

"The Pakistanis will probably find someone else to pin the blame on. How likely is it that he's already back in India?"

"I don't know."

The MP's phone rang, his devotional Bollywood ringtone filling the room.

"Go now."

Garah hesitated. "The treaty. Can we still stop it?"

The MP gave him a terse grunt and proceeded to answer his phone.

50

1700 HOURS

FACING the dying embers of the invisible sun under a deeply coloured evening sky as he prayed, Javid almost forgot the purpose he was here for. It was colder now, and he was grateful for the thick overalls and socks provided to him. The silence of the camp set against the unending magnificence of the blue and purple hued sky did nothing to distract him. As he touched his forehead on the rocky ground in *sajdah*, his focus on the namaz was total.

Once he was finished, as he folded his prayer mat in slow movement, Ahmed's speech came back to him. The commander had said all the things Javid believed in. And Khurram was on his way to leading the closest notion of what was a 'normal' existence. *It will cost you your life* – that's how Ahmed had finished. At that moment, his deepest fears had come true; they expected him to become a martyr. Yet, taken in by Ahmed's words, he had agreed without delay.

They did not trust him still, he knew. He had not been told any specifics. Ahmed had asked him to think about their conversation, and told him he could leave. He had a hurried word with Shaukat as Javid waited some distance away, and then Shaukat had led him back to the camp.

"You rest now, we'll speak in the morning," Shaukat had told him.

People like him had no means to wage an honest battle, he had to accept that. If giving Khurram a better life meant fighting politicians, then who decided what was the right way to fight? If violence was not the answer, then what was?

He did not know the answer. Yet, he had come. The justifications followed thick and fast. The picture of Khurram at the New Delhi station flooded his vision.

2015 HOURS

Night fell quickly. A nourishing meal made him feel stronger against the bitter, cold winds. Someone started a fire and the small platoon gathered around it to warm their hands. There was little talk and an odd comfort in the rhythmic crackling and popping of hot timber in the freezing darkness.

Thick bedding and rugs were laid down on the floors of the barracks, serving as beds. Shaukat showed him the section he was assigned to. Javid was not surprised to find Afzal positioned next to him.

As everyone settled in silence, Javid lay on his back and closed his eyes. But that didn't stop Afzal from starting a conversation.

"Do you know why Ahmedbhai has got us here?" he asked Javid, whispering to avoid waking others.

"No. Do you?"

"I heard other people say that he's going to choose

one of us… for something important. All my friends in the camp made fun of me, they said I was stupid… that I couldn't remember anything… that I was the slowest amongst them all. But Ahmedbhai picked me to come here. Now look who has outsmarted them!"

"I saw you eat dinner. There's no way you're a slow one," said Javid, eyes still shut.

"Wait till you see me run. I am faster than the wind. My sister used to tell me that."

They did not speak for a few minutes.

"Did they kill your family too?"

Javid opened his eyes and turned to face Afzal, resting his head on the crook of his arm. He could barely make out his outline in the dark.

"I have a son. His name is Khurram. He's about your age. He also runs, but I'm not sure he's as fast as you are. Can you catch a runaway goat?"

"Oh, that's easy. We had to catch roosters in our training camp. The others would just run and catch one and then wait outside, tired. I was the one chasing the rest. I caught every one of them," he said, unequivocal pride in his voice.

"That's quite something. Well, you're clearly a very talented young man. I think the reason the other boys made fun of you is because they were jealous."

Afzal giggled. Javid could just about make out the whites of his teeth in the dark. This boy was only a little younger than Shaukat. *Witnessing the death of one's parents would have a great psychological impact*, thought Javid. Perhaps that's what stunted his mental growth.

Javid felt lucky that Khurram would not witness his death. He found himself unable to hold back the tears that rolled down his cheeks.

51

2220 HOURS

WAGAH – on the historic Grand Trunk Road, one of the world's most secure border points – on a daily basis catered to a mere handful of actual people using it as thoroughfare; primarily officials and the odd European tourist. Of course, Wagah was most famous for the goose-stepping soldiers participating in snorting and staring contests during the sundown beating retreat ceremony, as the flags were lowered. A vestige of separation, the mirrored spectacle was beginning to wear down even those in uniform. The Pakistanis called for a toning down, but if the Indians didn't lower the intensity of their high kicks, were their enemies going to buckle? Like the ceremony itself, it was a matter of who blinks first. A massive suicide bombing on the Pakistani flank that had cost fifty four lives had upped the security ante on their side. This incident was soon followed by a crazed NRI, a Canadian citizen, driving his SUV through three gates and barriers on the Indian end before crashing into the Pakistani gate. The media talked of it as being a security breach. But the truth was the man had been allowed to live. Even the bomber, whatever his intention, hadn't made it past the parking lot, well before the first checkpoint.

Wagah's impregnability was multi-layered and covert.

A thirty-person elite squad, sifted from the Punjab Police and with tactical combat training from Israel, was on constant alert. They were the second line of defence, out of sight from the public. In the forefront were some of BSF's finest recruits (though the best were reserved for Kashmir.) Both teams were armed with multiple weapons including the likes of the Belgian FN MAG machine gun, and for strategically positioned snipers, the Steyr SSG 69. The SWAT also had state-of-the-art night vision thermal imagers that could spot targets up to five kilometres away. Every square inch was covered by CCTV and monitored closely.

This was just the Indian side.

There was simply no sneaking in.

Vikram's advantage was that he already knew all this. He had hopped off the bus in Lahore, on the Grand Trunk with a vague sense that he'd have to travel a straight line to reach his destination. He found a bicycle stand and easily freed what looked like would be the quickest pair of wheels of the lot. It was too risky to take any other mode of transport. He pedalled the distance of twelve kilometres furiously, ignoring the searing pain of his phantom toes, and less than forty minutes later was within sight of his destination.

Getting rid of the cycle in a deep ditch, he was back on foot for the last stretch. About a kilometre away, towering lights had the area lit bright as day.

This was unexpected. And much to Vikram's surprise there was significant activity at the border zone. A military drill? That would be disastrous.

But then he noticed that the parking lot was half full of civilian cars. He limped up to a chauffeur and putting on his best Punjabi accent – imitating a man he had overheard rambling on the bus – he asked what's going on.

"Don't you know? There is a treaty being signed on Friday between Pakistan and India."

"Is it happening here?"

"Don't be stupid. For three days starting today and leading up to the event, they have organized a festival at Wagah, where artists will be performing on either side of the border. Agam Sood has come from India."

"That Bollywood singer? Can we listen for free?"

"Sure can."

"You got some water I can have?"

The driver gave him a dirty look and handed him half a plastic bottle.

"Keep it."

Grinning, Vikram hustled away.

He had heard of peaceniks gathering at midnight betwixt the independence days of the two countries. One of the gates would open, allowing for physical contact between the citizens through the bars of the second one, amid music and cheers. Often, a few citizens would be selected to go to the other side and interact for a brief period. All under strict vigilance of course. This seemed a similar, controlled set up. By all reckoning, it looked as if his task had just gotten harder. Vikram was willing to fall back and reassess and try another route if required. This time he wanted to leave nothing to chance. To get a sense of what was possible, he would first have to recon by getting closer to the action and that meant crossing the security checkpost. After taking a sip from the plastic bottle, he washed his face and smoothened his hair. He got rid of the shawl and pulled up to his height. He needed to look as different as possible from the picture splashed on national – by now in all likelihood international – television.

The security team here would have got a special alert. But it begged the question of how seriously they would heed it; for a fugitive to attempt a crossing at Wagah was nothing short of suicide, a mouse trying to cross a roomful of hungry cats and an equal number of mousetraps. He was counting on them to not even consider such an event.

He queued up behind a few people. Vikram could hear a singer finish a popular track on the loudspeakers. There was applause and sloganeering. Suddenly, it was his turn.

The guards barely looked at him as they patted him down and let him pass. He tried his best to keep his eyes on the ground and turned away from the CCTV. It was unlikely but not impossible that Pakistani intelligence had the camera feeding its images into a national global facial recognition system. And the system would be looking for him.

He was less than four hundred metres from India, and indeed he could see its flora bathed in the milky glow of the floodlights. Yet, he felt farther than even when he was in Islamabad. Now that he was at ground zero, he realized his original covert plan was futile in present circumstances.

The stands lining both sides of the border, used by citizens during the sundown ceremony, were all but empty. But there was a throng by the gate. It was an informal setting. And it seemed a lot more lax than he had imagined. People sat on carpets with picnic baskets, vendors moved around serving hot cups of tea. Vikram thought he saw a couple of troops joining in; were they getting carried away with the peaceful intentions in the air?

The gate on the Indian side was open and the local

contingent – a crowd of about two hundred people – had been allowed to walk across the zero line and interact with the Pakistanis gathered in similar numbers. The only barrier between the people of the two sides was a single gate. A band accompanied classical and pop singers on either side. The atmosphere was festive with people sitting around the artist on the asphalt, singing along; others standing by.

The song came to an end. There was more sloganeering.

"Pakistan India Zindabad!"

Not the usual refrain in these parts, thought Vikram; on a regular day chest-thumping patriots would line the stands and hurl unsparing abuses at the other side. These folks were different… an idea began to take shape in Vikram's head.

The Pakistani Rangers were keeping a stringent watch on either side of the gate. Their firm, alert stance indicated they meant business. Vikram had no doubt that their guns were locked and loaded. Meanwhile, another song came to an end. There was a smattering of applause, the stray 'zindabad'. Vikram seized this opportunity.

"India!" he yelled in a voice hoarse, earnest, intense, all at once.

"Zindabad!" came the instinctual reply from the crowd.

"Pakistan!" he continued.

"Zindabad!"

Now even more fervently he repeated the names of the countries. Again, the response was swift and matched his vigour. He picked up the pace. The crowd followed suit.

Every guard's eye was on him. He did not have long before he was identified.

He motioned to a few people to join in and take over his cry, pointing to his throat indicating it wouldn't last.

They heeded.

The singer next in line was looking on, bemused. This was a welcome interruption. She herself had joined in with a few 'zindabads'.

Vikram took a few steps towards the gate. He encouraged the people around him to do the same by spreading his arms and sweeping them up with his movement. They in turn got the attention of others and there was a surge towards the barrier.

Somebody shouted something about bringing down the gate.

The Rangers were wary now. Vikram could sense that they were battle-ready for any eventuality.

The mood was shifting. The passive tone of proceedings was giving way to aggression. More people joined in the sloganeering.

The gate rocked slightly with the push of the throng. Stirred by their neighbours, on the other side, the Indians were getting similar ideas. They pushed towards the gate as well. But because the BSF guards were behind them, they had a freer hand. One Indian tried to climb up.

The moment Vikram had hoped for was here.

The Rangers sprang into action – two of them rushed to the gate and used the butt of their rifles to push back and bring down the Indian man, screaming for him to stay on the ground.

The artist standing closest panicked and ran for cover. The crowd looked on in a stunned momentary silence. The Indian guards were working their way through the gathering on their side. Vikram played his final card.

"Is this the way to treat someone trying to meet us?" he yelled. "Let's go meet our brothers and sisters!"

The war cry was picked up by a group of youngsters around him.

"Let's go meet our brothers and sisters!" rang out. There was another strong surge towards the gate. Vikram was swept in its current. Pushing aside the soldiers, they rattled the barrier. The Indians were not to be left behind. They too lined up at the gates and pulled it towards themselves.

A guard fired a shot in the air, causing the crowd to check its zeal.

"They can't hurt us. They can't touch us," yelled someone. Vikram repeated the cry and the effort was back in full strength.

Vikram knew that the guards were a little too well-equipped. This was a demonstration. To subdue this, you needed water cannons, tear gas, rubber bullets. But they only had real, deadly ammo designed to take down terrorists and their ilk. Using any of that on peaceniks would result in a global howl of the likes not seen before.

It happened as if in slow motion. The gate broke open nice and smooth as if made of cardboard. People from either side, whooping with joy, crossed over into waiting arms. And in the bright sun-like gleam of the floodlights, with some of the world's best soldiers looking on, Vikram slipped across the most dangerous checkpost in the world and dissipated into the darkness on the road to Amritsar.

52

2220 HOURS

RAJVEER Yadav asked his cab driver to pull up a few gates away from Vikram's residence.

He had been in Gurgaon at a colleague's house for a beer and dinner when the news broke. He was pouring his drink when he saw the images on television; his hands had frozen in the act and the beer overflowed from the mug and onto his shoes. As it is he had no answers for Bani's frantic calls when Vikram had disappeared and the next day here he was, his face all over the news channels. He had dissuaded her from filing a missing person's report with the police, hinting that it was a highly classified mission, even though he hadn't the slightest idea of his friend's whereabouts. All he knew was that Vikram wouldn't do anything irresponsible and was much too competent to be in trouble. He prayed his conjecture were true; if nothing else, it had helped calm Bani down.

What really troubled Raj was that there was neither any precedence nor any explanation for such a disappearance. Vikram's last known location was Jaisalmer. After that he had vanished into thin air. Raj had reached out to a CO at the Rajasthan base, who confirmed that the heli had indeed taken off with him inside, presumably to carry him back to Delhi. Raj had been trying to track down the pilot of the chopper, but had not gotten very far. Forty eight hours later, the Pakistani government claimed Vikram was involved in an assassination attempt. Raj just could not make sense of it. For now, he knew he had to reach Bani. She needed support. He had immediately requested for a taxi and headed to the Rathore residence in South Delhi.

Outside their gate, an SUV was parked in plain view. He could tell it was an army-issued vehicle from the ubiquitous upward-pointing arrow on its licence plate. Unsurprising, he thought; best he didn't reveal himself yet.

Raj asked the taxi driver if he could borrow his phone. When the man hesitated, he gave him a currency note that covered his fare and more. Phone handed over, he dialled Bani. No doubt their conversation was being tapped.

"Hello madam," he spoke in rapid Hindi when she answered, hoping she would recognize his voice. "I'm outside your gate. Outside 21/11. Isn't that your address?"

There was a long pause. Would she be able to put together what he was trying here, given her state of mind?

"Yes, okay. I am coming."

"Waiting madam."

Without a doubt, the control centre would relay the message to the stakeout car. But hopefully, he would have enough time before they took a call to follow them. And he hoped they wouldn't suspect it was Vikram making the call.

Bani emerged and walked over from 24/11 to the taxi and got in through the back door. Raj told the driver to take a left into a lane and drive away. He turned to Bani.

He had expected her to be shaken, confused like he was, but her eyes were burning with intensity. Bani was livid.

"What is this garbage, Raj? Why the hell would Vikram

go to Pakistan?" She yelled at him in an accusatory tone, as if he were responsible.

"I don't know Bani, I am surprised too."

"You knew about this!"

"No, I did not."

"You knew he was on a mission."

"Not really."

She understood immediately that he had been cosseting her.

"Can this be true or… have the Pakistanis just posted a random picture? Did Vikram really do what they're… It can't be!"

"It shouldn't be true. There is no reason for such a… I mean the NSG's job is internal national security; we just don't get assigned offshore jobs."

"So it's a set-up?"

The army vehicle was on their tail, inching closer. Raj sank into his seat. He did not want them spotting another man in the cab.

"What are you doing?" demanded Bani.

"I don't want them seeing me. Could you look ahead while talking?"

"Why?"

"Bani, Vikram's a wanted man. I have done the math. If Pakistan wants him, India probably does too. The good news is that they don't know where he is. The bad news is that you are probably under full surveillance. Your phones are tapped. I want to be off their radar in case he tries to make contact."

Bani looked ahead and tried to make sense of all this new information from Raj. That Vikram was on the run and wanted in two countries was not conjecture that he had voiced without analysis. And if he was right, if Vikram did try to make contact, it would be with Raj. She needed to keep her anxiousness at bay and do what was best for Vikram's safety.

"Stop the car," she said to the driver, tapping his shoulder.

Startled, the driver heaved hard to the right, the car getting on and off the pavement and stalling.

"You're an idiot risking being seen with me. I'm getting out and going home. It's absolutely essential that you are not in their crosshairs. Let me know what happens."

Then she was out the door and gone.

The tailing vehicle stopped. Enough confusion in their minds to get away, thought Raj as he asked the driver to move on as quick as possible. Silently, he prayed that Vikram would not call home.

The army car turned around, opting to follow Bani who was stomping off in the opposite direction.

53

2230 HOURS

ADITI'S hands shook a little as she pried open the frame. It had taken all she had to steel her nerves in the presence of Bhushan, when she had noticed that the top left edge had a fine crack that ran down its length. She had driven home in reckless haste after leaving his house, blood pounding and her mind whirling with the possibilities of what the artwork would reveal.

She had latched and locked her door as soon as she entered home, realizing only a few seconds later that it was something she had never done before. Her face was flushed. She threw her sweater on the sofa. When she was on Bhushan's bed all she could think of was returning to the comfort of her shower. But she felt rejuvenated, focussed on unlocking the mystery of the painting. It was a silent night, with not a hoot or a bark to break the stony silence that surrounded her. She shook off what she recognized as a spurt of fear running down her spine.

Get a grip, she told herself. She felt she had reached the end of her chase; that the final clue was before her. She pulled apart the frame from the canvas. An unassuming envelope dropped out of the gap on the floor. She let it lie there for a second, absorbing its significance, the lengths she had gone to reach it. In a few seconds, she would know its contents. Would it have been worth cutting short her vacation, illegal trespassing, duping Scotland Yard, committing cybercrime, bartering her body with a sleaze for the prize, all this while telling herself that this is who she was? That the story and her ambition were paramount?

Aditi pushed the painting away to make place on the table, and set the envelope in front of her. Never before had it felt so lonely sitting in her own living room. She started with fright when her phone beeped. A text.

Where are you? Soumik was asking. "Oh fuck you," she mumbled.

She composed herself once more. Then carefully turning it over, she flipped it open. The flap came apart easily, indicating it had been handled recently. Bobby Bhullar, no doubt. The letter inside, however, must have been sealed in decades ago. Aware that her fingerprints were all over and knowing that it did not matter as she was unlikely to give whatever came out of this to the police, she stared at the pages. The aged sheets were cream-coloured, the typewriter ink now green but distinct against the powdery paper. A communiqué from a different era. The thought sent another twinge of excitement down her back. She unfolded the top half, her eyes scanning the first line.

Her hand went to her mouth as she dropped the letter on the table. There was no way for her to know if it was genuine. But her instinct confirmed it. The enormity of what she had discovered overwhelmed her completely and she had to hold on to the edges of the table to keep from shaking.

THURSDAY

54

0550 HOURS

"JAVIDBHAI," said an unfamiliar voice.

Javid pulled himself out of the deep dreamless sleep he was in and opened his eyes. It was still dark.

"What's happening?" he mumbled.

"Come."

Javid staggered to his feet as the man helped him up. He seemed to be in a hurry. Javid looked around. Afzal's bed was empty. Most of the others were sleeping undisturbed. He grabbed a pheran and put it on before stumbling out of the barracks. His legs were numb from being curled deep into his body, as protection from the cold. As the icy blast of the morning chill hit them, his senses stirred awake.

"Where are we going?"

As he plodded on in front, the man didn't even acknowledge the question. Javid followed him on the rocky path downhill. The rushing river was the only sound besides their heavy footsteps. A light appeared in the distance.

Holding up torches was a circle of men covered in woollen layers. They were all from the camp, but Javid could not identify them right away. He thought he had just about distinguished Shaukat's lean frame when a hand caught him by the shoulder.

"Javid," said Aziz coming up behind him, "it's time for your initiation."

"Initiation? What is to be done?"

"Before I tell you, I would like to show you something."

He held out his smartphone. It had a large screen that lit up as he pressed the button. An image of Khurram flashed into view so bright, Javid's eyes hurt. The boy was standing in front of a modest though modern apartment complex, all shades of brown, in a city he assumed was Delhi.

"Your friend lives here now. This was taken moments before we dropped your son off. Hit play," said Aziz.

"Play?" Nonplussed by his son's sudden image, Javid was having a hard time keeping up.

Aziz bent over and touched the screen. A video, Javid realized.

"I am fine, Abba, they have brought me to chacha's house in Delhi," Khurram said in halting words. He paused and looked up at the man shooting the video who said something Javid could not hear. "Please do as they ask, it will be good for both of us," Khurram finished before the camera turned towards the ground. Javid could tell that Khurram was merely repeating the words he was being fed.

Now the camera focused on a worn, unremarkable blue canvas bag. A hand entered the frame and unzipped it. It was hardly open for more than a couple of seconds, but that was enough time for the camera to shift its aperture so that the dark insides brightened into focus and Javid saw an unmistakable sight. Currency notes. Several wads.

The video froze in an out-of-focus frame of Khurram's profile. Aziz pried the phone out of Javid's hand.

"What do I have to do? I have already agreed to everything."

"Just… it's a small matter. A proof of loyalty. And commitment to the mission. Take this–"

Aziz pressed something cold, heavy and hard into his hands. Javid brought it up to his face to see what it was. A small handgun.

"Here," said Aziz herding Javid towards the circle of men. They made way as he approached. On the ground in the middle was a waist-high figure covered entirely by a large pheran, swaying slightly but of its own accord. Aziz pulled away the cover.

It was Afzal. On his knees and bound, emitting wordless whimpers through his gag.

"Shoot the boy."

55

0610 HOURS

TOSSING and turning in bed, Raj gave up his efforts to sleep when he saw the sun peaking between the buildings in the distance. Groggy after having caught almost no shuteye, he had spent the better part of the last few hours in bed holding up a book, but barely turning a page as his thoughts wandered to the same question over and over again: *Where was Vikram?*

Was he in hiding in Pakistan? In that case, there was little Raj could do. And what if he was in India? It was absolutely necessary for him to reach some sort of safe house.

Raj's phone rang with a shrill old school tone, shattering the silence. He reached for it without getting out of his bed, grabbing it from the table where he had left it to charge. *An unknown number.*

"Hello?"

"Mr Yadav!" chirped the unfamiliar voice in a thick Punjabi accent at the other end. "Are you hungry?"

"Who… who's this?"

"It's your good friend of course, don't you recognize me?"

Raj stayed silent.

"Come, let's get some butter chicken. You know, the

best butter chicken in all of Delhi. I'll be there by 7.30. Wait for me outside. Bye bye!"

Raj sprang into action. A quick change of clothes while he brushed and he was out the door. He hopped into his Hyundai sedan and started driving towards central Delhi whittling through the smog.

En route, he dialled the NSG HQ in Manesar and requested to speak with the Deputy Inspector – General Dahiya, a man Raj was close to and knew was on duty at the time.

"Arun, is there any update on Vikram?"

"There's a communication from the CoAS's office that came in late last night stating that Vikram is acting on his own and is no longer to be considered associated with any government agency, specifically the NSG…"

"Is he up for a court martial?"

"No… Raj–"

"What?"

"There is a shoot-at-sight order. They think he's a terrorist!"

"Fuck. This is crazy. Labelling him rogue just to muzzle him."

The DIG hesitated, "What if he *did* go rogue?"

Raj stayed calm. "You knew him, Arun. Do you think he'd go rogue? Do you think he's so stupid?"

After a beat: "No, you're right. It doesn't add up."

"Keep me posted."

Even though this communication came as no surprise to Raj, he was dismayed at how quickly the authorities had jumped to conclusions. In a way he was no different, taking the other extreme view, but he *knew* Vikram. And in any case, the truth would come to light soon enough from the horse's mouth. But would it be too late for the government to roll back orders?

Raj dialled another number that was answered after six long rings. Raj addressed the man on the other end in Hindi.

"Tony, meet me outside your shop. Bring two phones with sim cards… yes, right now."

He took a slight detour and pulled up at a small store in Connaught Place. A big bleary-eyed Punjabi man in a leather jacket and a monkey cap emerged from the haze and shuffling up to the driver side window, handed Raj the phones–utilitarian, old Nokias. He also gave him two sim cards and a couple of chargers.

"Hard to find these chargers nowadays. But these are at almost hundred per cent. The battery should last three to four days."

"The sim cards?"

"Unregistered."

"Thank you, here you go."

Raj handed over a slim wad of ₹2000 notes, worth much more than the value of the phones, which Tony pocketed without counting.

"Thank you, sir."

In under ten minutes, Raj had reached Pandara Road. He was much too early, the rendezvous hour still some time away. But he didn't care. He parked his car right opposite the row of five famous Mughlai restaurants. Of course, they were all closed at this hour. It was one of these – Khan's – where Vikram and Raj had found their perfect butter chicken. Or at least, the best amongst all they had tried, after months of evaluation and consuming scores of skewered birds, cooked in the celebrated tomato and butter gravy.

He watched hawk-eyed from behind the wheel as the street came alive with activity; runners getting replaced by officegoers. It was almost time.

At five minutes to the hour, he stepped out the car and made his way to the shuttered restaurant, taking a seat on a bench outside. Ten minutes later, a man on a motorcycle – a classic RX 100 with a Haryana licence plate – pulled up close to him. The rider had a helmet on; it was impossible to see his face behind the darkened visor.

At the very first glance, Raj was sure it was Vikram. With a sideways look and the slightest of nods, he walked around the restaurant to the back. On the narrow path, flanked by high walls on either side, a garbage truck and its crew of two were loading the waste belonging to the five restaurants. Kites circled overhead and a pack of dogs with their tails wagging pranced around the men begging for sustenance.

The man in the helmet waited until the truck pulled out of the lane. Now, it was just the two of them and the foetid stench of putrefying food.

Vikram took off his helmet as he limped towards Raj. There was an audible sigh as Raj realized he had been holding his breath. They grabbed each other in a bear hug and stayed there for a long time. When they let go, Raj's eyes were moist.

"Vikram. Thank goodness," Raj's words wavered with relief and delight.

"How's Bani? Did you meet her?" Vikram was no less emotional.

"She's holding up. Putting on her feisty face. Were you really in Pakistan?"

"Yes."

"Attempting assassination?"

"Yes."

"And the rest of it, all true?" Disbelief was writ large across Raj's face.

Vikram shrugged.

"They said you were acting on your own."

"You know that's bullshit."

Raj smiled, "How did you cross the border so quickly?"

"Came through Wagah. Had some luck."

"*Wagah*?" Raj had the most incredulous look on his face that now brought a smile to Vikram's.

"Thanks to some peaceniks. These guys get riled up so easily… once I was across, I convinced a trucker – the same guy who called you – to get me to Haryana, where I had to steal myself a bike. And here I am."

Vikram took a step back and spread his arms. Raj was quick to notice his hobble.

"What's wrong with the foot?"

"Lost a couple of toes."

"What? Wait. Wait… You want to tell me the whole story? From the beginning, please."

Vikram dove right into it, starting with the sortie to Rajasthan with Garah. With every turn of the narrative, Raj grew more wide-eyed. *MFA? Taliban? I still can't get over Wagah.*

"Now you tell me what's the status on ground here. I guess they're waiting for me at home, which is why I haven't gotten in touch with Bani yet. I'm expecting a court martial. But I guess someone in the chain of command will get that sorted…"

"No Vikram. The situation is not good. Your house is

under watch. Your phones are tapped. There is no way you can meet Bani…"

"What? Why? Surely the army and the government…"

"The army and the government have distanced themselves from Pakistan's accusations entirely."

"But that was to be expected as far as public knowledge goes. This was a top secret mission that went awry. They have a responsibility…"

But Raj was shaking his head. "They've declared you rogue… a terrorist. And there is a shoot-at-sight order. There is going to be no court martial. This is not from the media, but a memo they sent to the NSG."

Vikram felt a sharp, physical rush of anger. It was as if a part of his brain short-circuited and every fibre was on fire. Could the country really disown him after what he had agreed to do?

"What? That's fucking inane! How the fu- this doesn't make sense. This is a government-authorized mission–"

Vikram stopped short of completing the sentence. It struck him – what if this was *not* a government authorized mission?

"Where is Garah? This is all on him."

"Vikram, we need to get you to a safe house first. We can strategize the next move from there."

"What safe house?"

"I… don't know… we'll figure it out. Let's think this through. You're at high risk out here on the streets."

But Raj had lost Vikram who was trembling with the rush of adrenaline. "I need to see Garah first. Where can I find him?"

"Vikram, look at me, that's just about the most unsound plan. You'll be walking straight into your worst-case scenario. Wherever he is, there's bound to be some serious security."

"Well, I guess they don't know what's going to hit them."

56

0650 HOURS

JAVID'S first reaction was to throw his hands up in protest.

No one said a word. Surely they were not expecting him to go through with this?

"No."

"Sura 8:12," said Aziz quoting from the Quran in Arabic. "Cast dread into the hearts of the enemy and strike at their head."

"But this boy is not our enemy!" protested Javid, looking around for support, but only finding grim faces staring back.

Afzal was in a daze. Javid wondered if he was drugged.

"Allah has given him the chance to be with us. But he cannot keep up. He often loses his way."

Javid knew what he had agreed to wasn't going to be easy, but this was the monstrous reality of what he had accepted. Unable to think straight, he was unwilling to accept the logical answer: that they needed proof of his loyalty and dependability. That he would not chicken out in the last moment. That spilling blood was not everyone's cup of tea, especially not a man whose very reasons for volunteering were to shield his progeny from violent participation of any kind. And what better way to do this than thrust him into the deep end, have him kill his only friend in these parts? By giving him constant peeks into Khurram's happiness, they had brilliantly orchestrated this trap. He was an investment, and this mission was critical to them. Ahmed's pitch about saving the sons of Kashmir flashed in his mind. Taking strength from it –

"No," repeated Javid. But it was a lot less firm this time.

Aziz came close to his ear. "Do I really have a to spell out the consequences for you? Ask yourself if you really have a choice. Take a moment. I'll give you another minute. Though if I were you, I would just get done with it and move on."

Javid took his minute. What Aziz had said – about not having a choice – rang true. From the beginning given their financial predicament, Khurram's inevitable participation in the brewing revolution, his fear of loss, his lack of options. He never really had a say. All he could've done was turn a blind eye and then it would be his son in his place. No, this was better. But what about Afzal? In his short life the young boy had experienced nothing but suffering, yet he could still eke out moments of optimism. Maybe, his retardation was a blessing. But how long could he go on? Once the group shunned him – and clearly he was but a dispensable tool to them – where would he go? And how would the rest of his miserable life play out?

The sun's first rays were clawing their way past the eastern peaks. Javid had made his choice. It had been Khurram's life over his own. And if this were the price of that decision, so be it.

"No," he said one last time. But it wasn't a refusal. It was denial of the act he was about to commit. He brought the gun to the back of Afzal's head. The boy stared at the ground, barely moving.

His heart galloping, Javid pulled the trigger.

Click.

Nothing.

The relief brought a sudden surge of nausea and turning around, he doubled over and vomited last night's dinner. Aziz patted his still-convulsing body.

"Just a test, Javidbhai; just a test. You did well. Come with me now; it is time for the real mission."

57

0830 HOURS

CoAS General Garah was a man of ritual and because he was a VIP, his routine was public knowledge. That he was President of the Army Golf Club in Dhaula Kuan, that he used to personally train his thirteen-year-old daughter, Heena, in the sport (and she had gone on to win various junior titles around the globe) was warmly and well-covered by the media, one that thrived on sporting and service heroes.

At the ninth green, Heena Garah had landed herself in a spot of bother with her second shot. The ball had dribbled into one of the three greenside bunkers. A bogey looked certain on this par 3 hole if she managed to scoop it out of the cat box efficiently. Her father was fussing over her grip of the sand wedge and they had spent an inordinate amount of time passing the club between each other as he demonstrated how to ease into the swing and she tried to replicate it in her practice.

Vikram had positioned himself at the refreshment hut, a permanent circular structure lined with red plastic chairs, and was watching the father-daughter duo strategize getting out of the predicament.

Both Raj and he were members of the club, though

he had barely been there a couple of times. Golf was not a game he had ever quite managed to get into. Raj on the other hand was a regular with his handicap steadily dropping. Garah's location was an educated guess. Raj had driven them to the club and they had cruised the parking lot until they had spotted the General's car and impressive security detail: besides his private vehicle, a Mahindra Marksman, a Maruti Gypsy and about a dozen juniors in uniform, including the drivers.

Vikram had borrowed Raj's membership card and scanned his way inside without anyone even raising an eyebrow. The guard manning the card machine was distracted on his phone. Making a beeline to the pro shop, Vikram purchased a cap, glove, and a polo shirt. He paid with Raj's credit card. Then he'd casually asked if the General had been coming these days.

"Religiously. Probably almost done with the front nine."

Vikram had stepped on to the ninth and waited. The cap kept his face shadowed from passing groups of golfers. Not that anyone was alert and expecting a fugitive in golfing gear at the high-profile club. It wasn't long before Garah had teed off at the hole with his daughter following suit.

Heena finally took the shot and the ball skidded downslope and landed only a few inches from the hole. She went and finished off with a confident single-handed putt.

Garah and his daughter began to make their way to the clubhouse. To keep out of sight, Vikram broke into a light run and circumvented them by taking a longer path that cut through the thickets where the last remnants of the morning's fog still clung on.

Back at the clubhouse, he waited inside the functional

yet elegant changing room, one that was dominated with wood panels and mirrors. There were only a couple of senior golfers inside. Vikram acknowledged their nod with a smile. He went towards a urinal and pretended to relieve himself while scanning the area.

Garah soon appeared in his line of sight, walking to the showers. Vikram watched him go into a cubicle. The CoAS's tall muscular frame and flat abs were the result of an unfaltering fitness regime that he had maintained all his life despite the high-stress desk job of his later years. There was confidence in his every move. His deep-set eyes and their unwavering gaze exerted his superiority with ease. And with his hair dyed black, he looked younger than his years; coupled with his rank, he was all about power that was warranted.

The two senior men were on their way out. As they exited, Vikram saw the opportunity to lock the main door behind them and have the entire space to himself. This would buy him maybe five minutes before an alarm was raised, probably out of annoyance of prickly members if nothing else. He decided against bolting the entrance.

Instead, he entered the shower cubicle next to where his antagonist was, scaled the partition and jumped in next to a soaped-up Garah. Turning off the water, Vikram swung the door open and dragged the naked, startled general into a supplies' storage area. His protests were feeble and confused. The door was thick and aluminium-coated, with a glass porthole and Vikram hoped that it would soundproof their conversation somewhat. He flung Garah into a corner and the man went sliding, crumpling against the wall with a jolt. He tried to wipe his eyes, only getting more soap in them.

"What the fuck is going on?" he demanded to know. His voice was still authoritative. It took a lot more to rattle the general.

"I should be asking that."

"Who are…"

Vikram wiped Garah's face so that he could open his eyes. On seeing his assailant, his face went pale and his eyes filled with shock.

"Rathore!" he whispered.

Suddenly, Garah began to scream for help. Vikram slapped him across the face and flipped him around in a choke hold, severely restricting Garah's ability to breathe.

"Shut up!"

Garah could barely move as Vikram balled his hand into a fist and held it close to the face of his foe, ready to strike. Garah blinked to show that he understood.

Vikram marginally reduced the pressure on the grip, just enough to let Garah breathe a bit and speak. "Tell me," said Vikram, "what the fuck is going on? Why have I been made a scapegoat? Why is the army and the government not taking me in?"

Garah said nothing, avoiding Vikram's gaze.

Vikram reapplied pressure. He bent over so Garah could see him clearly and spoke in a measured tone laced with menace.

"I am going to kill you, you understand? You've put me in a position where I have nothing to lose. Even if I snap your neck right here and by some miracle manage to get away undetected, everyone with an army-issued gun is looking for me and will not hesitate to put a bullet in my head. Now, if you answer my questions, I might still be inclined to let you live. So I'm going to give you one last chance to speak the truth. Make it count."

Garah took a sharp breath as Vikram loosened his grasp. And this time, the general didn't wait for a prompt.

"This..." Garah croaked, "assignment... it does not have the sanction of the army or the government."

"This was your idea? You were acting out on your own?"

"Yes. Well... there are others."

"Why would you ..."

"Remember Kargil..." Garah spat. "Remember how those bastards stabbed us in the back? They will do it again. They will sign this treaty and we will be forced to withdraw troops... and they'll walk over us again. We're handing them this opportunity on a platter. You know them, those bastard Pakistanis. You understand, you're a soldier."

"How could killing a minister solve anything?"

"If we killed the MFA, there would be no treaty. There would be more aggression and posturing. Maybe they'd mount an attack. I hope they attack. We'd be ready. More than ready. We'd make those incursions in PoK that we held back from in '99. A peace treaty would set everything back, we'd stop being relevant. Funds would dry up. It would affect the economy. We need Pakistan as an enemy. And ask yourself – do you truly believe that we will ever be secure from those snakes?"

Vikram was aghast at how blinded by hate this man was. Hate for an enemy whose context time had changed. This man was willing to create a narrative of falsehood to justify war. Vikram was not going to let this pass. He held Garah at the neck with both his arms and lifted him off the ground.

"You made me an accessory to your private war over Kashmir..."

"Every war in Kashmir is a private war, young man," scoffed Garah, "make no mistake about that. What I tried… was to give it legitimacy."

"This plan would never work, no one in power would allow this."

"I had someone on the inside. A politician. He had his own benefits from the treaty not going through. He said he'd handle the cabinet, the PM. But assassinating the Pakistani minister would be enough."

"Who? What the hell are you talking about?"

"I…"

"Who. The. Fuck. Is. This. Man?" Vikram applied pressure on the choke hold.

Garah gagged. "*It's… it's the Defence… Minister. Ajinkya Ranade.*"

58

0900 HOURS

CAPITAL *News* had its reporting and broadcasting HQ in a towering office building just off Kasturba Gandhi Marg in Connaught Place. Unlike the contemporary, freshly minted Gurgaon and Noida constructions, CN Media House was a classic Delhi building. Early postmodern, fifteen stories tall, and built of brick and stone; it was a rising complex in the heart of the city. This was where old school power met new age power brokers. The solid exteriors were designed to keep inquisitive glances out, in complete contrast to the inviting, modern glassy facades. In every way, the building faithfully followed the Vitruvian ideals of being solid, useful and beautiful, in that order.

At this hour, it was relatively quiet. Producers, editors, journalists and research staff of the primetime shows had only just started trickling in and the beautiful chaos of a media building was a long way from peaking.

For Soumik Sen the day started at 6 am every morning. This, more than anything else, marked out his transition from being a reporter to a business owner. It helped him focus on the corporate matters when the markets opened, leaving the rest of the day for prepping and pushing his broadcasting team towards their daily goals.

Today however, he sat in his luxurious and spacious

cabin on the top floor with a curious matter dominating his attention. Usually, when he had a problem to solve, he would use the giant Amrita Sher-Gil canvas covering the wall across his table as a focal point to organize his thoughts. But on this occasion, he was concentrating on a much smaller frame that he had propped up on the wall by his chair, a construal of the Sunderbans by an artist from his own home state of Bengal of whom he had – much to his incredulity – never heard.

Five floors down, in her small (but still impressive by journalists' standards) cabin, Aditi sat reflecting on her meeting with Sen, and the events that led up to it.

She had read and re-read the document a dozen times the previous night, a cocktail of emotions flowing through her. One moment she was euphoric at the thought of the eminence that awaited her, and at another, she was terrified just holding it. It had taken her two straight shots of Old Monk to calm herself. Her tryst with Bhushan was a minor blip in comparison. She realized she needed to hide it. But where? Her four-bedroom apartment seemed to have shrunk around her, too small to accommodate this piece of paper. The only furniture with a key in her minimally designed residence was a cupboard in the master bedroom.

Before going to bed, she stashed the envelope in a drawer and covered it by tossing clothes over it. It had been an effort to sleep and her eyes were fixed on the cupboard. Finally, the combination of alcohol and jet lag came to her rescue, knocking her out until daybreak.

The first thing she did on getting up was figure out a better place to keep the letter safe. It had to be somewhere unsuspicious; somewhere that would be, as the cliché went, the last place anyone would look for it. When the answer dawned on her, she felt pleased. It was perfect under the circumstances.

She showered and called Soumik just before 8 am, certain that he would be in the office.

"I've been trying to get in touch with you for over twenty four hours now. Where are you?" He repeated his question in the quiet tone reserved for times when he was not happy. Soumik seldom raised his voice or spoke with aggression and was harder to deal with when upset.

"Wait, wait, don't be mad. I'm in Delhi. I got back only yesterday," she paused, avoiding mentioning the time she landed. "I've been following a lead on the Bobby Bhullar case. I saw your message but you know, I got home and crashed. I was knackered."

He said nothing for a couple of seconds.

"What did you find?"

"A bunch of things. I am not sure what it adds up to. But it's a long story. I'll be there soon… let's talk then?"

"Fine. I'm waiting."

Duty done, she put her phone back on charge, and retrieved the document from the wardrobe.

She knew that she was holding in her hands the biggest break of her career, way more landmark than 26/11. If the Mumbai attacks had made Aditi Shenoy a media phenomenon in India, this could catapult her into the orbit of global figures of broadcast journalism. Pulitzer, Cronkite, Anderson, *Shenoy*. Every journalist worth their salt had that one story that defined them, that made them who they were. Wars created journalism legends, scams unearthed reporting stars, conflicts carved out celebrity anchors. There had been a secret, nagging feeling that 26/11 had been her moment, and that maybe nothing would ever surpass it. *Except this*, she thought looking at the treasure she held. *Nothing would surpass this.* All she had to do was plan her next moves with precision. She buttered her toast mechanically, going over her next steps. She needed time. This was a once-in-a-lifetime opportunity, there was no reason to hurry into a decision.

She had a vague idea of how to leverage this document. The big question was whether Soumik and *Capital News* were needed at all in its execution. She liked Soumik, and she was grateful to him for giving her a break. But wasn't it true that he and his company had benefited just as much from her? News broadcasting was no different from the entertainment business, and she was *Capital News's* showstopper. Her looks, her social media reach, and her easy and earnest reporting style had made her a celebrity. And *Capital News* had been the biggest beneficiary of Brand Shenoy.

She decided she would not tell Soumik about the letter. Not today for sure; possibly never. She would let him know the other details related to Bhullar's death as she had promised.

She booked an Uber to work, and spent the half-hour ride going over her story. She was carrying the painting with her, carefully sealed back as best as she could manage. She had to make sure that there were no inconsistencies in her version of the investigation.

It was 8.30 am by the time she reached CN Media House. She went straight to the fifteenth floor.

"He's waiting," said Sen's equine secretary.

Taking a deep breath, Aditi entered his cabin.

"Okay fine, I'll do that piece on Bollywood star homes.

Would that make us even?" she started with her rehearsed line, hoping her attempt at humour would seem natural and help lift Soumik's mood.

"Good. We'll air it next Friday, so you've got a full seven days. Now let's talk about Bobby Bhullar. Every channel has got their spin on his death out there yesterday, except for us. We had nothing. I've got our social media team showing me memes with monkeys in them mocking our choice of stories. So this better be good." He pointed to the painting.

Aditi launched into the chain of events, and for the next half hour narrated what she hoped was a convincing version of what happened, starting from the call from Soumik while she was smoking outside that pub in London all the way up to the night before.

Sen was impassive. He heard her out, interrupting her only a couple of times for clarification. When she was finally done, he fell silent. He pulled the painting towards himself. He examined it, much like Aditi had the night before at Bhushan's house.

"So Bhushan had no qualms handing this over to you?" he finally asked.

"Let's just say we struck a deal. It's not important."

Soumik looked at her, wondering how far she had gone. He didn't have to inquire, in his silence she caved instantly.

"What? He's a fifty-something-year-old lech. I took him to a fancy restaurant, had a few drinks with him, and that was that. He's not daft, and he knew the painting must have some significance. But he didn't care about it as long as he got something in return. I told him that as far as the case goes, it's worthless. But being a news channel, we can create some story around it, it will help our TRPs, the public will love it and so on. And to sweeten the deal, I promised him an interview. We put him on air, increase his prospects since he's out of a job... Maybe even give him some money. The rest I managed, thanks to the fact that I don't have a penis."

Long explanations made Sen suspicious. They almost always turned out to be excuses. Or worse, lies.

"Okay. Whatever. I guess I don't care so much about how you got it, as much as I do about how it is linked to Bhullar or his death. If we can't make a connection, there's no point of this entire exercise and you'd have made a friend you don't want. So let's evaluate. One, Bhullar did not seem to have any plans to buy this art. It was precipitated post his meeting with Lord Cecil. Two, he bid for it anonymously and set up a temporary bank account to pay for it, so he took a bunch of precautions for an object that in any other situation he wouldn't care for and three, he seems to have sent it to India without even as much as seeing it. Who spends hundreds of thousands of dollars and doesn't check what he's paying for?"

"Probably someone in a hurry," offered Aditi.

"As in you think he knew he was going to die?"

Aditi shrugged.

"It's not adding up. Why did Bhullar buy this painting? Nothing you have told me answers the question. Did Cecil ask him to bid for it? But why? And why send it to India with such haste?"

"Maybe it was meant for someone in India? As in, Cecil wanted it to be given to someone in India, and Bhullar was the go-between?"

Soumik looked unhappy. He wasn't convinced, but it looked as if they were at a dead end for now.

"I guess we'll never know." He then turned his chair in Aditi's direction, got up and looked Aditi in the eye.

"Are you sure there was nothing else besides the painting? I mean… in the package that Bhushan gave you… was there anything else at all?"

"Yes, I'm sure." She didn't say anything else for a few seconds and then added, "Trust me, there was nothing else. I can speak with Bhullar's wife, maybe she can put us on to a fresh lead."

Soumik sat down. Aditi had no way of knowing if he had bought her version.

"Drop this painting. I can't see a story with it. We're going to go with what we have on Bhullar. Even though it's utterly unsubstantiated, maybe we can work on the Russian angle. Hint at it."

"Suits me. Right, I'll see you later."

When she left the room, Soumik took the canvas and propped it against the wall. He slouched a little on his chair, thinking. That Aditi had not given him the full story was apparent. It intrigued him that she may have hidden something from him. Why? She had done it in the past, but it had always been obvious that she was hiding some details – she would tell him it's better for *Capital News*, protecting her sources, her methods. Those were understood, swept under the carpet. This felt different. She wasn't just hiding something, she was lying. He was sure of it.

He perked up, sitting ramrod straight. It's someone else's puzzle to solve now, he thought. He dialled a number from his cell phone.

Somewhere, a contemporized devotional ringtone started to chime. Defence Minister Ranade answered his phone.

"The painting is with me…"

"Good, Soumik. And what of it?"

"Nothing… I can't tell what's so special. Except its value. Aditi said there was nothing else with it."

"She's lying," said Ranade, matter-of-factly. "She's found it. And she's keeping it for herself."

"Found what?"

There was a pause on the DM's end. John Steele had connected Ranade to the Marquess of Hertshire. Lord Cecil had apprised Ranade of the deal struck with Bhullar. "It was meant to be in your hands, please find it before someone else does," he told him.

The DM chose not to answer the question. The editor knew it was a shot in the dark.

"Okay, never mind," said Soumik, "but there's no way for me to prove that Aditi has done anything wrong at the moment. Do you want me to push her for a confession? I didn't think it would be a good idea, but whatever you want."

"No, you're right. It's not a good idea. She's smart, and she'll suspect you know more than you actually do and this will implicate you in the matter."

"What should I do then?"

Silence for a few seconds. "Continue to keep me informed if there's any more information about Bobby. I'll take it from here."

"Uh… okay. I mean… I can speak with Aditi again, we're friends… I just… she doesn't know how important this may be, so I can explain it to her. I… don't want her to get hurt."

"I'm sure you don't. Neither do I. She will soon

understand the consequences. What happens after will be entirely her decision."

He hung up. His cold tone and the implication of his words hit Soumik hard. He wondered if he had made the right move. Cultivating politicians was not a new strategy for media houses. The biggest ones curried equal favour from those in power and those in the opposition. With the defence minister's blessings, though under the board, *Capital News* had a lot to gain. After all, he was potential PM material. It was insurance on many fronts – especially early access to breaking news and impunity from government scrutiny whether it was I&B or the Income Tax department. At first, he had thought nothing of Ranade's request to run by him whatever information he had on the case as he was taking personal interest. Bobby was his guy. Defence deals, kickbacks, the buck stopped at Ranade. But the situation got murkier as Soumik realized that Aditi was missing from the office and they had had no updates. The tone of the request had turned instructive. The DM wanted to handle Aditi on his own.

And now Soumik wasn't sure what he had put his best reporter up to.

59

0915 HOURS

AJINKYA Ranade! Vikram was reeling. He relaxed his hold on Garah by a trace.

"Why? Why would he…"

"It was his idea. But like all politicians, his motive is money. Defence contracts. That's big money. The arms dealer, that Bobby Bhullar fellow was his man."

Vikram tried to piece it together. One man motivated by profit. Another by nationalism. Between the two of them they were endangering millions of lives…

There was some hubbub outside. He peered out of the porthole. Garah's daughter Heena was peeping into the changing room, calling out to him. He had heard enough.

"I'm going to let you live. But I'm going to expose this hare-brained plot and your involvement in it. And I'm warning you; if you touch so much as a hair on my family's head, I will find you again and we won't be exchanging pleasantries."

"It's too late," wheezed Garah, "the wheels have been set in motion. One more life means nothing."

It took him a moment to realize that Garah was not talking about himself, but of Vikram.

Vikram made a slight adjustment in his grip and instead of the airway, shifted the pressure on the carotid and the jugular, cutting of blood supply to the brain. The blood choke was an advanced judo technique he had learnt in training. In five seconds, Garah had lost consciousness.

As he exited the room, he saw Heena in the hallway, talking to her mother on the phone with frantic gestures. He wanted to tell her that her father would be up and with her soon enough, but then he spotted her signalling to a man in uniform. Possibly someone from Garah's security detail. Vikram walked right past them, looking down at the burner phone in his hand as he dialled Raj.

He thought he saw the man look in his direction.

"Hey…" called out the man in uniform.

Vikram ignored it.

"Hey!" louder this time.

Raj answered the call. "Start the car, I'm driving."

Vikram pulled the Hyundai out the gate, unrushed, trying not to raise any alarms. Maybe the guard would not react to his ignorance. Raj was looking behind.

"What happened back there?"

"I may have been recognized."

Vikram kept glancing into the rear-view mirror every few seconds, still pulling away from the AGC campus. With every few metres of distance put between them and the club, Vikram eased his grip on the steering a little more.

But just as he started to relax and about to recount what Garah had told him, suddenly in the wing mirror he saw the Mahindra Marksman from Garah's security motorcade speed out of the club gate, pivot and turn in their direction.

This was followed by a Maruti Gypsy. Garah's men were onto them.

"Shit!"

Vikram floored the accelerator.

Having grown up in the city, Vikram was well acquainted with Delhi's streets and its motorists. The traffic was surging, but there was still time until it hit peak. If there was going to be a chase, he would have to end it quick. The longer he was out there, the more forces would be on alert and lesser the chances of escape.

Vikram headed east towards central Delhi weaving his way through the smaller lanes of Chanakyapuri, hoping to lose the 4x4s, but they stayed in sight and were beginning to close in. Vikram swung into the buses-only lane on the BRT to try and put some distance, but both chasing vehicles followed his lead. Now with the road clear, they began gaining on the Hyundai rapidly.

Coming up ahead was a bus stop with two buses pulling in and beyond that a traffic signal. On the right was a flyover. Vikram veered to the left, narrowly missing the first bus and then switching to a lower gear for acceleration, he pushed the car to its limit to force it between the bus and the pavement. Waiting passengers jumped back in shock to avoid being mowed down. Vikram just about managed to squeeze past the bus – he busted his side-view mirror in the process – and then zoomed through the red light before taking a sharp, ninety-degree turn that the Hyundai had great trouble coping with. The car cut across a garbage truck that lost control and came hurtling through and blocked the BRT exit. The sprightly Gypsy was sandwiched between the bus and truck with nowhere to go. The Marksman though, using its bulletproof shell, punched its way through the BRT barrier and cut across, finding itself on the tail of the Hyundai once again.

Vikram zoomed up on the flyover, opting to go in the wrong direction because he gambled that there would be much less traffic to deal with, even if it were oncoming. The Marksman did not hesitate and it too plunged straight up with cars speeding directly towards them.

"O… kay then," said Raj pulling on his seatbelt.

"Did you just put on your seatbelt right now?" asked Vikram, looking straight ahead.

"I've survived worse scenarios with you calling the shots."

Vikram dodged past a dozen cars whose drivers freaked and hurtled out the way seeing this onslaught in their lane. The Marksman stayed in the Hyundai's slipstream, relatively shielded from danger.

At the base of the flyover it caught up and started tailgating the sedan. It bumped into the car's rear maintaining contact and causing it to lose control. Vikram simply couldn't seem to outrun the vehicle.

"Hang on!" he yelled. "It's going to get hairy."

"Been a walk in the park so far," mumbled Raj to himself, and closed his eyes.

Vikram pulled hard on the handbrake, locking the rear wheel. The momentum from the chasing car nudged the Hyundai, causing it to fishtail in a most delicate manner and, along with Vikram's expert handling, made a complete U-turn to end up on the right side of the road.

The Marksman skidded and made a clumsy U-turn itself, but by this time the pursued car had put a significant distance between them and was on its way back onto the flyover.

Vikram slowed down.

Raj had opened his eyes and was looking over his shoulder.

"They're gaining on us, you haven't lost them yet. Mind speeding up a bit?"

"I will."

One thirds of the flyover in, the Marksman was within touching distance once more. That's when a shot rang out and shattered the Hyundai's rear windshield. They were taking aim! Vikram and Raj ducked in case there was another round. The car remained steady.

"Shit! Didn't think they'd do that."

The Marksman was almost parallel now.

Vikram swerved to the left and bumped lightly into it, bouncing back almost immediately, barely being able to waver the sturdy Marksman from its path.

"What did you do that for? That's a 4000 kg bullet-proof armoured vehicle. You aren't going to be able to nudge it off." Raj was incredulous that Vikram would even try such a manoeuvre.

"I know. Just giving them an idea."

"What's that?"

As Vikram had predicted the chasing driver decided to give it back. If he did crash into him, the Hyundai at one-fourth the weight would get crushed between the railing and the Mahindra. He had but one chance.

The Marksman widened the gap between them, driving parallel at over 100 kmh. A gun stuck out from one of the rear windows, but they weren't pulling the trigger yet. Perhaps, the possibility of hitting a civilian stymied their finger.

Then heaving with all its heft, the 4x4 came hurtling on

a path to converge with Vikram's car at full force.

Vikram swerved to the very edge of the flyover and slammed the brakes.

The Marksman sailed past them in the front and with its armoured momentum went right through the railing, careening off the flyover and falling onto the street below.

"I really, really hope there was no one under that," muttered Vikram. And as for the occupants, as long as they were wearing their seatbelts, they would have survived, he thought. He calmly shifted to fifth gear and the car shot forward.

As he aligned east once again to get to central Delhi, there was a familiar whup-whup-whup sound overhead. Raj rolled down his window and stuck his head out, looking up.

"Yup, that's for us."

"Sounds like a Pawan Hans Dauphin."

"Spot on."

"Just a tracker then."

A tracker heli in such a situation was deployed only to tail the car and relay information to checkpoints, and wouldn't be aggressive in any manner.

"Let's try and lose it."

Keeping off the busy routes, Vikram took various unsystematic turns in trying not to give away a specific direction. He guessed the police must've started deploying all over their quadrant of the city. But he had to make sure he got rid of the heli first.

For the next ten minutes, they were unable to shake it off. It was only a matter of time before they ran into authorities on the ground.

"Look there–" Raj was pointing to a car that resembled

his own silver Hyundai. Vikram started tailing it, hoping the copter pilot hadn't seen it yet. They turned into Amrita Sher-Gil Marg. Delhi's greening program had been flourishing and there was significant tree cover that kept their car from the copter's view for a large part. Here, the canopy had them covered altogether. The car they were following exited from the other side on to Humayun Road. The copter continued to hover for what seemed like a long time.

Vikram and Raj had already gotten off and were hoofing it across a large house's compound perpendicular to either exit, scaling walls, jumping fences. Vikram had collected his helmet.

The copter finally moved in the direction of the decoy car.

"Looks like they bought it."

Vikram spotted a middle-aged man on a Vespa knockoff. He stood in front of him, forcing him to stop.

"I'll give you my car keys if you drop us to Pandara Road," said Vikram. "It's over-parked at Amrita Sher-Gil."

The man was still deciding how to react to this strange barter request when the two strapping men wedged themselves on the backseat.

"Take it through the market," said Raj. This allowed them to skirt past one police post, but the cops were more interested in checking cars and didn't bother with them as they took a narrow service road. Finally they reached Khan's, where Vikram's bike was parked. As promised, they handed their car keys to the rider who still didn't quite comprehend what was happening. Raj politely asked for his helmet and the two took off with Raj riding.

"Well, that was fun. What now?" asked Raj.

"We need to go to the media."

"Who do we know?"

"Aditi Shenoy."

"Ah, of course. Your girlfriend. Good idea. And by the way, if we get out of this alive and don't end up in prison, you owe me a car."

60

1020 HOURS

ADITI was in her cabin. On her instruction, her assistant had ensured there were no meetings or appointments scheduled for the day. She had wanted some quiet time to think. But the breaking news had occupied most of her morning so far.

Newsrooms across the country were trying to source all the video footage they could of the wild chase that just ended on the streets of New Delhi with an army vehicle driving off a flyover. From people who had shot bits of the pursuit on their cell phones to shop owners who had it on their CCTVs to the traffic police, an informal search-and-auction was on between news channels.

A colleague had texted her to find out if she could help with her contacts in the Transport Office to identify the owners of the cars from the number plates. Not wanting to get involved, she had passed on her contact. That there were army vehicles involved made this already uncommon event newsworthy to a whole new level.

But her mind kept circling back to her conversation with Soumik. He had not questioned her further, and this had her worried. *He knows I haven't been honest.* But how much did he know? She had been unable to focus on work after her meeting and was becoming paranoid about the document's safety (Was her secret place safe enough?). Soumik's accusing silence had magnified the feeling several times over. A wave of anxiety rose in the pit of her stomach. She wished she were back home.

Home. Where she could retreat to and plan her initiative. Amidst her fears, the idea of what her future held was like a constant glow at the end of a dark tunnel. The thought eased her mind a little.

The story of the single largest revelation in the history of independent India was hers to break to the world. With implications that would change the direction of subcontinental politics – and with it, the larger politics of the world – forever. And every time, every time anyone looked back at how all this started, it would trace back to Aditi Shenoy.

Her office extension rang.

"Yes?" she barked into the phone; she was rebuking herself for daydreaming, building castles in the air again.

"Hey Aditi, your contact checked out. They've identified the car on the run belonging to a Rajveer Yadav. We're looking him up now. Just wanted to inform and say thanks."

"Yeah, no problem."

Aditi hung up. Now why did that name ring a bell? It had almost come to her when her cell phone chirped. Unknown number.

"Hello?"

"Hello, is this Aditi Shenoy?"

Most likely a crank caller who had managed to get hold of her number. Still–

"Who's this?"

"Rajveer Yadav. From the NSG. I need to meet you

right now."

It all came back to her. This man was part of Vikram's squad in the Srinagar operation. What were the chances.

"You were the man being chased?"

After a beat: "Yes."

"Vikram Rathore's colleague?"

"Yes. Listen, we need to meet somewhere private. Trust me, this is worth your time. Where can we do this?"

For the life of her Aditi could not in that instant think up a place that was not public. And for some reason she believed him.

"My place?"

"Where is it?"

As she recited her home address, she couldn't help but feel that the universe was signalling and history beckoning her to acknowledge it and leave her mark forever.

61

1110 HOURS

VIKRAM hadn't slept since Tuesday. His limbs, already impaired in the Taliban attack, were throbbing with pain and threatening to cease functioning. His mind kept turning to the burning question: with his entanglement in the matter so deep, what was the endgame? What was his best case scenario? Taking on the defense minister one-on-one would be rash. He was much too powerful and shielded. A stronger case could be made if he went public with Aditi's help and exposed the conspiracy. He'd be perceived as the victim, and rightly so. But the law could still sneak up on him to implicate him in myriad ways. And what protection did he have from the state's shadow machinery? If they could put him up to assassinate a Pakistani politician, how difficult would it be for them to find someone to finish him? Could he get witness protection as a whistle-blower? Bani… he wanted to drop everything and rush to meet her. But he would be jeopardizing his life if he did that. And Raj's. And Bani's. And their child… he hoped it would be a girl.

"We're here," said Raj, as he turned the bike around a corner. Vikram snapped awake. They were in Noida. He didn't recall crossing the DND Flyway across the Yamuna. He had dozed in and out of sleep while holding onto Raj. *Stay alert*, he told himself.

The news anchor's residence was within a recently developed, exclusive gated community with all the creature comforts of the modern suburban lifestyle from multiple swimming pools and a putting green to a walking track suspended thirty floors above the ground. She owned the penthouse in the tallest building within. But as with most housing societies, security was incongruous to the amenities. Vikram had no trouble filling in a fake name at the register with the security guard and a brief intercom call later, was on his way up to the top floor. Raj had elected to wait in the palatial lobby that was no less impressive than a fancy hotel's and had comfortable couches disbursed, one of them in front of a television. Raj decided that watching clips of the chase was all the entertainment he needed while keeping a lookout as Vikram finished his business.

"Get straight to the point with her," he warned him.

Upstairs, Aditi had set up her Canon 5D camera on a tripod pointing at a chair in front of a featureless grey wall that could service as a green screen if required. She checked focus a few times and was ready for her guest. There was not much prep to be done. Instinct told her that the questions would ask themselves once Raj Yadav had revealed what it was that was 'worth her time'.

When she heard the elevator, she opened the door before her guest had a chance to ring the doorbell.

"Raj?"

"No, I'm Vikram Rathore. We spoke on the phone after the Srinagar op. I have just escaped from Pakistan, where I was sent to assassinate the MFA. I want to tell you my story."

As Aditi prepped the camera and Vikram sipped from a glass of water she had brought him, she couldn't help but steal furtive glances and stare at the man who was now wanted in two countries. Yes, the picture the Pakistani authorities had released was him all right.

"Do you want to tell me in brief before we start recording or would you like to get straight into it?"

"We should start. It's not safe for me to be in one place for too long," he said. But he changed his mind instantly, "But so you know: the Chairman Chiefs of Staff Committee, CoAS General Garah in cahoots with Defence Minister Ranade hatched a conspiracy to kill Mohammed al-Bashir, Pakistan's foreign minister, to jeopardize the peace process, specifically the treaty to be signed tomorrow. They sent me in disguise as a journalist in a covert operation. The mission went awry. I crossed back. Now the government has issued a shoot-at-sight order. I want the truth to come out so that I may find protection and justice is carried out."

Vikram's words were measured and he watched Aditi almost fumbling with the camera as she heard this explosive divulgence.

"Wow," she exclaimed, recovering. "Okay… let's just get into it right away. Be thorough, and start from the very beginning. Let's say from Monday, since I spoke with you."

She discreetly readjusted the field of vision of the lens and pulled another chair into the frame. She wanted the world to associate her with this revelation. Two of the decade's biggest unrelated stories falling into her lap. Goodness, her fortune bordered on the absurd. *Capital News* could have this one as a farewell gift.

Vikram was twelve minutes into the story, stalking the MFA in Margalla and about to be clubbed by the double agent Jamal when his phone rang.

Only Raj had his number. This meant there was trouble. He was already up and heading to the door as he answered.

Raj was talking in whispers. "Six men are on their way up. Four are taking the elevator, two are taking the stairs. They're in plain clothes but they're army, possibly ex-army as they look older. Could be mercs. I'm still in the lobby. There are two people outside by their cars parked right out front. Call me when you're down. They looked right through me, so I should be okay."

Vikram stopped in front of the elevator. The floors were ticking up. It was on the eighth storey right now. Aditi had rushed after him.

"What happened?"

"They've traced me."

"Stay inside, I'll send them away."

"No. They won't leave without searching the house. I'm a terrorist to them right now. They'll be ruthless."

Fifteenth floor. Half way there.

As Vikram saw it, he had two options: the balcony, find a way down using the plumbing system or take a chance with the stairs where there were men on the way up.

Twentieth floor.

Vikram shut his eyes weighing his options. Aditi was still at the door, looking nervous, biting her lip. This was a new building, the drainage was probably all concealed, he couldn't remember seeing anything from the outside except a staggered layout of square balconies. Even if he risked jumping from one to another, there was every chance he would be spotted by the men on the ground who would raise an alarm. If he took the stairs, he would undoubtedly run into those working their way up. One would be stationed in the landings, while the other swept every individual floor. He could take them out, but then again, the window would be small for his escape as their disappearance would not go unnoticed for too long.

The elevator was two floors away.

"You need to hide the tape you were recording on. Shut the door, go!"

At once Aditi slammed her main door shut. Vikram pushed past the egress opening up to the stairwell and turned behind a wall just before the elevator opened. He crouch-walked down the first flight and then, putting his helmet back on, started making his way down with stealthy but rapid strides.

Aditi rushed to the camera and ejected the microSD card. The doorbell rang. She looked frantically around the room for a place to conceal it.

On the seventh floor, Vikram was certain he was about to run into his would-be assailants. There was no option of sneaking up on them, he would have to take them head on. As he turned the corner, they were right there staring up at him, this man in a helmet. Vikram tightened his fists.

Aditi's doorbell rang incessantly. They were getting impatient.

"Coming!" She shoved the media storage into a potted plant, hoping it wouldn't affect the footage, and rushed to the door.

"Who is it?"

"Open up!"

Aditi, not the kind of person to be cowed down and still exultant at her fortune, decided to take them on. She opened the door and stared down the barrels of multiple guns. The men entered and pushed her roughly into the house, closing the door behind them.

The two men walked right past Vikram. *What the hell?*

He had already dialled Raj by the time he reached the lobby.

"Waiting outside."

Vikram spotted him on the bike. The Gypsys the men had come in were parked not too far off. Again, there was not even a flicker of interest, a look in their direction as Vikram got on behind Raj.

Aditi was outraged at her manhandling.

"What the fuck is going on?"

"Madam, you have something that came in a package with a painting. Please hand it over," said the tallest of the five men. The rest were already fanning out in her apartment searching with ruthless efficiency for the document.

Aditi realized in that instant that the men had not come for Vikram, but for her.

62

1230 HOURS

COERCED at gunpoint, Aditi sat on her sofa and watched as every square inch of her house was searched with a merciless, professional dexterity straight out of the movies. Drawers and cupboards were emptied, chairs and tables upturned, every upholstered article ripped apart, walls drilled into where they sounded hollow, every page of every book flipped through. They even slashed open every item of clothing with lining. For a minimal home, Aditi seemed to have a lot more secret spaces in there than she had ever imagined. They would not find anything. The papers were simply not in her house. They missed the memory card in the soil of her potted mini bamboos as well.

The seven men – all of a sturdy built, but none younger than forty – convened for a short meeting. Aditi had insisted she had no idea what they were talking about and that the painting itself was in her office, specifically with her editor Soumik Sen. The broad-shouldered leader dismissed what she had to say and had proceeded with the search.

Satisfied that he had covered the house from every angle, he went to a corner and dialled his phone for a brief, private conversation, every now and then glancing up at Aditi. Then he walked up to her and held out the instrument for her.

"Speak."

"Hello?"

"Hello Miss Capital News."

Aditi recognized the voice and the salutation; it's what he had called her in jest on a couple of occasions. She had interviewed the man on the other side multiple times and over the years they had become familiar with each other. He had earned her respect. Though outspoken and opinionated, his POV had always been one of reasonableness, epitomizing the modern and moderate politician. This made him a favourite of the media. That he had Prime Ministerial ambitions was no secret, but he never displayed any signs of insubordination internally or in public. As one of the chief fundraisers and guarantor of multiple Lok Sabha seats with his team of loyalists, he enjoyed tenure in the party. Now he was on the other end of the line. And because he had come up in the conversation with Vikram, the image of this eminent man was fresh in her memory.

"Mr Ranade?"

"Yes, it's me. I know you are hiding something, Miss Capital News. Something that belongs to me. Please hand it over to my men and we can forget any of this ever happened."

Aditi realized that the defence minister was aware of the document. Of course, Bobby Bhullar was the connection. An arms dealer at the end of the day was working for the Defence Department and the perks had to go all the way up the value chain.

"This is ridiculous, Mr Ranade, I don't know what the hell you're talking about and I assure you, this intrusion into my life is not going to go unquestioned in the media.

In fact, you calling and talking to me–"

"Shut up. Just shut up."

Aditi was taken aback by the vehemence of the order. His tone was unlike anything she had ever heard from him.

"Let me be forthright with you: I don't think you understand… the severity of the situation. Of what I can do to you. You have family in Mangalore, don't you? You have friends…" he let his threat remain suspended, pulsing for a few beats. "You listen to me," he continued, "my boys tell me what I'm looking for is not at your house. I'm going to give you until 3 pm. I won't harass you. You bring it to me. And… like I said… we'll put it all behind us."

The broad-shouldered man ripped his phone out of her hand. He instructed his companion to collect her iMac and all the hard discs they could find.

Then they marched out the door, leaving the house and her thoughts in disarray.

How was Ajinkya Ranade mixed up in both these plots? Was there a connection between an assassination attempt and a historical document? She had never envisaged that her discovery was not merely anthropological, but part of a deep, murky political conspiracy with a trail of corpses.

Aditi could not afford to hand over the document right away. It was not as if she could take a picture on her phone and pass it along. The information itself was irrelevant, in a manner of speaking, given the circumstances. What was critical was that the text existed at all. The conduit she chose – Indian broadcast media or an international publication – would want to authenticate the basis of her story. Document forensic scientists, typography and typewriter experts, dating technicians; a host of specialists would have to verify that it was not a forgery. All this would take a lot more than the few hours Ranade had given her.

How could she buy more time?

She brought out her second phone, her secure private number that she had kept hidden even from Anmol, her hacker friend, and used only to make the most sensitive calls. She dialled the number Raj had called from earlier.

"Raj…"

"Aditi? It's me. Are you safe?"

Aditi recognized Vikram's voice.

"Uh… nothing. It's… they were here to talk to me."

"Oh? You okay?"

"Yes yes, it was all very civil. Listen, we should finish the interview. But not here. My house is probably under surveillance."

"Hang on."

After half a minute Vikram returned to the phone, "Okay, so there's an empty apartment on the Yamuna Expressway that belongs to Raj's family. Note down this address–"

Even as she scribbled into a notepad, a thought gnawed at the back of her head until she allowed it to take over her consciousness. She was opening up to the possibility of making a deal with the devil.

63

1330 HOURS

VIKRAM finished his interview with Aditi. Every detail of what had transpired with him was now on two small storage cards. It was the only record that existed, solitary proof that he was innocent and incriminated by the powers that be. At one point, he even showed the camera where his missing toes used to be.

Aditi seemed distant during the interview, approaching it with a mechanical indifference. It surprised Vikram that she had no further questions and seemed less than enthused. She had even stayed out of the frame this time around.

"Was it okay?" he asked at the end of it.

"You did well," was all she had to offer.

"Now what happens?"

"I put this on air as soon as possible. But before that, I want to know your plan. Where are you going to be? Here?"

"I didn't think so far ahead. I'll have to have a word with Raj…"

"Listen, why don't you come with me? *Capital News* has a safe house for whistle-blowers in the heart of the city. It's something Soumik set up when the Haryana education scam news broke. No one knows of it. I've already got the requisite permissions. It's where you should stay for the next few days. You and Raj of course."

The idea appealed to Vikram.

"Let's go then," she said wrapping up her gear. "I'll drive. You can follow me on your bike."

1420 HOURS

Forty minutes later, Aditi pulled up her car outside one of the several entry points into Sainik Farms. Raj stopped about fifty metres behind her. Aditi called Vikram; it had been agreed that if they wanted to talk they would use the phone.

"Sainik Farms?" said Vikram, surprised. He thought it odd to create sanctuary in the midst of what was essentially an illegal colony, the continuance of which was fuelled by hundreds of wealthy private citizens and corrupt government officials. But then again, this would be the last place a fugitive was likely to be found.

"I'm going to go in first and make sure everything is in order. You guys should stay outside the perimeter but in the vicinity. I'll call you again."

She eased into the gates of the colony and wound her way to DM Ranade's palatial quarters. She had played the scenario several times in her mind and its likely outcomes. It was a huge risk from every angle. She had no idea how the MP – in this hitherto unknown avatar – would react to her offer.

She was escorted by his security straight to Ranade's study, an expansive room dominated by luxurious leather couches and arcing floor lamps with French windows that opened up to the swimming pool. He was sitting behind his handcrafted crocodile leather desk.

His gaze went up from her feet to her face, as she trooped in with confidence, her heels making a racket on his wooden flooring. She was in a fitted pair of jeans and a simple black blouse that outlined her tall, slim figure, accentuating the right places. Her poker-straight hair was cut blunt with a fringe, framing her high cheekbones and downturned eyes that she had emphasized with a deep eyeliner.

Despite her striking looks and assured poise, Ranade was utterly dismayed.

"Empty-handed?"

"No. But I wanted to have a discussion first, sir."

The *sir* didn't go unnoticed by Ranade, but he chose not to acknowledge the cajolery.

"What a pain in the neck you are, woman. I have much more important things to do with my time than discuss–"

"I have Vikram Rathore," she cut him off, "and I can hand him over to you."

Ranade stayed impassive. She knew he was trying to gauge if she was telling the truth. *Did she really have the man he wanted dead?*

"I don't believe you."

Aditi let fly at him. She spoke rapidly, trying to overwhelm him, trying to drive the bargain hard:

"I know what you put him up to, you and General Garah, sending him to Islamabad, the planned assassination of Pakistan's Minister of Foreign Affairs, the sordid details. I have Vikram's confession. And it's on video. You can guess the implication if this video makes the news, right?

Your life and career… I don't need to spell it out. Instead this is what we're going to do: I need one month with the document. With that, I want a guarantee for life you won't go after me or anyone connected to me. This guarantee will be in the form of the video evidence that I have. I will keep that too. I have buried many stories in the past – from politics to Bollywood – under the guise of responsible reporting, but we both know the right price can cover any exposé. I'm offering you Vikram now, and all I'm asking is for a month. After that, the document is all yours."

Her proposed arrangement was laid out. There was little room for negotiation. Aditi hoped that in her zest she would rise in her host's estimation and reap due respect.

Ranade turned away from Aditi and faced the windows. The pool glittered in the afternoon light like constellations of citrine. Parrots circled overhead. This had all gone so horribly wrong for him.

"I have a question for you," he addressed her, in almost a whisper. "What was in Bobby Bhullar's package?"

Ranade didn't know what the document was!

"It contained a few British-era documents, letters from squabbling politicians."

Aditi tried to sound confident, believable.

"And you'd rather give up Vikram Rathore's story for… this?"

"There's exciting history in there for a journalist. Shows our national icons in a whole new light. It'll make for hours of primetime TV, help advance my career."

Ranade had heard enough. There was no more reason to trust her.

"You lying bitch."

Defence Minister Ranade had pulled out a shiny,

compact Glock 43 pistol from his drawer and pointed it at Aditi. Already on the brink with his anger and pride being battered by this woman's demands, his senses and perspicaciousness were overwhelmed by rage.

Aditi's felt her muscles bunch up, and her heart was pounding. She tried to speak between rapid breaths. "There's no need for this Mr Ran–"

"This confession, who else has seen it?" asked Ranade, in almost a whisper.

"No one."

That was all he needed to know. He squeezed the trigger point blank.

Aditi was thrown back by the force of the bullet, her head bouncing on the floor. She held her stomach where it hurt and when she brought her hand to her face, she saw it covered in carmine blood. She looked down, unbelieving, at her already damp blouse, unable to pull it back. She knew the damage was instant and complete.

In the distance she heard Ranade barking orders: "Vikram… in the area…"

As her eyes started to defocus, she reached into her pocket and felt for her phone. With great effort she pulled it out and dialled the last number, visionless.

She did not have the strength to bring it up to her head. She hoped it had been answered on the other end even though she had lost sense of time.

"Where… you… sent… the phone." She struggled with the words. It was going to take a lot more force than this to get her message across. So she tried again, putting every last vestige of her remaining life into it.

"Where you sent… the phone!"

The mobile was pried out of her hand. Ranade was upon

her. There was no way to know if Vikram had heard her.

"Hello? Vikram? Where are you? Hello…" he snarled into phone.

Ranade cut it off and looked at Aditi without emotion. As the last flicker of life left her being, Aditi's final sensation was a rush of remorse for Vikram Rathore, the man whose life she had tried to trade for personal glory.

64

1420 HOURS

VIKRAM and Raj had found a corner under the shade just inside the Sainik Farm gates. Raj had even managed to wangle them a couple of cups of tea from a corner stall. As the minutes they'd spent waiting for Aditi's call piled up, Raj could see Vikram – even with his face half masked by the helmet – starting to look agitated.

"I need to meet Bani. It feels as if it's been months."

"Yes, I can imagine… let's look into that once we are settled in the safe house." Raj was trying to think up a new subject to steer away the conversation but was drawing a complete blank at the moment.

"No, listen. I need to do this."

"I hear you."

"We should do it now."

Raj had seen the 'now' from a mile away. When it came to Bani, his friend transformed into an illogical loon.

"Look, Aditi asked us to be around here…"

"We should at least formulate a plan so that there's no time wasted."

"Don't you want to lay low for at least 24 hours? Get some food, sleep…"

"First, she's got to shake off the unit tailing her. "

"Yes," said Raj. No point fighting him once he's made

up his mind. Might as well go along with what he hoped would be an academic discussion for now. "But don't forget that any communication by us from our end will reveal our location and number."

"What if we use the burners?"

"They'll triangulate it to here, plus we'll have to lose the phone."

"Same if we use a payphone, if we can find one; they'll know we've been here..."

"... and potentially track us using public CCTVs and witnesses. The cameras are so new, they must be all still working too."

Over twenty thousand new CCTV cameras had been installed all over the city recently as part of a major upgrade.

A boy in a tattered shirt from the tea stall, no older than twelve, came up to Vikram and Raj to collect their empty glasses. Raj opened his wallet to pay up. He was pulling out twenty rupees when–

"How much do you have?" Vikram interjected.

"About two thousand."

"Give him all of it."

"What? Why?"

"Just do it."

Incredulous at his own actions, Raj emptied his wallet of the cash and gave it to the boy who was as confused as he was.

"Is this my tip?" he asked in a daze as he took the money.

"Yes," said Vikram, "but you have to do a job."

"What?"

"I'm going to give you an address. I want to you to go there and talk to my wife Bani and give her a message. Can you do that for me?"

"Where is the house?"

"Not very far. Take a rickshaw from the money we've given you. When you come back after delivering the message, I will give you more."

The boy looked into the distance, giving the offer some consideration. He looked at his stall. "I guess we are not that busy. I'll make up some excuse for the boss. Okay, what's the message and the address?"

"Give me your phone, and hold on to this," said Vikram to Raj, exchanging their Nokias.

Vikram took him to a corner and started to explain. Raj was suitably impressed, but he wondered what the actual ploy was.

He was still watching Vikram squatting down to the boy's height and making him memorize the instruction, when Aditi called.

Raj waved and called out to Vikram. The boy was sent on his way and Vikram bounded over. Raj had already hit the green button and put it on speaker.

They caught her mid-sentence, barely audible. Vikram's senses were on full alert. There was every indication that all was not right.

For one Aditi didn't sound herself and was struggling to speak. They could barely make out the what she was saying. Someone was yelling in the background, Vikram thought he heard his name. And the tone was aggressive, almost malicious.

"What the hell?" Raj frowned. Vikram shushed him.

Then they heard her again and this time her voice had more force and clarity. *Where you sent… the phone!*

"Who is she talking to?"

Then the vicious voice again at the other end, addressing

them; demanding to know where Vikram was.

The line went off.

"We need to get the hell out of here."

Raj was already kick-starting the RX-100.

"What happened there?"

"I don't know but it didn't sound good for Aditi," said Vikram. "She sounded incapacitated. Do you think we should…"

"No, Vikram, it's probably a well laid out trap."

"But she was trying to help us; she's here because of us."

"I know. But we have no idea where she went or what has transpired. And another minute spent looking for her is another minute endangering ourselves. And it will turn out to be a situation where everyone loses." Raj was forceful with his words. He wanted to halt Vikram's train of thought there and then.

Vikram knew he was right. He could only hope she was okay. But for now, there was no way to know.

Raj chose to mingle into the traffic to stay incognito. If needed, he could always dodge his way out. The RX-100's ebullient engine matched the most powerful bikes of its time, managing a 0-100 in under five seconds.

"What was Aditi saying?" Raj hollered through his helmet and over the honking, "about sending a phone?"

Vikram was thinking about it at that very moment. She had dialled him. What she had said was meant for him. *Where he had sent the phone.* He hadn't sent any phone anywhere. But she had given him one. Back in Kashmir. On Monday. For the telephonic interview. He had insisted on wanting to return the instrument. She had given him a PO Box number. He struggled to recall it. Shutting out the clamour of the traffic in his mind and closing his eyes, he tried to imagine himself back in the armoured vehicle's seat; back to the moment when she had called him–

"This phone, uh, how do I return it?"

"Don't worry. Trash it. Give it to a nephew."

"No, no. It looks… tell me how I can reach it to you."

He thought he heard her chuckle. "Fine. Post it to PO Box 1500, New Delhi. Easy enough to remember?"

PO Box 1500.

He was sure that's where she was asking him to go.

But why?

65

1500 HOURS

PO Box 1500.

It took precisely two phone calls and five minutes for Raj to figure out the physical location of the post box. The first was to his local police contact who in turn got in touch with the Postmaster General who gave him the details. The mailbox was hanging on a wall at the Lodhi Road Head Post Office.

The postmaster in charge, however, was in no mood to entertain two hulking men who refused to take off their helmets. When Raj insisted the short, frail gentleman with the toothbrush moustache call the Postmaster General himself, contrary to expectation, he did not hesitate. He dialled the New Delhi GPO board line and worked his way through the ranks until he reached the PMG's secretary.

All this while the white and green trapezoid container with *1500* freshly repainted was right behind him in plain view of the commandos.

After requesting to speak with the PMG he heard out the secretary and then disconnected the call, much to the exasperation of the two men.

"What the hell?"

"I'm sorry, the PMG is out for lunch, post which he will be in a meeting until 5 o'clock; we can take up the matter once he's available."

"5 o'clock? Mister, we need to see the contents of the box right this minute… you don't understand…"

"You listen to me, *mister*. This is the Indian Postal Service. We are the most widely distributed postal service in the world and, if I may add, the most reliable as well. We didn't get here because we allow erratic youth like yourselves to ransack our post-boxes at will… a billion people depend on us because…"

As the man droned on about the salient features of India Post, Raj looked around. Employees were still straddling in after their lunches, putting away their boxes, some pacing up and down the length of the customer waiting area as a post-meal exercise regime. Most waiting customers were not amused watching this routine, others were following the conversation between the diminutive postmaster and his unusual guests.

Raj decided that the employees were all on the brink of a siesta and would not put up much of a fight. And he had been far too nice for far too long. So he jumped over the counter, pushed the postmaster aside, grabbed the PO Box, heaved it off the wall and tossed it to Vikram.

They scooted out the entrance much to the horror of the employees and amusement of the customers and the tumultuous rage of the postmaster.

Back on the road and on the motorcycle, Raj headed south with the mailbox wedged between him and Vikram. No one gave them a second look. A couple of minutes later, he turned into Kidwai Nagar, a colony where considerable on-going construction work would provide them cover for the interim.

Vikram picked up a short rebar from the roadside and,

using a smooth rock as a fulcrum while Raj held down the post box, he pried it open without much difficulty.

An envelope caught the wind and took off towards an earthmover.

Vikram and Raj chased behind it, grasping it inches from the ground as it almost plummeted into a pit of sludge.

It was Raj who brought out the sheaf of papers first. He scanned them with what Vikram thought was the most intense frown he had ever seen on his friend's face, though his expression didn't give away any emotion. From the back, the paper looked aged; brittle and yellow-stained. Then Raj looked up and held them out for Vikram.

"I don't understand."

Vikram took the papers. The title on the first sheet started almost halfway down.

NEW ACCESSION TREATY

Around him, the sound of jackhammers and rumbling excavators, the blinding sparks of circular saws cleaving steel, everything faded into an obscure existence as Vikram and Raj stood there coming to terms with the contents of these papers:

An alternative, later version of the Instrument of Accession that Hari Singh, the ruling king of Jammu and Kashmir, had signed. It was a reimagining of the Kashmir situation, and attested by everyone from Nehru, Mountbatten, Patel, Gandhi, and Jinnah. The key to the greatest conflict on the subcontinent and the destiny of nearly two billion people was now in their hands.

66

1550 HOURS

THE house help answered the door and informed Bani that 'a street urchin' was asking for her and should she 'shoo him away?'

Bani was consumed; ferreting between news channels, burrowing for more information on the morning's car chase, now that the perpetrator's vehicle had been identified as belonging to a Rajveer Yadav.

Without looking, she nodded to her maid.

On being told off, the boy had shrugged and had almost gone all the way back to the gate of the house, when the maid hollered for him to come right back.

Bani was at the door and waiting all alert, the television's irresistible spell broken.

"Who sent you?"

"Superstar sent me."

Bani yanked him in and gave him a mammoth hug that surprised him and disgusted the maid in equal measure. 'Superstar' was what Vikram's juniors had nicknamed him at the Manesar NSG HQ. He had hated it, especially when Bani teased him about it.

When she let go of the boy, there were tears streaming down her face. The maid had disappeared into the kitchen.

"Did he seem fine?"

"He was very animated. And he smelled a little."

Bani chuckled. The boy held out the phone.

"He asked to give this to you. And he's sent a message."

"What's the message?" she asked, accepting Raj's old Nokia cell. Her heart was pounding.

1630 HOURS

The instructions from Vikram were brief: *Get on the metro. Keep changing trains arbitrarily. Try to lose whoever is following you. I will call.* The last three words sparked a single-mindedness in Bani that refused to wane over the hours. She was going to be resolute in following his directive. There was nothing more important to her at the moment in time than to hear his voice.

She had put on her most comfortable cotton pants and sneakers and rolled up a hoodie to carry in her hand. She stuffed some cash into her pockets along with the Nokia and jogged to the metro station. Her own phone she had left behind, well aware that its location could be easily tracked. There were two army cars staking out now and one of them kept pace with her. Breaking into a light run, she ducked out of sight, bounded up the escalator to the station, bought a token and jumped aboard the first train she saw pulling into the platform. There was no way to tell if someone had managed to follow her, though she suspected it would be easy to monitor her movements through CCTV. But it gave her a lot more time. The more frequently she changed trains, the more effort it'd take them to keep abreast of her movement. After the first change of trains, she put on her hoodie, potentially buying herself even more leverage. Not bad, thought Bani, for a chemical engineer she had picked up a few cloak-and-dagger capabilities from her commando husband. And, she guessed, with some additional credit to Hollywood.

Now she was on the Blue Line, clutching on to the phone, checking every few minutes if the battery was healthy. She was heading towards Central Delhi again. She intended switching to the Green Line at Kirti Nagar, head north and then take the Red to go either east or west, depending on what train arrived first. She was thinking as few steps ahead as possible so that even if a mind-reader was tailing her, they wouldn't know where she was going.

The phone beeped.

"Platform 2, Rajiv Chowk."

Bani took a deep breath. Rajiv Chowk was on the very line she was on right now. She wrote a text back saying "ten minutes". It remained undelivered.

The air was thick with the commuters' acrid fetidness when she alighted at Rajiv Chowk, the busiest of all Delhi Metro stations. She cautiously made her way to Platform 2, her eyes darting from face to face, hoping to catch sight of her husband.

She placed herself roughly in the middle of the perpetually crowded platform. One train came and departed. The throng thinned out momentarily, but was back to strength within the minute. Another train approached. It slowed to a halt, the assemblage surged into the doors as they opened. Bani kept waiting. How many more trains would she have to see go by before someone suspected something fishy? Suddenly, a hand hooked her arm and guided her into the stream of the boarding passengers. She tried to look around, but she could not move her head as she was swept into the waiting train's compartment.

As the doors closed, the grip on her hand loosened. She turned to see a tall man, his face masked by sunglasses, a beanie, and a red scarf wrapped loosely around his lower jaw. Vikram!

"Look away, put the phone to your ear and pretend you're talking on it" he said. She didn't see his lips move and no one else around them heard him. She followed the instructions.

"Are you okay?" He asked after a few seconds.

"Besides waking up every day and puking my guts out… yes, but what about you? What's happening, Vikram?" It took Bani a monumental effort to not look at him, to not grab him and hold on to him. A tear appeared, she wiped it away in haste.

"It's a long story. I am sorry I left without informing you. It was stupid. I… I… should have never left, Bani."

"It's okay, V. What's done is done. Tell me what I can do to help you now."

"Just stay safe. I'm sorry I've called you out here… I needed to see you."

"Enough with the apologies," Bani admonished him. "You know I'm here for you. And listen, I know you're doing the right thing."

"But I'm putting you at risk here."

Bani wondered how grave the risk was for him if she was in danger for just meeting him.

"I'll be okay if you are. But when do you think you can come home?"

"I… need to sort this out."

"Is there anyone helping you?"

"Well there's Raj every step of the way. Look to your right."

Bani turned. It took her a few moments but she managed to pick out Raj on lookout duty two doors away, wearing an oversized grey windcheater similar to what Vikram had on now.

"Say hi to him," she said looking out the window again.

"I will."

"But what now, Vikram? It seems everyone has it out for you. Is there someone, a higher-up who can bail you out from the situation?"

"Y… yes" he stammered. "There is someone. I… just hope it works out."

"So there's a plan?"

The answer wasn't instantaneous. "Yes."

Bani nodded, unconvinced, as a sense of foreboding rose in her chest. The train pulled up at the Chawri Bazaar station. Bani and Vikram maintained their positions as commuters rushed past them in either direction. A teenage couple seized the adjacent vacated seat and – finding ironical anonymity in the public around them – wasted no time in locking in an embrace and plunging into an endless kiss.

This broke up the tension somewhat. And to ease into lighter banter, Bani identified the perfect object for the job on Vikram from the corner of her eye.

"What's with the bright red scarf? It's even got Christmas trees on it."

A soft chuckle. "Just a change we got ourselves outside Palika."

"Well I hope you haggled; this was on its way to the

dumpster."

"Well, I just came from a dumpster."

"What do you mean?"

"Well Pakistan was rather rough."

Bani snorted into her phone – V had never been adept at political correctness; "Overrated," he would say.

They still hadn't looked at each other.

"I'm going to have to get off at the next station. You change a few more trains before heading home. Get rid of the phone."

Vikram let go of her arm and took a step away to align himself with the door. Bani couldn't help herself any more. She turned and looked at him. He caught her eye. Their eyes locked into each other's, an outpouring of love expressed sans words. Vikram put his hand on her abdomen.

"Have you thought of names?"

"That is literally the only job the father has during these nine months. While I do all the hard work, you are supposed to present options for me to pick from."

"Consider it done."

They drew close. Vikram squeezed Bani's hand. Bani leaned into him and stayed there as the train continued to hurtle.

"Bani," he whispered in her ear, "I have a quick question."

She arched her brows.

"Why is India holding on to Kashmir?"

"Kashmir? What do you mean?"

"Tell me – when the majority of Kashmiris want azadi, why are we hell-bent on claiming their land as our own, crushing all resistance?"

"Because… I guess… because at the time of

independence they *chose* us? And I suppose it is our duty to honour the agreement?"

"Right. That's what I thought."

The train started to slow down, the station appeared outside, blurry commuters coming into focus.

A woman shrieked. Vikram looked up, instantly detaching from Bani. Three cars away there was commotion; a buzz of surprise. Raj was already running in their direction.

"Shit. They tracked you," said Vikram as he pushed Bani into the seat, almost into the laps of two teenagers, breaking up their lingering kiss. She turned in the direction of the clamour, catching a flash of a gun held up above people's heads and making its way past like a bobbing shark fin. Three men in plain clothes were pushing their way through a crowd that was panicking on seeing the weapon. Vikram and Raj were already out by the time she looked back again. The men exited a parallel door. Consumed with guilt that she had led Vikram into this predicament, Bani couldn't help but chase after them. Whatever her fate, it couldn't be worse than what her husband had in store.

She tried to keep up with the chasers, taking a safer path, as they vaulted across tracks in pursuit. She couldn't see Vikram and Raj any more.

People were mercilessly shoved out of the way by the men with guns. A walker was knocked out of a limping grey-haired man's hands and unable to keep balance, he fell on the platform. A group of young boys rushed to help him up. Bani threw away her phone in the melee and continued to dash after them through the station.

They raced up the short escalator towards the Chandni Chowk exit. Bani pushed past the chaos, losing her line of sight as they left the station. She clambered up, about ten seconds behind, only just about seeing past the top stair when she heard the unmistakable sound of gunfire ring out. Just the one, single shot. She exited into near-blinding daylight in silence. As her eyes adjusted she saw masses of people scampering out of the way of the attackers, screaming for their lives. Not fifty metres away were the armed men, fast approaching a figure that had slumped over in the middle of the street.

Once upon the scene, one of the men turned the body over. Through the pandemonium Bani could just about make him out pulling the lifeless body by the neck, a red scarf with Christmas trees on it.

67

1600 HOURS

JAVID'S lunch remained untouched in a corner. He had spent the last few hours sitting in the ammunitions barracks, facing the wall, repeating an unspoken mental apology to Afzal. The anguished wail that had come from the boy's chest when the gag had come off had sounded not of the living. Thinking of it even now, a chill went down his spine.

"Ahmedbhai will be here by afternoon. He will arm you. And then we plan the mission. Until then you can wait here, no need for any interaction with the rest," Aziz had said after bringing Javid up to the same place, where he had met the sphinx-like Arab the day before.

Weapons. Javid guessed it wouldn't be unwieldy and conspicuous like the firearms that the uniforms carried, perhaps grenades and smaller guns that they had put in a backpack with other essential supplies like they did with fidayeens who were sometimes holed up in places that they attacked for days.

Light sneaked inside as the doors opened and outlined Ahmed al-Hashem's arrival in the shadows it cast.

"Well done, Javid. You have proven your loyalty," he boomed.

Javid offered no reply. He wanted to get out of here.

The incident had driven out the last shards of curiosity left in him, only a burning impulse to end this charade. As he turned around, Ahmed stood before him, smiling. Shaukat and Aziz were present too.

"Perhaps, you are angry with us. I assure you, in due course you will change your mind."

"Due course? Isn't the mission tomorrow?"

Ahmed didn't hesitate, "It is, it is. But your whole life remains between then and now. There is much you will experience until the moment is upon you."

This was the first instance of a confirmation that Javid was on a suicide mission. The realization felt like a mallet pummelled into his stomach, driving the wind out of him. Without warning and without restraint, tears flowed down his cheeks. What was happening to him? Why was he crying? His mind had not acknowledged the message, yet it had reacted in a physical way. He wiped them off hurriedly and looked up at Ahmed.

"What do you want me to do?"

"The weapon you'll carry is an IED. Short in English for 'Improvised Explosive Device'. However, this particular IED has some very remarkable aspects to it." He put his hand in his pocket and, holding it between his thumb and forefinger, pulled out what looked to Javid like a six-inch glob of washing soap with wires stuck on it. "Our well-wishers in Saudi have gone great lengths to acquire this explosive. It is made by the one and only Ibrahim al-Asiri, a man without whose genius our fight across the world would be a lot less restricted and without the teeth we have now. Our brothers first in Al-Queda and then in Daesh have been using this bomb to great effect. One man almost took out Prince Nayef, Saudi Arabia's counter-terrorism head, inside his own house. This particular device is one of the smallest IEDs in its class. The Americans have a phrase for it, 'more bang for the buck'. But the best part – the USP, if you please – is that it has no metal parts. And this means…" Ahmed walked towards a self-supported frame that Javid only now registered was present in the room, "…that this bomb is undetectable by a metal scanner."

Ahmed took out his watch and placed it on a table. Then he stepped through the scanner he had just turned on and backed up. He did this a couple of times. The frame remained impassive, no alarms. He put his watch back on and stepped through again. This time there was a distinct beep-beep.

"Wow," said Shaukat and Aziz almost in unison.

"Is this it?" asked Javid, cautious.

"This is all you will carry."

"How does it trigger?"

"By remote. We will give you a cell phone that will be the trigger."

"Then… wh…" Javid did not know how to phrase the question. If this were so small and passed through metal detectors and had a remote trigger, why did he need to die?

Ahmed knew exactly what he wanted to ask.

"Because Javid you will not carry this bomb on you. It will be *inside* you. That is the only way we can ensure you will make it past all the security at the event tomorrow to allow you to get close enough to do the damage that needs to be done."

Ahmed fished out a packet of condoms from another pocket.

"You know what these things are?"

Javid knew what they were. But he did not know how

to react to the theatrics that were unfolding before him.

"The IED will go into one of these. And then you will insert it in your anal canal," he paused, as if daring a reaction from anyone present in the room. When there was none: "It's common practice in prisons across the globe to use this technique to smuggle in drugs and knives. So there's nothing to worry about. It will hurt a little. But then, what's a little discomfort at the threshold of martyrdom?"

68

1730 HOURS

IF the odds are stacked against you, if you're unarmed, and if you're the target, and if a shot is fired… you don't turn to look. You run. You run as fast as you can. You get out of the shooter's sight. You get behind cover; a building, a wall, anything at all. You take a breath, you plan your next move. There is only one next move: you get out of the shooter's territory. That is what you have to do. Get out of there. Don't. Look. Back.

Drilled into his head in a classroom from his training days, these were instructions that had saved his life on more than one occasion.

But Vikram had looked back.

The very fact that they had pulled the trigger in itself signalled two aspects of serious consequence. The first, that the perpetrators were going for the kill. Two, they wanted to do this at all costs, even if it meant taking aim through a thronging area like Chandni Chowk. Collateral damage was acceptable. This was high stakes. When the bullet hit the intended mark, more hypotheses got confirmed: that the shooters were professionals, with high-level training. The margin of error was miniscule. At three metres, a gun that's not precisely aimed, even if it's five degrees off, it will miss its target. Here the distance was a lot more, and the target was moving.

One shot. One strike.

Vikram and Raj had accounted for the three scenarios that would play out when the meeting with Bani was in progress: nothing would happen; they would be tracked and followed; they would be attacked.

They bought identical windcheaters, beanies and red scarves. They would wear the jackets. But Raj would keep the beanie and scarf out of sight. If they were spotted, they would confuse and divert the assailants by switching their big visual clues. Vikram would lose his beanie and scarf, Raj would pull them up. Misled into thinking they were chasing Vikram, they would eventually catch up with Raj, not the man they were looking for.

It was a good plan. But Vikram had not accounted for the one scenario that did play out – that the assailants would be willing to eliminate their target in broad daylight. And succeed.

The sound of gunfire and with Raj tripping the very next second, Vikram knew he had been hit. He looked back, calculating if turning to assist his friend was tenable, but the momentum had already carried him. Going back would be suicide. So he had continued to run, hoping that Raj was merely hurt. And that their plan had worked and that they had managed to detract them with their deception.

Vikram ducked into the crowd and vanished. The attackers had stopped giving chase, convinced they had got their man.

Vikram circled back in an hour, stealthily, careful to stay in the shadows. He sidled up to a balloon peddler who was in the midst of an animated conversation with a man minding a juice stall.

"… I tell you, I saw one of their faces. But I'm not going to tell the police. No one in their right mind would want to get mixed up…"

"A glass of sugarcane juice please," interrupted Vikram.

The man nodded and got to work, grabbing a few sticks and running it through the crusher, making a racket.

"What went down here?" asked Vikram, looking over at the square of activity with cops.

It was all the prodding the duo needed.

They gave Vikram a blow-by-blow account of how Raj had fallen. The assailants had crowded around to finish off the job. They held up the victim's head as if to ID him. Their other target had got away. The shooters dispersed moments later, leaving the body half-slumped on the ground on its knees, its head dripping blood, pooling around him on the concrete. They had him in the first shot. A bullet straight in the back of his head. Gone, they said, just like that in an instant.

The men spoke with glee and gusto, like seasoned raconteurs, while Vikram's innards churned. He felt dizzy and sick in the stomach. By the time the two men had reached the point in the tale when the cops had arrived – a good half hour after the shooting – and a glass of freshly squeezed sugarcane juice had been proffered to the customer, Vikram was barely in control of his emotions. He staggered away mid-conversation. His world was blurry. Only his best friend's smiling face loomed in the foreground. There was a physical sensation, a stinging his chest that made him choke up.

Had his hubris killed Raj? Why had he agreed to the plan? How could they not account for what had happened?

He crumbled into an external recess carved into the boundary wall of Jama Masjid, losing himself amongst the homeless as the azaan rang out from the minarets. He stayed there a few hours, uncaring if he were found, his thoughts with his friend.

2000 HOURS

Vikram uncurled himself from the fetal position he had withered into and stood up. The market was buzzing, there was no trace of the shootout from earlier that day. Life had moved on.

He thought he should too. Raj's last favour should not go in vain.

He dialled a number they had located and stored in the phone earlier that day. Fifteen rings. No answer. Vikram redialled. Another fifteen rings. Again. Finally, on the fourth attempt, the voice he intended to reach crackled to life on the other end.

"Hello?"

"Thank you for answering, sir. This is Vikram Rathore. We met in your garden on the night of the NSG operation in Srinagar. You... you showed me your rhododendrons."

After a long silence, the CM of Kashmir, Obaid Sheikh, spoke again; his voice guarded, unforthcoming. "You are a wanted man, Rathore."

"Yes, sir. And I'm calling because you, of all people, know a conspiracy when you see one. I am just another dispensable soldier in the machinations of politics, a victim. And I need your help."

The CM took his time. And when he spoke, he was equivocal. "What do you want?"

"I have something to show you. And we have to meet for that to happen. I have the… solution."

"What are you talking about? The solution to what?"

Vikram had pre-decided that the only way he was going to convince the CM to agree to see him was if he told him the truth.

"Kashmir. The instrument of accession signed by Hari Singh is invalid. I have the *actual* document. It's in my possession. It explains itself. I don't know what to do with it. And I trust only you."

The CM snorted, his voice carried a tinge of irritation. Had the soldier come unhinged? "Sounds like a hoax, young man."

"Sir, an NSG commando, Squadron Commander Rajveer Yadav, was killed in broad daylight today for no fault of his. Bobby Bhullar, the arms dealer, and journalist Aditi Shenoy; they have all paid a price for this. The Pakistani MFA was almost assassinated. And all this while the real target is me. So please. Trust me. This is not a hoax."

There was a sharp intake of breath on the other end. Vikram knew he'd gotten through.

"Come. I will be in Uri for the treaty signing tomorrow. Send word via my people when you arrive."

"I will use a code name so you may identify it's me. Tell no one I'm coming, sir. "

"I understand."

Vikram hung up and went in search of a vehicle. An eighteen-hour journey lay ahead of him. And he was planning to do it in much less than that.

FRIDAY

69

0230 HOURS

JAVID was accompanied by Aziz, Shaukat, and Afzal as they trekked back towards the LoC. They had been ascending for some time and were amongst the clouds now, with only a few feet of visibility. Both Aziz and Shaukat carried AK-47s. Afzal shouldered a bagful of dry fruits, biscuits, and flasks of hot, salty tea. Every half an hour or so he would ask the company if anyone wanted any of the fare. Mostly he would be turned down, but when Aziz finally gave in and called for a five-minute halt for a cup, Afzal was all smiles. He treated them no differently, the events of the morning forgotten and forgiven.

Javid, who had been spared from carrying any weight, was trying hard not to think about what was wedged into his body. Inserting it in had been the most painful experience of his life. He tried it first on his own, but had to call for help when he couldn't make any progress. Biting into a piece of cardboard and lying face down on a table and letting go of all modesty, he let the others do whatever it took. It was short-lived and now, with each step, the pain eased.

The lights of the fence were visible up ahead: a wide string of floating luminescent orbs that disappeared into the fog on either side. Aziz walked on ahead to determine the positions of the Pakistani Rangers. While he was gone Afzal suggested another round of tea and a biscuit packet, and Shaukat informed Javid that the Rangers were not in the plan. Usually, the authorities knew of their every move, their camp location, every aspect of their operation. Free passage was a given. But not this time. The governments were going to quell the dream of a free Kashmir once and for all, and the Rangers and the BSF are in cahoots in their stand against insurgents.

Aziz's footsteps telegraphed his return.

"One patrol of two soldiers that are crossing by on a ten-minute interval. Come with me. As long as we are quiet, this should be easy to time."

They hid behind trees, each behind a towering deodar, and watched as the two rangers ambled by with their torches. Their voices carried in the silence of the woods. Javid picked up bits of their discussion: on the state of their uniforms and how they could use an extra pair of snow boots. "We won't need it," said one. "We're done here."

With no fence on the Pakistani side, all they had to do was tiptoe into no man's land once the soldiers were well out of sight. The complication was on Indian territory. Getting out was easier because they weren't looking in that direction. Their sights were trained on infiltrators.

"They haven't mended the fence yet."

They had reached the same spot from where Javid had been brought in. It looked altogether unfamiliar from the opposite view in the veil of the billowing fog.

"Wait here," whispered Aziz moving up ahead.

This time Afzal didn't offer tea. Like the rest, his gaze too followed the big man as he vanished from view. No one spoke. The wait was inordinately long. Once again, Aziz's form took shape in the mist.

"Let's go."

He led the way to the fence. They filed across one at a time, Afzal bringing up the rear. He was almost through when the lights on the fence – the ones that were supposed to be damaged – switched on in their faces, blinding them. This was immediately followed by the abrupt sound of gunfire that shattered the silence. *The Indian Army was onto them.*

Javid's first reaction was to drop face forward to the ground. He got on his fours and crawled as fast as he could, trying to keep up with Shaukat who was screaming and returning fire while trying to get behind a tree. Against the background of ear-splitting bursts of bullets, yelling, and his own grunts, Javid couldn't assimilate a visual of what was happening. There was no way to tell where the enemy was or where even the members of his own company had gone, save for Shaukat, behind whom he clambered to be within touching distance.

And then as suddenly as it had started, the guns fell silent and the wind in the trees were the only notes to be heard. Shaukat crouched next to Javid; the heat from the gun perceptible on his face. No one moved. Not a word was said.

After what seemed no less than an hour, they heard a hoot. The signal, recalled Javid. Immediately, Shaukat hooted back. A minute later Aziz was with them. They followed him for a time until in silence they were deep inside Indian territory.

"I had them in my sights. Their search party left in the other direction. That's when I signalled. I got one of theirs. A head shot. But…" Aziz paused and looked Javid in the eye, leaving the next part of the sentence unsaid, forcing him to phrase the worst.

"They got Afzal?" asked Javid. He had already guessed it given that the boy was nowhere in sight.

Aziz put his arm around his shoulder. "Yes. The uniforms got him. I'm sorry. I know he was special to you."

For a while they trudged in silence. As he mourned mentally for Afzal, Javid took the lead. Aziz slowed down and let the gap between them widen, making sure Shaukat stayed behind too. When there was enough distance between them and Javid, he turned to his younger companion for a private conversation.

"I should have told you earlier, I knew about the attack. I didn't realize you'd go on the offensive," said Aziz.

"What do you mean?" asked Shaukat, bewildered. *How could Aziz have been aware of the attack and still ask them to go through with the crossing?* His muscles tensed up.

"Shaukat, you are yet to learn the ways of the world. The truth is that the Indian Army knows of every infiltration. It is not possible to go back or forth without their knowledge. In fact, it was they who had cut and widened the fence for us. Before I had entered on Tuesday, I had made a deal with the CO. For us to slip the two of you out that day and back in today. We paid a heavy price. A big amount to feed everyone in the upper hierarchy from the CO all the way to a Colonel. Of course, their jawans have no idea."

"Does this really happen?"

"All the time. Colonels manipulate their postings in Kashmir. The government needs to spend and take lives to keep the propaganda machinery churning. Infiltrators killed to show their prowess, jawans martyred for sympathy. What no one knows is this is all pre-decided. What is most disheartening is the exchange. A life for a life. A staged encounter…" and then he added as an afterthought mostly to himself, "As if there is any aspect of Kashmir that is not staged."

"So Afzal… and the jawan you killed…"

"News items. Part of the gimmick that legitimizes the Indian Army's occupation."

"Afzal was going to die in any case…" Shaukat thought aloud.

"What other need would our commander have for a handicapped kid?"

Up ahead Javid heard none of this. He was in deep thought, considering Aziz's words from earlier. Just that same morning he had put a gun to Afzal's head and pulled the trigger. He had made up his mind to kill the boy, who as Aziz had perceived, was special to him. Now in a cruel twist of fate the enemy had taken his life. Was he supposed to be angry? Or was he to resign to the fate that Allah had in store for Afzal today and him tomorrow?

At this point Javid realized that he had been on edge all his life grappling for survival; in constant worry for his son and his own future; fearful of the uniforms and their unpredictable violent ways; anxious whether his herd was well and producing enough to sustain their modest lives. In essence, he was fighting death. But now that death was at the doorstep, and he knew when exactly it would strike, and that he was the master of his destiny, he could be free of these concerns. A sense of calm pervaded his consciousness as Javid realized he simply need not worry anymore.

70

0700 HOURS

OBAID Sheikh had woken up early even by his own standards. At 4.30 am, he ran a couple of laps of his estate, huffing against the glacial morning wind that cradled occasional snowflakes in its flux. On his final round he stopped and attended to his gardens, where he was particularly enthused to note that an entire ailing section of his plants had finally revived after days of cajoling and the first of its exquisite Tyrian purple flowers had bloomed this morning.

He had gotten ready and driven out in his modest convoy to Uri, taking just over two hours to cover the stretch on NH 1A. His father had, predictably, refused to accompany him. With the Pir Panjal Range in full view on this clear day, he thought about Vikram – a face he was still struggling to recall – and what he had said the evening before. Too conspiratorial, he thought. Sheikh was born into a political family, he was a politician all his professional life. Macabre crimes, implausible corruption, swashbuckling scandals; in his time, he had seen and heard more than most. There were outrageous stories and then there were stories that had transcended into myth. Vikram's case leaned towards the latter. He recalled having a long, monological conversation with the man and opening up on subjects he, in hindsight, probably shouldn't have. What was this crazy conspiracy Vikram was bringing to him? Sheikh hoped the soldier wasn't suffering from some form of PTSD and that he was in a rational and sound state of mind. But there was an aspect of it that intrigued him. Much to India's infuriation, Pakistan had continued to harbour terrorists. So when a man became a person of interest and a joint target for two countries who had never seen eye-to-eye on such matters, if nothing else, the story would be worth hearing. It was this curiosity that had led him to agree to give Vikram audience.

Sheikh was the first major politician to arrive that morning and even the hordes of media personnel were caught unawares. Jolted out of lethargy brought upon by the cold and the long trek to Uri – a town so poorly equipped to handle visitors, that there wasn't a single lodging to house them the night before – they scrambled to get their cameras switched on and rolling as he slipped right past them until the Trade Facilitation Centre came into view.

Cross-LoC trade had restarted in 2009, after the Lahore Declaration, when a handful of trucks carrying goods crossed paths on the Aman Setu, the bridge linking the two Kashmirs in what remained a brief, symbolic gesture. But 26/11 had come soon after and the reception at the trading post had remained deserted for a long time until ops had picked up again. Twice a week, three Pakistani trucks would roll into the TFC with goods and Indian trucks would cross the Aman Setu to a similar setup on the other side. The joke was that the two countries had spent more on building infrastructure for this exchange than they had ever hoped to recover from the value of the goods exchanged.

Same place, similar sentiment, thought the CM. Only this time, he hoped the effects would endure political vagaries and regime changes. It remained to be seen what his heart told him: that it would only take a single crazed decision or act to revert to square one. The Sharif-Vajpayee Lahore Declaration and the subsequent Kargil debacle were testament.

Sheikh's company tracked the road by the river until the hydroelectric power station off which the TFC was located. The area had been transformed. The ground had been levelled and sloping construction on the banks with seating and fort-like ramparts on the side opposite the dam made it resemble an extravagant and mammoth medieval cycle race track. This was made for the benefit of a thousand Indian citizens who could witness this historic moment, a perk for hosting the summit that the Pakistanis did not get. Ring-round teams of security forces radiated outwards from the epicentre, creating a sterile sector in the nucleus where the leaders would meet. Snipers armed with Mausers were poised atop strategically placed towers linked by electric fencing. Overhead, the IAF's Sukhois left contrails that betrayed their vigilant flight paths.

The two cargo halls had been razed to create barracks-style constructions to house the leaders and their retinue, the media, backup protection, and supplies. *Newsweek* reported on the rumour that India had spent upwards of $150 million on security arrangements for the signing. Sheikh had been baffled by the entire tamasha. Why host it in this geographically hostile territory? Why spend this kind of money? Why not sign in Delhi or Islamabad? It's not as if they were going to get shots of the local population celebrating. One of his aides pointed out that there were no tanks or mortar guns. India is keeping a low profile, offered Sheikh. The irony of the statement was not lost on the acolyte.

The Uri plan had necessitated taking steps that were contrary to the spirit of the accord. Because the treaty was a bilateral agreement making the LoC a permanent border and thereby sealing the fate of Kashmiris as either Indian or Pakistani citizens – leaving no scope for self-rule – eruptions of violent protests were imminent. Afraid, thousands and thousands of additional forces from all over the country were brought in. The police had arrested hundreds of 'potential troublemakers' in the preceding weeks: youth leaders, locals with a record of participation in organized demonstrations. There was expected backlash and a stone-throwing teenager had died when a BSF tear gas canister had been fired in his face. This had led to a chain of events where government buildings and vehicles were torched, there was retaliatory gunfire, more casualties; it all came to a head with the Srinagar hostage crisis.

The 'clean-up' operation, as the Northern Army Commander had distastefully put it to the media, was now complete. The CM had watched it all from the sidelines, unable to act or intervene. How the pro-freedom factions were going to react in the new era could only be speculated. The eyewash that this was a demilitarization exercise was ineffective on the locals. They knew that with this move, their chants of azadi would be heard by even fewer people. But – and this was what Sheikh really hoped for – their lives would be transformed in an army-free environs. With equal rights, media freedom, and a boost in development, maybe they would reconcile to the future thrust upon them and accept their nation. Even as he had this thought, deep inside he felt empathetic for his people in a manner even he didn't know he was capable of. Their dreams of autonomy were all but over.

71

0730 HOURS

TAP *tap tap.*

Vikram stirred.

Tap tap tap.

Vikram lurched in his seat, stifling a cry as he was taken aback by the ghost-like face in the window. It took a second for him to register where he was.

It had been fourteen hours straight on the road when the Scorpio Vikram was driving had started veering to the side. The car's metal body gnashed against the mountainside and the wretched sound of metal crumpling against rock woke him up with a start. He had fallen asleep at the wheel, it couldn't have been more than a two or three seconds, a micro nap, but it had felt like a lot more. He was lucky the car had gone left and not right, where a sheer drop of five thousand feet would've meant certain death. The damage too was only cosmetic.

Once again, he had come close to accidentally killing himself because of lack of sleep. *Not an option*, he told himself. His fuel gauge – like his body – was running on empty. Now alert and driving conservatively – mostly on neutral gear, coasting downhill – he pulled up at the first village in a transitory valley. He asked around and was directed to a modest hut. A woman in a burqa emerged.

From her gait, he could tell she was aged. Behind her, he could see a stack of ten jerrycans taking up most of the space in her little cottage. It was not uncommon for tourists, especially motorcycle enthusiasts, to run out of gas and make unscheduled stops. Almost every village would have households stocked with varying emergency supplies. The more remote the village, the higher the price. The exchange of money and diesel was almost wordless.

Refuelled, he drove a few kilometres away from the village before sharply turning a right angle and going deep off road. Amidst a thicket of chinars, he yanked the handbrake, pushed his seat back and settled into a comfortable position. One hour. That's how long he could afford to sleep. Even though he was within striking distance of the valley and Uri, he knew that a lapse of a few seconds could be disastrous. This was going to make him late for his appointment with the CM, but he needed his senses to be functional at the very least, if nothing else, to protect the piece of history he had folded in his back pocket.

Tap tap tap.

A middle-aged man with deep creases on his forehead, fair skin and a gauzy beard, stood outside the car. The angular lids of his bright green eyes carried the weight of his world's troubles. His headgear let on his Muslim identity. His clothes were ill-fitting, multiple sweaters over a pathani that billowed with the slightest gust of wind. Either they were not his or he had lost a lot of weight suddenly. When he saw Vikram wake up, his gnarly fingers spread as if saying 'hello'.

Vikram rolled down the window.

"Salaam alaikum," said the man.

"Wa-alaikum salaam," replied Vikram, confused, still

struggling to emerge from REM sleep. Was he asking for alms? Why was this man so far off the road in a deserted area?

"Do you have water to spare, sir? I've been walking a long way, and my canteen is dry."

There was a refilled bottle lying in the cup holder in the Scorpio when Vikram had jacked it. He gave it to the man. He took a long sip.

"Thank you, sir," he said, handing the bottle back.

"Keep it."

"Do you have some for yourself?"

"I will get some."

The man nodded and accepted the bottle from the window and put it in his sling bag.

"Thank you," he said turning away.

Vikram looked at his watch. His power nap had lasted less than half an hour, but he was feeling better. Then he had an idea. He started the SUV and honked as he pulled up next to the man.

"Where are you going? I can drop you to Uri."

The man stopped. He smiled at Vikram.

"I am indeed going that way, but perhaps it is better I walk."

"But surely it'll be easier if you came with me. I need the company, someone to talk to, keep me awake."

The man hesitated. He thought long and hard about the proposal.

"Okay, if my presence will keep you safe, I will accompany you."

"Great. Get in."

The man walked around as Vikram leaned over and opened the door for him.

"My name is Vikram," he said, as the man climbed in and sat leaning forward, his back unsupported by the seat.

The man nodded. Vikram thought he was being shy, deferential.

"What's yours?"

"Javid, sir. My name is Javid."

72

0745 HOURS

FOR all the congeniality the brawny young man had shown, there had been unexpected silence on the drive so far. Not that Javid was inclined to converse; he had been staring blankly out the window. He wanted to take in the magnificence around him; the sweeping pristine peaks of the Pir Panjal Range, their caps glistening with snow, bulbuls in flight, the deodars reaching for the sky, meadows with fluff that kept turning out to be sheep; images he knew he was witnessing for the last time. But what crowded his thoughts was an unfiltered fear of his impending death. At this moment, all he had been told, the promises made of paradise in the afterlife, he desperately needed them to be true.

Perhaps, thought Javid, a conversation with a stranger would be a welcome distraction. Also, maybe he would ask his friend not to drive so fast. He wondered why this man was so anxious and in such haste. He chose a moment to speak when the road was straight and open.

"I assume you're going to Uri to attend the event."

"Yes."

"But it will be hours before…"

"Don't want to miss it," Vikram interjected in a manner that forced Javid to change the topic.

"You're familiar with Kashmir?"

The creases on Vikram's forehead eased out as he let out a small grunt of a laugh.

"I wouldn't say that."

"But you've been before?"

"As recently as earlier this week."

"Business?"

"That's right. Business."

"So where are you from?"

"Delhi."

"Ah. My son… he's in Delhi."

"Oh, that's nice. How old is he?"

"Twelve."

"You sent him away young."

"Kashmir…" Javid left his comment incomplete but knew Vikram had caught on. Again, he steered the dialogue away, "You have children?"

"One on the way."

"Oh… that's nice. Congratulations."

"Thank you. I believe you're the first person I've told. My wife had asked me not to mention it until we were three months in."

"Sounds like a modern, city decree."

"I wouldn't know. I'd never thought about kids. I wasn't even very good with them."

"It all changes when your own comes along."

"So I've been told."

"Children… they transform you. And they also complete you. They're like keys that unlock concealed facets of you that you didn't know existed. There is a very real, physical sense of this. It's hard to explain."

"Was it easy then? To send your son away?"

Javid couldn't find the strength to reply to this query.

"No," he whispered, holding back his tears. He looked out the window, hoping Vikram would get the drift and leave him alone for now.

"You've stayed in Kashmir all your life?" Javid sensed it was Vikram now who was trying to distract him.

"Yes."

"And what do you do?"

"I'm a goatherd."

"Are you happy?"

"I don't know any Kashmiri who is happy. Our smiles vanished a long time ago. Our children…" Khurram's image was still fresh in his consciousness, "their idea of happiness is but a pale shadow of moments that I knew when I was their age. It's a small miracle every time they laugh."

Vikram stayed silent. So Javid continued; Ahmed's spiel had given him perspective. He had realized what he was angry about, ordering his thoughts and finding words for his reason.

"And what are they to do? Can you blame them? The only valuable lessons I've taught my son is to be cooperative with the Indian army. To submit to them. To do as told. To be home before curfew. To not disappear on me. To not end up in their hands or in a grave. Before he turned ten, I had to tell him about how the uniforms use torture. I told him what they did to my brother: rubbing chillies in open wounds, burning his skin, electric shocks to his head and genitals. He had returned home with chunks of his flesh missing. I described all this to my son in great detail to put the fear of the uniforms in him."

"I'm sorry," whispered Vikram. As a soldier, he had no choice but to overlook or even doubt such accusations directed at his fellow men in uniform. But he had never met a victim. Suddenly the stories seemed all too real.

"Why are you sorry? You don't need to say sorry. You're not one of them. And I got him out in time."

"Your sacrifice... so he may lead a normal life."

"No sir. I hope he does not lead a 'normal life'. I do not want India to assimilate him. It's true I didn't want him to fight India with stones and bullets. But fight he must. And he will, I guarantee you this. But he must do so with words."

"Why didn't you leave with him?"

"Kashmir is my home. I will die here."

"You'd rather stay because of your relationship with your home than be with your son?"

"It's more complicated than that. As I said before, most Kashmiris are not allowed too many choices. I made one. And I will pay for it. And it will be the reason my son will crusade for his land."

"Do you think Kashmir will be glorious again?"

"It is glorious now, sir. We are in the midst of an eclipse that is all. Overnight, the troops came. Overnight, they can leave. It is the only difference. It might be a long fight, but every Kashmiri is in it for the long haul."

"Maybe it won't be as long a haul as you imagine," said Vikram, his attention shifting to the pages in his back pocket.

The car turned a corner and a town materialized into view: hundreds of small white houses speckled on a green valley with the mighty Jhelum curling like a moat around it and garrisoning the settlement from the hills of Pakistan.

A milestone indicated that Uri was now a mere five kilometres away.

73

0815 HOURS

VIKRAM ditched the Scorpio in a lane full of brick houses in Uri. Javid and he walked towards the river downhill together.

With all forces assembled at the venue, the town itself was devoid of security. There was just the odd local police patrol, who let them on their way when they pointed out they were heading to the event, a sign of confidence that anyone with ill intent would not get far past the fortress.

Once they reached the perimeter demarcated by the fence, Javid and Vikram split up without ceremony, only a simple shaking of hands. The goatherd stood in a long winding line that went upslope; the soldier went in search of a supervising officer who could take him to the CM.

Javid thought he would be early. Driving with Vikram would have saved him at least two hours of walking. But he was wrong; at his position at the end of the line he was nowhere near the primary checkpoint.

Javid's mission was to disrupt the signing. But there were several caveats to this. The closer he got to the leaders, the more effective the message he needed to deliver would be. It was certainly unlikely that he would be able to take out both or even either of the PMs. But he had to get inside the staging area at the very least. He had heard of stories of suicide bombers who had managed to take only a single life: their own, leading to mockery in the press. Such an event, Javid imagined, would only anger his handlers and might even jeopardize Khurram's future. And if he was going to do this for a cause – even if his cause was his son's safety – he would at least try and be effective.

Once he got past the upcoming body search, he would take his place amongst the crowd. Then he would assess if it was better to blow himself wherever he got a seat or if he could move into a better position.

As he shuffled ahead, the heavy-duty metal detectors came into view. He tried to observe the procedure, especially the pat-down that every entrant was receiving. Not unlike airport security, thought Javid. Or at least how he had seen it done once on television.

But then something curious happened. A man was asked to empty his pockets. Javid couldn't make out the individual items he extracted, but after an examination and some back and forth, the man dropped out of the line with his female companion and headed up the line. Javid waved to him.

"What happened?"

"They're not allowing phones. There's an open box you can deposit it in, but that's just asking for trouble. We don't need our phones stolen by the police. Mine is new too... no sir, we're heading home."

But Javid had stopped listening. It felt as if an icy hand had grasped his heart and it squirmed, struggling to beat. The phone was his trigger. Without it, and without a manual alternative, there was no detonation. This had not been anticipated. The line seemed to be moving briskly all of a sudden. He stayed on course, undecided on his next move. Did he have to end it all at the checkpoint itself?

Though his phone had finally run out of juice, Vikram was confident it wouldn't matter. After all, Sheikh had given him an assurance that he had alerted his team to his arrival. He finally located a tall, whiskered security guard radiating an air of authority and an extra stripe on his rank insignia. Standing still with his arms on his waist overseeing proceedings, he was the first man in uniform Vikram had found with no proactive participation.

"Captain Dhillon?" he asked, reading off the name badge.

The captain turned slowly and sized up the person in front of him: at 6'2" they were of equal height. A thick, dark stubble only enhanced Vikram's distinctive features: crow's feet at the edges of grey-brown eyes on a symmetrical face, a thin but muscled neck and short-cropped hair. Vikram looked filthy; dust and grime stuck to his face and hair. And he reeked as if he had not showered in days. But Dhillon could tell that this was not his usual state; that this man with his athlete-like body and soldier-like posture and conduct who had interrupted his duty was someone he couldn't dismiss right away. The captain took a step back.

"What do you want?"

"I'm NSG. I need to see Obaid Sheikh."

"NSG? The NSG is not supposed to be here."

"I know, but he's expecting me."

"Do you have your credentials?"

"No, I was… I was in an accident," he lied. "Please. Can you call someone from his detail? It's urgent."

"I don't know anyone from his detail or how to reach them. This is my post."

Vikram considered pleading some more, but he was running out of time. He decided to use his ace. Except that it was a bluff. Raising himself to his full height and taking a step forward–

"Captain Dhillon. This mission is critical. I have come all the way from Delhi. There is verified information about a security threat to his life. There's an additional SPG squad en route but I got here first via helicopter, the permission to land, as you can imagine, was available only in Srinagar, not to mention that I was in an accident on the way here. Now it's up to you, sir, to hamper my access to the intended target for additional protection or not. My phone battery is out. All you need to do is get in touch with him, his PA, or anyone from his team and inform them of my arrival. That is all. If you don't and if something happens to him, be assured of your court martial."

Dhillon stared into Vikram's eyes. Then he wavered. And blinked. He took out his walkie and asked for backup for his post.

"Come with me," he said and walked in the direction Vikram had just come from.

Javid was next in line. His head was still a muddle. He was unable to think straight. One finger was on the cell phone deep in his pocket, ready to trigger the bomb. He knew that he wasn't going to get much farther than this checkpoint. There was little chance they wouldn't confiscate his mobile. What he should have done was dropped out of the line when he first got hint of what was to follow. Now it would seem too suspicious. If he wanted out, then it would be best to make the scene like the man had earlier and walk out in a huff. But that would be effectively shutting the door on a re-entry. But here was an opportunity, he realized. The post was buzzing with personnel keeping strict vigil. He counted the people the blast radius would contain: eight policemen, at least two civilians. Was ten an acceptable number? Acceptable for innocents who would lose their lives, acceptable for the men he worked for so that they may leave his son alone?

It was his turn next.

His hands were still in his pockets. The man asked him to spread them wide. Javid looked at him for a moment, closed his eyes and muttered under his breath "Allahu Akbar".

74

0850 HOURS

JAVID wasn't sure if he had pressed the '+' volume button – the remote trigger on the phone for the IED – because he could hear commotion around him, but he hadn't heard the blast. Also, how could he hear the effects of the aftermath if he hadn't been torn apart yet?

He opened his eyes. Everyone was looking up at the heavens. And the commotion was really an emphatic cheer from the crowd. He followed their gaze and the din that had been clouding his senses was now a visual: two identical massive helicopters – VVIP rigged AgustaWestland AW101s, the kind that heads of states of the first world, including the POTUS, used – were courting each other overhead after materializing from behind mountains on either side of the border and preparing for descent.

The prime ministers had arrived.

A sense of purpose pervaded the ground; lounging TV crews outside ran helter-skelter to appropriate ideal positions for the action, guards stood at attention, visitors stirred in their places.

Amidst all this activity, Javid spotted Vikram walking with a uniformed officer. Was it possible…

"Excuse me," he told the distracted guard who was still looking up, mesmerized by the spectacle of the landing helis, "I'll be right back."

Javid lopped off towards Vikram, waving his arm, trying to catch his attention.

"Javid! What happened?" Vikram was surprised seeing his driving companion again. Dhillon shot him a glance, but his walkie squawked and his attention was diverted.

"Nothing. Are you going inside?"

"Yes, why?"

"Oh, I was just… maybe I'll meet you there."

Javid gave him a courteous hug and slipped his phone into his layered jacket's outer pocket without him realizing. Captain Dhillon was still coordinating with someone on the walkie.

Vikram was bewildered at what had just transpired.

"Okay, yes. Maybe we will."

Javid returned to the post and smiled at the guard who let him cut the line.

"Sorry, just spotted a friend that I hadn't seen in a long time."

After giving him a once-over, the guard asked him to step through the scanner. Javid held his breath and took a long stride through.

No beeps or blips.

Relieved, Javid offered another smile to the guard and went on his way, following the designated pathway leading to the public stands. Javid followed it until he was out of sight of security and cut across trying to follow Vikram from the inside. The helicopters had touched down, and even though the choppers were well out of sight, people were still clamouring to catch a glimpse, rushing to the edges, craning their necks.

Vikram had stopped outside a non-civilian entrance.

There were armed guards, but no scanners. They seemed to be waiting for something or someone. Javid didn't know how long he could stay in one place before he was spotted out of bounds and questioned, or worse, ejected.

It was about five minutes later when an officer joined them and after a quick word with Vikram and Dhillon, led them inside.

The trigger and the bomb were in.

Now all Javid had to do was bring them together.

75

0900 HOURS

THERE was a roar from a section of the crowd, though not all were cheering, as the PMs embraced and waved in all directions after alighting from the helicopters.

Vikram could see them – tiny figures in the distance – camera flashes creating a glittering ring of light around them.

"Can't we hurry?" he asked Captain Dhillon.

"No, we literally can't. All movements are being tracked. If you run, you could be mistaken for an assailant and will be shot. There are snipers every thirty feet."

"Haven't you alerted them?"

"Who exactly do you think you are? You should be happy that the CM's PA has okayed your request and has let you in. We are keeping this low-key. NSG or CBI, you're under my jurisdiction and will follow orders accordingly."

Vikram kept quiet. He knew Dhillon wasn't bluffing. Even a minister would have to toe the line and observe protocol.

"Who was that man you met outside?" he asked.

Vikram didn't want to raise any alarm bells so he offered the minimum possible information, "Him? Just an acquaintance."

"Looked like a local. You're not."

"Just someone I know from Srinagar."

"And he's here to attend? All the way?"

Vikram shrugged.

A low fence and gate separated the leaders' barracks.

"We have to wait here," said Dhillon, once again unclipping his walkie and speaking into it.

Vikram unconsciously reached into his pants' back pocket and felt for the documents, making sure they were still there. In a few minutes, this would all be over. At least his part. He didn't know if he would be safe from the authorities yet and there was much to answer for. Aditi's plan had gone awry and his story was yet to see the light of day. There would be accusations and counters. But by then the treaty would have been long signed and the new chapter in Indo-Pak history, he hoped, would drown out old denouncements. The CM would cover for him for now. Maybe, he could stay in Srinagar with him until all charges against him were dropped. Bani could join him there. As for the document, what impact it would have if revealed to the world, he had no idea. He guessed the politicians would have a go at it, debating its consequences, before the press and public got wind of this discovery. There was every chance it would be buried. But he had more faith than that with Obaid Sheikh. Empowered, he would act in the best interest of the people. It was why he had made this arduous journey in the first place.

A balding, white-haired man emerged from the barracks and looked around until he spotted a gesturing Dhillon. Vikram correctly assumed he was the CM's personal assistant.

"Is this the man?" he asked the Captain.

"Yes sir. Says he's NSG."

"What's your name and business?"

"I'm Squad Commander Burunsh," said Vikram, using the Hindi word for rhododendrons.

"And what do you…"

"What's the matter with you people?" Vikram had exhausted his last ounce of patience, "Dial that phone, right now!"

The PA hesitated for a fraction of a second before complying. "Please wait," he said as he punched in a number and walked away to speak in private.

A minute, then another. They weren't going in, and no one was coming out. Vikram raised an eyebrow. The PA raised his hand to indicate he should hang on.

Then he saw the CM emerge.

And a second later, following him was Ajinkya Ranade.

Vikram's jaw dropped in shock. Were Ranade and Sheikh working together and on the wrong side? Had he completely miscalculated?

He needed time to reconsider, but there was none. They were walking towards him. Ranade's eyes were fixed on him. They were within earshot now.

"Squad Commander…" said Sheikh extending his arms for a shake, even though he was still some distance away, "Defence Minister Ranade was curious to meet you when he heard my aide inform me of your arrival. I'm sorry I…"

Vikram spun around looking for an out, when another shock awaited him. A familiar figure was sprinting in his direction.

"Javid…?"

He was barely ten metres away and closing in, when there were the two distinct sounds of a muted, distant rifle going off and of a bullet finding flesh.

Javid stumbled and fell. A sniper had taken him down.

Momentarily forgetting Ranade, Vikram instinctively stepped forward to help his friend. When he tried lifting him, his hands felt warm. Javid's shoulder was a bloody mess.

"Vikram. You have my phone."

"I... what?"

Dhillon was moving in.

"What the hell is happening here?"

"In your pocket," stammered Javid.

Vikram was confused. His heart was racing. His mind couldn't put together what was happening. Behind him, the two politicians had stopped in their tracks. Time had started to stretch. He could sense there were more people converging

"Vikram... in your pocket. Put your hand in your jacket pocket."

Javid's face didn't seem to reflect the pain he must've been in. Vikram followed his instructions as if hypnotized.

"How did this..."

Javid plucked it out of his hand even as Dhillon watched the exchange, unable to act on what seemed a harmless action.

"Run," Javid said simply.

"Run?"

The CM and Ranade were upon him. Vikram turned around.

"Run," he said again to him, but Vikram heard nothing and only saw his lips move. How could a man's face who had just been shot be so serene?

Vikram got to his feet. He reached into his back pocket and took out the document. All he knew was that he had to deliver it to the CM. That was the mission. But when he turned around, he saw that Ranade was straightening his arm, a small handgun clasped at the end of it, taking aim at him from not two feet away. The DM pushed Sheikh to one side. Javid lunged past Vikram's feet in an attempt to come in between the muzzle and the intended target and held up his own trigger. Vikram held out the document towards the CM. But the papers slipped from his fingers and scattered in the air.

"Allahu Akbar."

Javid pressed the button and detonated the IED that was deep within his body. Those around him first felt the heat. Their skin was already melting by the time they perceived the all-consuming white incandescence that blinded them. Most perished even before the sound of the blast reached their scorched ears and the smouldering flesh from the bomber had become one with their own.

THREE MONTHS LATER

THE school bus lurched for a couple of metres and stopped again. The kids groaned. What was going on ahead? They had been stuck in the same spot on the road for twenty minutes now, a sea of cars idling around them. A senior student who had jumped off to go and check ahead made a dramatic re-entry, bounding onto the bus in a single leap. Curious eyes turned to him. Had he managed to find out the cause of the hold-up?

"I spotted at least two fucking politicians, including that Ajit Seth bugger unveiling a plaque. They're renaming East End Road," he announced in a triumphant voice, eliciting more expletives from the older students.

"What is the road called now?" asked a voice from the back.

"Ah, fuck knows. Oh, wait wait. I know. They're naming it after one of the guys who died in the Kashmir blast."

"Which blast? Isn't there one every day?" came an attempt at humour that only a couple of schoolgirls chortled at.

"Ah, you know," said the teenager, dodging the sarcasm, "the one that fucked up the peace treaty signing with Pakistan."

"Good that happened. No one wants to be friends with Pakistan."

"Yeah," piped up another voice, "but it's caused this traffic jam now."

In the very last row, a twelve-year-old boy caught enough of the conversation to comprehend what was going on.

The new school had been hard on him since he enrolled a couple of months ago. His local guardians had warned him that he would be bullied and that his identity would be the root of it. But a clique of influential girls had taken a liking to him and this most unexpected occurrence had shielded him from the worst of the ragging. Still a passing classmate would mock him, calling him a 'Pakistani' and this would elicit a round of chuckles. He weathered it, but it had affected him, making him quiet and ponderous-looking. He found a friend in his older cousin whose mattress he now shared. The local boy had been accepting of the new family member from the very first day, taking it upon himself to ease his newfound brother into this new world. He had his own fading memories of another life in his first few years in a village in Kashmir and – with empathy rare in a boy of his age – knew that such a transition was not easy. They took the same bus back from school and he sat next to him now.

"Khurram," said his cousin, "looks as if we'll be here for a while. Are you hungry?"

Khurram shook his head. "They're renaming the street after the CM who died?"

"Obaid Sheikh? I suppose so. Or could be the other fellow. The defence minister…"

"Ajinkya Ranade."

"That's right. The blast was in Uri, right? That's close to home."

"Yes. Close to home. And a day after I arrived here, in Delhi."

"Close call then."

"I guess so."

Khurram looked away, out the window, trying not to

think of his father. He knew he would never see him again. That hope had extinguished in only a few days after he had arrived.

The futile, frequent honking of the cars around them signalled their rising impatience. Every car had their windows up; and in their temperature-controlled pockets, while their drivers looked for opportunities to make up the inches, every passenger had their head buried in their phones.

Except one. Khurram shifted his vision to try and get a better angle. She was a striking woman. Her poker-straight hair was bunched up with a lazy elegance, a hair stick holding it all together; she looked straight ahead, her eyes unblinking and her skin radiant, as if she were a source of illumination herself. Khurram wondered about this for a split second when the woman shifted, adjusting her position; that's when he realized she was pregnant.

Bani moved in her seat with some difficulty. Her back hurt, her legs – cramping earlier – were now falling asleep, she was feeling hot though the AC in her Uber was on max.

It was mere instinct but she had little doubt that Vikram's fate was linked to the suicide bomb that had killed the CM and the defence minister, whose memorial installation was holding up the traffic. She had refused to accept Vikram's disappearance as anything more than just that. Every few hours her mind would play back the memory of the last day they had met: on the metro, him asking her about Kashmir, Raj executed before her eyes.

It had taken her a while to recover from the trauma of Raj's death; she had taken the initiative of funeral proceedings until his parents had arrived from Ranchi.

Bani had tried to piece together what had transpired in Kashmir on the day of the treaty signing. The media, reeling from the death of one of their own, Aditi Shenoy – whose body had been washed up on the filthy banks of the Yamuna with untraceable bullet wounds – had very little to go on. With multiple claimants, they did not have clarity on which terrorist organization had orchestrated the attack; neither was there any consensus on the number of people that had perished in the bombing. The story had moved with haste; a leaderless J&K thrown into disarray and the PM taking over the defence portfolio, while putting the CBI among other agencies on to the case. The peace process between the two countries had reached a cul-de-sac, and with the burden of blame on Pakistan, India had wasted no time inking multiple international arms deals, including one with Mikoyan, Zakharov's Russian firm, for fifteen attack and fifteen heavy cargo helicopters. The timing of the attack, theorized analysts, would alter the geopolitical paradigm for decades to come.

On an impulse, Bani had bought a ticket to Srinagar, with the intention of tracking her husband down. She was in the midst of packing her suitcase when it struck her that Vikram would either be in hiding and impossible for her to find or – she tried to be apathetic here – in smithereens. The flight had taken off without her. It was also the day she felt her baby kick for the first time.

Her cab had gotten through the bottleneck and was soon pulling into her lane. The army vehicles staking out around her house, a sight she had become accustomed to, had driven off one evening a month ago and not returned the next. She wondered if they had simply given up or had news on Vikram that she didn't. There was no way to check.

Bani grabbed her shopping – three pairs of new shoes to accommodate her swelling feet – and, not quite used to the change in her body's centre of gravity, got off the car with some awkwardness.

She turned the key and entered through the main door. But the moment she stepped in, she sensed something was not right. Had she left the windows open? Was it a burglary? No, the house was how she had left it. Just as she was bending to keep her shopping bags down, her eye caught the newspaper that she had set in the corner of the dining table. It wasn't how she had left it. The order had been altered, the tabloid was on top. And a pen, out of place from its stand on the sideboard was next to it. She cautiously checked every room, her pulse racing. There was no one.

She came back to the table and turned the pages of the newspaper, one by one, examining each square inch. Then she saw it – on a page carrying a minimal advertisement that accommodated the words without constraint – a note in Vikram's handwriting.

If it's a boy, we'll call him Raj.

EPILOGUE

JULY 1948

Nehru was the first to arrive. The last time he was in this room, it had seemed a lot smaller. And noisier. The stewards of the Congress party, the Sikh faction, Jinnah and his cabal, and on occasion the press at the fringes had spent hours every day with Dickie Mountbatten as they bickered over the June 3 Plan, the conclusive blueprint of independence and negotiations in the last days before August 15th. Despite his nemesis Jinnah's presence, the air was electric in those final days. That he had fought on the behalf of hundreds of millions and lived to see and lead a sovereign nation was a life not many men in all of history could claim.

Now the room looked vast, much like the way the country he was presiding over had started to seem. The first year had come at him like a battering ram. His enthusiasm in taking up the reins had met with a feeling of being tossed into the deep end of a freezing lake. The shocking, bitter truth was that the new government was out of its depth. It comprised of fierce fighters who had won India's freedom, but they had no idea what to do with it once attained. They had driven the colonizers out, but forgotten to ask for the instruction manual: how were they to administer the country?

On an old bureau a countdown calendar lay rolled up. Nehru blew away the gathered dust and unfurled it. Large numbers in the centre counted down from 30 to 1 with the text 'DAYS LEFT TO PREPARE FOR TRANSFER OF POWER' right after. He had come into the room in the days leading up to independence and his eyes would first fall on the number – as if to ensure the person in charge of it had flipped the page; that indeed August 15, 1947 was edging ever close; and their dream was inching towards reality.

He looked up and saw Mountbatten standing close.

"Dickie… another month and then you're gone."

"It's long overdue. India is yours. Raja is a capable man. He will take care."

"I'm going to miss you," and after a beat, "and Edwina."

"We'll all be the worse for it."

Nehru flopped into a chair. Mountbatten thought he looked tired. Pre-independence Nehru had spark, a fireball of energy; his skinny legs and small frame buttressing a storm of a man always up for a challenge, even a physical one. Now his shoulders drooped as if crushed by the nation's weight upon them. He stared vacantly at the table, a shadow of his former self when he used to tower over the rest, sitting in the same chair.

Their relationship had become strained in the last few months by virtue of their differences on how to tackle Kashmir. In his fierce fight to portray himself as an inclusive man, the PM was willing to go as far as adopting a militant route and make incursions into Pakistan to attack what he called the 'nerve centres' from where insurrectionists were rolling in. Mountbatten, at the behest of the British government, had worked hard to remind him that this was illegal and would not stand up to international scrutiny. It would lead to war and that Jawahar had to 'stop the fighting' and live up to the promises he had made to the UN.

Could today bring about a change? The meeting had been set up after months of to and fro with neither party willing to concede on a location or agenda. So he had called for an informal talk, off the public record so that there was nothing lost if no headway was made. At least they would've tried.

An aide rushed in.

"Pardon me sirs, but he's here."

Mountbatten turned to Nehru, "You want to go and receive him?"

"Not really."

"Come now."

Nehru reluctantly got up from his seat. Then he sat down again.

"No. I can't get myself to do it. The blood of everyone dead in the Partition holocaust is on this man's hands."

Mountbatten sighed. "That is not true. You know that is not true. We are all to blame. In fact, he himself has repeatedly blamed me and me alone."

"At least we tried to stop it. I…"

"Tried to stop what?" Muhammad Ali Jinnah stood at the door, his arms extended wide, resting on the frame for support.

Nehru shot him a glance, his face all frowns. There was an uncomfortable silence, then he slowly got to his feet. But there was no greeting forthcoming.

"You call me all the way to Delhi and you aren't even outside to say hello?"

Nehru had a response ready, but Mountbatten

intervened.

"Good sir, we have talked about this. We agreed it would be easier to meet here in Delhi and keep this low-key."

Jinnah considered this for a moment and decided to accept the explanation with a shrug. He pulled himself a chair at the table.

"Whose idea was this, to have this meeting in this room?"

"Oh, it was mine," said Mountbatten.

"If there's a message in this, I haven't understood it yet. This is where you proposed partition – as if it were a British idea – and this is where we agreed. And I suppose you haven't put up an updated map just to make a point," said Jinnah pointing to the large canvas on the wall behind him with a coloured portrayal of pre-independence India.

"Oh, I don't know… it didn't even cross my mind. We chose this room because we have always met in this room."

"Didn't even cross your mind?" said Jinnah, mock-aghast. "This right here is the reason you chaps are running your country into the ground."

"Why do you say that?" asked Nehru. He always took such accusations to heart.

"Details, Jawahar, details! You and your sweeping statements and declarations; your overflowing love for all people – except for me of course – and your brash, romantic sense of patriotism that has no place in the real world… this is what has led to the mess of partition and now Kashmir. Your principles and actions are never aligned… as I have always suspected, you're still the Brahmin behind a veneer of western edu… are you feeling well, my friend?"

Nehru had gone from a quiet seething to shaking in anger. Jinnah had gotten under his skin once again. Yes, he had been brash, he had acquiesced to the idea of partition – whether it was Jinnah's or Attlee's, he didn't care – just so he didn't have to deal with this toxic man. When his own friend Bapu had suggested that Jinnah be made head of the interim government in April of '47, it had pushed him to the edge with paranoia. If the Congress leadership had not backed him, he would have been isolated and uncoupled from the future of India.

Mountbatten put an arm on his shoulder in a feeble attempt to calm him down and Jinnah decided to use the opportunity to change the topic.

"Say Dickie… you didn't call me all the way here to not even offer me some whisky? It's such a chore in Pakistan… to pour a drink on the sly. It's getting tiresome."

"I had some put in the cabinet over there."

Jinnah walked over and pulled out a bottle, while Mountbatten whispered to Nehru to stay on course with the agenda at hand.

"Anyone else want a glass?"

Mountbatten raised a hand to indicate no, Nehru looked away.

Jinnah returned with his drink. "To our health," he said and proceeded to take a sip.

"Gentlemen, we should get on," said Mountbatten.

"For a moment there I thought you said get *along*," chuckled Jinnah. "Okay, so where do we begin? Oh, I know… how about we talk about why your leadership has not come to its senses yet and let the Kashmiri people have their say? They have been through enough. News has come in that over 200,000 Muslims were butchered by Hari Singh's troops right before you forced him to accede…"

"That number is exaggerated and we had no idea of

the atrocities and then your tribesmen–" started Nehru. Mountbatten intervened before it got out of hand.

"I think what Jawahar is trying to say is that Hari Singh acted out on his own. He is no friend of ours. We *really* didn't know. And still don't have the details of what transpired. Overall, the situation is complicated–"

"Then simplify it!" thundered Jinnah. His fiery eyes coupled with his pale skin stretched over his protruding bones were innately intimidating. "I am dying, gentlemen. You already know this. Now you're hearing of it from me. I know my friend Jawahar regrets not knowing earlier. Maybe, he would have allowed Mr Gandhi to have his way. I don't know what I would have done. Would I have accepted? Prime Minister of a united India? The truth is–"

Jinnah paused. He was staring at a spot on the wall, thinking aloud, now detached from his listeners' reactions. Nehru shifted in his chair and leaned forward. The answer to this hypothetical question meant a great deal to him. It was extraordinary for Jinnah to be so candid. Would he–?

"I don't know," said Jinnah finally. His eyes flickered into focus and he took another sip, watching the two men before him. His lips curled as he spoke, rancour returning to his voice. "I don't know because the two of you have turned out to be vipers, agents of betrayal. And I don't know what you would've done to me if I had accepted. What you did in Junagadh and what've you done now in Kashmir… is proof enough of your duplicity."

"What are you talking about?" growled Nehru. "In both cases, there is a legitimate–"

"*Legitimate?*" Jinnah clenched his glass so hard, his knuckles turned white, alarming Mountbatten that he might shatter it. "In Junagadh, you threatened the Nawab's life so much so that he fled and fell at my feet in Karachi, begging for shelter. And this after signing the Instrument of Accession in favour of Pakistan!"

"We had a plebiscite!" countered Nehru.

"Nonsense! You invaded and occupied the Nawab's state and then you ensured a Hindu vote for accession to India."

"200,000 votes for India. 91 for Pakistan. It doesn't matter who the Nawab signed for in the Instrument…"

"Precisely!" yelled Jinnah at the top of his voice, slapping the table hard with his hand. "Precisely, my friend. So if the Instrument of Accession that a Muslim ruler signs in a Hindu state is invalid, the issue is apposite in the case of Kashmir, where Hari Singh presided over a Muslim population."

"It's not the same, you know it," countered Nehru, raising his voice too. "Abdullah has sway with the populace. And he wants India. We have offered to hold a plebiscite just like we did in Junagadh."

"No. You won't. Because you will lose the vote and Kashmir. So you won't. You will do it in Hyderabad despite the Nizam's valiant stand with his Razakars, because your Hindu brethren outnumber the Muslims, just like they did in Junagadh. Look at me, both of you, look at me in the eye and tell me I'm wrong."

The Indian contingent was not falling for the bait.

"We have to see how Hyderabad plays out. And as far as Kashmir goes, we believe the chapter is closed," said Mountbatten.

"Kashmir is not a closed chapter. And it never will be. Mark my words," said Jinnah.

"The accession has been brought about by violence and the violence came from tribesmen for whom Pakistan was responsible," countered Mountbatten.

"The Pathans were angry. They were responsible. And perhaps Liaquat was responsible. Not Pakistan. He made this move without informing me, on the assumption that I would agree. He was not privy to the information that I was; that the two of you were plotting a military takeover in any case. He gave you just the excuse you needed. Tribesmen! Ha. You countered these men with clubs with a hundred aircraft and thousands of troops in a perfectly coordinated move; a bit of an overreaction, perhaps? I beg you, sirs, do not insult my intelligence."

The accusations, coming thick and fast from Jinnah, were stacking up. Nehru knew they weren't all false. But he also knew this was not the man he wanted to be. His heart ached for Kashmir – the state of his birth, beautiful Kashmir, strategic Kashmir – to come into the fold. But above all, he did not want history to condemn him.

"What do you want?" he asked quietly.

It was a moment for Jinnah to absorb this unvarnished peace offering.

"I want Kashmir… to decide for itself. And I want us to work towards that. Abdullah thinks he can influence the public, so by all means let him. But Pakistan gets to campaign, too. Free and fair elections, under the UN's auspices. You have already promised this."

"It is a promise I intend to keep."

"The Instrument of Accession neutralizes this requirement. If you delay and I die, we're back to square one."

"Then we draw up a new agreement negating the Accession."

"Jawahar!" protested Mountbatten. His friend, on the

verge of militancy not a week ago, had backtracked in a matter of minutes.

"No, Dickie," said Nehru turning to him, "it's true. The people have a say."

"Good," exclaimed Jinnah putting his empty glass away. We're agreed then. I hope you've brought your typewriter, Dickie. Because I wouldn't want any of us to leave this room until we have an understanding. Just one last thing…"

"What's that?"

"Since this meeting cannot be made public knowledge for now, and we have no witnesses; I am putting my faith in you to produce this document in the event…"

"You'll be fine, Quaid-e-Azam," Mountbatten tried to reassure him.

ACKNOWLEDGEMENTS

First novels are made of a lifetime of influences, inspiration, and encouragement and it's impossible to list everyone who has played a role in shaping the culmination of what has been a persistent aspiration.

The concept was first imagined as a film with my friend and confederate, Saumil Gandhi. We felt a strong urge to express ourselves on the subject in the mainstream and set about writing a screenplay. None too soon we realized that given the current political climate of the nation, it would not be possible to release a movie on Kashmir that is short of propaganda. We thought instead we could go under the radar and novelize it and even though we would be bereft of Bollywood's auspices, at least our beliefs would be at large in the world. Saumil has graciously allowed me to take the author's credit, but let it be said here that as my primary motivator, a fountainhead of ideas when I had none, and recurrent drinking partner, Saumil's contribution to the novel is second to none.

I would like to thank my agent Kanishka Gupta for calling me out of the blue and insisting that I write a book. And Namrata Joshi for engineering this call. My publishers at Jaico – Sandhya Iyer and her team including Sanjana Parikh have been immensely patient with my shenanigans. Teesta Guha Sarkar for her insight and priceless feedback on early drafts. Sumit Purohit, who was on-call with his support.

A doff of the hat to my mentor Saeed Mirza with whom in many ways this odyssey began over a decade ago and my co-conspirator in all my screenwriting endeavours, Puneet Krishna.

I would also like to thank the scores of Kashmiris who let me peek into their hearts and minds, Ameya Sarda for accompanying me all the way to the literal edges of the country's border, the Arora family for a wonderful writing retreat in Jaipur, and of course my own brood who have believed in my journey and have motivated me with their support throughout – Manjul and Vineeta Sinha, Simone Anshuman, Gaurav Desai, and our mutts Max and Momo.

Above all, I would like to offer all my gratitude and love to my partner, Anuradha Sharma, who had to get through nine months with another human being inside her, hold on to a job she loathed, and raise little Zoë almost all on her own so that I could write a novel. You're my hero.